Then Came July

Cornelia Allen

outskirts
press

Chapter 1

As always, the worst things happen to the best people. Police Captain Rick Mora just never expected that the victim this time would be lively, charming, first grader, Claudia Tapia, the youngest daughter of his deceased friend, Carlos.

His jaw clenched, and he closed his eyes against the scene. He and Carlos installed this big picture window last year, just before the accident that took his old Army buddy's life. Now, morning light streamed through what was left of the window. The cheerful light felt wrong, insulting, mocking. It sparkled on shattered glass that mixed with blood from the child's punctured skull. He wanted to howl at the sun, to make it cover its face, to make it stop shining so prettily on the heartless scene. And he wanted to hurt whoever had done this. Hurt them terribly, permanently.

He remembered the last time he had seen the little girl, grinning at him as he pushed her in the swing on his mother's front porch up in Juniper Springs. She was missing one front baby tooth that day. Now her face was unrecognizable. A coloring book lay beside her, the picture of a giraffe partly finished. Her hand still clutched an orange crayon.

Glass crunched under foot as he moved into the kitchen. Claudia's older brother, Gordo, sat with hands clasped between his knees, staring at the floor. This was almost surely Gordo's fault in one way or another, and Rick wanted to hurt him, too. But not here, not now.

Rick spoke to the young officer on her very first patrol. "Officer Gateman, stay with Mrs. Tapia until her sister can get here. Remember not to touch anything. Your sergeant will maintain the perimeter until the team arrives." Rick gestured with his head, and Sergeant Huerta quickly obeyed the order. Officer Gateman, silenced by the grim scene and smells of death, swallowed convulsively.

Rick crouched in front of the grieving mother, her head bowed low over the kitchen table. "I am so very sorry. We will catch them, Sylvia. I promise. They will suffer for this." He took an ironed handkerchief from his inner jacket pocket, pressing it into her hand.

She wiped her eyes and grasped Rick's strong fingers. "I knew it could happen, but I never dreamed that it would be Claudia. Never dreamed." Looking into those startling pale eyes in his brown face, she asked, "Will you sing the *Ave* for her, Enrique? Like you did when my Carlos died? Will you wear the Silver Star?"

He hesitated for an instant. He hated wearing medals, as though what he had done that day in Iraq was a good thing. But Carlos had been one of those who campaigned for Rick to receive the award, and what mattered now was not Rick's feelings, but Sylvia's wishes.

"Of course, my friend. And I'll talk to Father Don about the music. Do you want to stay with my folks for a few days? Dad will come get you."

"I think I need to stay here in town. There will be more family coming. You know." Her voice trembled, and tears started afresh.

He gently squeezed her hand. There was no comfort that he could offer. "I will always remember Claudia, just as I do Carlos. I will remember all the joy they brought to our lives." Then pointing at the guy sitting as far from his weeping mother as the room allowed, he said, "Outside, Gordo."

"My mama needs me, bro!"

Rick's brows drew together and his fists clenched. He took a step toward the young man. "Out!"

Gordo struggled up from the chair, pulling his tight tee-shirt down to cover the heavy roll of fat that gave him his nickname. He lumbered toward the door with the policeman close on his heels.

"I am not your bro, Gordito. A worthless little prick like you survived and Claudia died. It's not too hard to figure out how that happened."

"Come on, Mora! Us brown guys gotta stick together. Don't take it out on me."

"Then who? You brought this on your family. You have had every frigging chance, and you chose the cartel over your own sister and mother. For what, Gordo? The few hundred bucks they throw to you once in a while? You think we should stick together? The only place a guy like you sticks is to the sole of my boot, like the piece of shit you are."

"You're so high and mighty! Hotshot Captain Mora in your fancy suits, trying to act like a white man. The Jalisco boys are going to get you, too. You shoulda died the time Aaron shot you, *pendejo*. I'll be flying high when you are rotting away, buzzard bait in some arroyo out there." Gordo motioned toward the surrounding desert with a gesture of his head.

Rick rocked slightly from foot to foot, controlling his rage, his desire for revenge, with difficulty. He wanted to beat Gordo senseless and leave *him* out there as buzzard bait. "So, if your mom was expecting something, she must have picked up on it from you. You knew they were planning this? You didn't do anything to stop it?"

"I didn't know! What was I going to do anyway, bro? Run to you cops? Tell you or Lieutenant Q? You wouldn't do anything, and I wouldn't live through the day!"

"You think I am going to let you live through the day? I think, one way or another, you are an accessory. An accessory to murder."

Rick felt himself grinning mirthlessly. The crazy coyote within him had cornered its prey. "You know, I am going to let you live after all. Killing is too easy, and would only hurt your family more. I want you to suffer like your mom is suffering. I'm going to lock you up until we sort out your role in this murder. You are twenty now, aren't you? It won't be in juvie this time. You'll be in with the big boys. I bet your cellmates will just love your fat ass. And I won't have to do anything to you, because your new boyfriends will make you suffer plenty. You know, in the showers, when the guards are maybe a little slow to respond? Oh, yeah. You will get hurt. So, which piece of shit pulled the trigger?"

Gordo crossed his arms over his heavy belly in a defiant gesture. "You got nuthin' on me. So, you going to scalp me or something? I hate to tell you, Crazy Hearse, Geri-no-mo, but the Anglos defeated you Injuns a long time ago. All you need is another dead homeboy on your record, and *poof,* like magic, no more Captain Mora. You'll be back walking a beat."

"Deja moo, Gordo."

"What?"

"You know, that feeling you get when you have heard this bullshit before? We weren't defeated. We just adapted to the white man's ways. And I'm only half Apache anyway." Sirens wailed in the distance, but at the moment, it was just the two of them there, face-to-face. Gordo looked like he was ready to run, or fight

"You son-of-a-bitch cop! If you were really my dad's friend, you'd let me go." He pointed to the tattoo on his neck, identifying him as a member of the Jalisco cartel. "You're a short timer anyway, 'cuz we are everywhere."

Rick saw the intent in Gordo's eyes, and braced himself for the looping blow that connected with his cheekbone. Needing only a step back to keep his balance, he grinned. "Now I have you for assaulting an officer, and that is another felony, *bro.* Go ahead. Run. I'll shoot you in the back of the leg, bust hell out of your knee."

Before Gordo could make his move, sirens died, car doors slammed. Lieutenant Elias Quintana, widely known as Q, approached with weapon drawn, unsure of the situation. He could see blood on Rick's cheek. "You okay, Cap?"

"Yeah. Gordito decided not to run after all, Q. Gave me a wimpy little punch instead. All we have now is Sylvia's description of the car. Gordo should get a nice long sentence though, because it sounds like he might have known about this drive by in advance.".

"Wait! I was just a witness. I didn't do nothin'. It was Charlie

Wallace. It was Wallace! Come on, man!"

"We'll see, Gordo. The truth will come out eventually. And just a witness? Sure. You can try to explain to all those guys in the county jail how you aren't responsible for little Claudia's murder since you didn't do anything. One or two of them might believe you."

Rick chuckled, a cold, frightening sound that matched the ice chips of his eyes. Gordo flinched as though he had been struck. "Maybe you should learn how to fight, Gordo. You think? You are safe from me for now, but if you show back up on the streets? Not so much. Book him for assault, Q," he said, as he strode away calling in his change of location.

"Don't test him like that, Gordo," Q said. "Rick is dangerous. He thinks like a rabid coyote. You are safer in lockup. "

"He's crazy! You cops aren't supposed to threaten citizens."

"That wasn't a threat. It was a promise. Yeah. He's crazy. So what? If it weren't for Mora, your dad and I and five other guys would never have made it out of Iraq. He almost bled to death himself, and he was only nineteen. You could have been a man, but you chose to be a cockroach. And now, you are about to be stepped on."

Chapter 2

The traffic light changed to green, and Doctor July Sullivan accelerated into the intersection just as a jacked-up pickup barreled across in front of her, running the red light. July slammed on her brakes, skidding sideways, missing the truck by inches. The frightened face of a woman stared at her from the passenger window.

"What the hell, Bubba!" she shouted at the driver. He squeezed into line at Starbucks, throwing her a finger as though she was the one at fault. Glancing in her rearview at the offending truck, she pulled into the next parking lot, shaken by the encounter. It took a few minutes to get her nerves under control.

"I should have smashed this old car right into his fancy new truck. Another guy who thinks he owns the world." *But not me. Never again.* A tear escaped, running into the corner of her mouth. She licked it away and took some deep breaths, trying to overcome old memories, the adrenaline rush, her racing heart. In the heat, her temper was even shorter than usual. She cranked up the air conditioner, but it still blew only feebly, barely stirring the red hair touching her sweaty forehead.

Peaks, reminiscent of a pipe organ's soaring tubes, towered to the east. Dusty-tan and gray against the bright blue sky, the unforgiving mass of the Organ Mountains' sharp rock spires held hidden nooks with seeping springs and lush vegetation. July wished she could be up there this morning with her feet in the pond at Dripping Springs. She sighed, already tired at nine a.m.

Fifteen minutes later, she pulled over to the curb down the street from El Rio Women's Clinic. Low-cost apartment complexes and one-story houses with faded stucco exteriors lined the street. She debated leaving the car windows slightly cracked to minimize heat buildup in the old Volvo, taking the risk of making it that much easier to steal.

"Damned if you do, damned if you don't," July muttered to herself. Dust coated the dash and collected in cracks around the speaker ports. "Maybe you look sufficiently derelict to make you uninteresting, old boy." She patted the steering wheel.

July wondered why she wasn't enjoying herself more. She should be happier, shouldn't she? She stared out of the pitted windshield for a minute, trying to dredge up some energy. A gust of gritty desert wind blew a sandwich wrapper across the hood of the car.

She jumped a little when the young mother pushing a baby stroller called to her. "Hi, Dr. Sullivan." Even in a halter top and shorts, the girl looked uncomfortable in the heat.

"Sure got hot early this year, didn't it, Shirley?' July tried to sound upbeat. "Looks like the pickets are out again, even with these temperatures. Sometimes I wish I had moved back home to the mountains instead of Las Cruces. What brought you and little Ralph to the city?"

"I don't want to raise Ralph around the rest of the family. Some of the cousins are pretty bad types. You know Aaron, Dottie's husband? He is a major crook, I think." The girl made a face and shook her head. "I want Ralphie to have a real chance in life, and my brother feels the same about his son, Gary. So, here we are, the outsiders in our family!" She grinned, making light of what must have been a painful experience.

July left an inch crack in the window and pried her sweaty cotton blouse loose from the worn leather upholstery. Climbing out of the car, she stretched and yawned. Her legs ached again. They felt tired and heavy. It seemed like she could barely walk the block to the clinic. She pushed the hair back from her forehead, remembering that it badly needed a cut. "How is Dottie, anyway?"

"Her acne has cleared up real well since she started taking that medicine you said was dangerous to babies, and I think she is pregnant. You know, they live across the border, so I don't see her as much."

July frowned, hoping that Dottie would be alright. There was nothing she could do now anyway. She smiled at her patient. Maybe it was the girl's voice, or stance, or her quick, curious mind. Anyway, July always enjoyed appointments with Shirley Gambino and little Ralph. "Well, come on, you two. I guess we have to brave the ravening horde sooner or later. It's too hot to stay out here." She straightened her shoulders.

They walked the block to the Clinic, a controversial center that performed abortions in the past. Heat radiating from the sun-drenched sidewalk penetrated the soles of their shoes.

"Long day yesterday?" Shirley asked.

"Oh, not so bad. Usually, I enjoy coming here to the clinic, but we had an emergency last night, and I missed some sleep." She put on an exaggeratedly tired expression to make Shirley laugh. With her rhinestone-studded dark glasses, slender build, and heart-shaped face, Shirley could pass for a starlet. July wondered if she was ever that young. *What the hell? I'm only thirty-two, and I think like an old lady already.*

July noticed Shirley examining her closely. "Wow, what diet are you on, Dr. Sullivan. you're getting real thin. I'm afraid that you will blow away one day!" But she spoke in a friendly way, so July skipped the usual sharp retort directed at people who commented on her small stature. She was acutely aware that she had lost too much weight in the last few months but just couldn't bring herself to eat much.

"No diet. I never have been able to gain much weight, and in this damn heat, I don't like to cook for myself."

July knew that with her delicate features and sprinkle of freckles, she looked like a teenager, too young to be a doctor. The giggle that she could never suppress made it worse. A bit of mild profanity helped patients relate to her a bit better. After all, she was from a ranch in the mountains north of Las Cruces, so maybe she was born in a barn, right?

"I hope we can get in without those people shouting at us," July commented. Shirley nodded in agreement. But there they were, a determined handful of activists trying to find some relief from the heat, clustered under the sparse shade of a few small crape myrtle trees.

July recognized some of the regulars. Athena, whose real name was Carolyn, dressed in her usual long skirt and embroidered blouse. She held up a beautifully painted poster of Gaia, the Earth Mother, the Greek goddess of life and fertility. Gray-faced old Mister Wilkins leaned on his cane, his worn Bible in the other hand. He looked like he might topple over dead at any moment. Mrs. Bond, in her usual striped seersucker blouse and shorts, wore a broad-brimmed canvas hat to shade her face. In the heat, the chants were pretty weak, but the brawny leader of the group moved to block the path as usual.

July sighed impatiently. "Step back, Mr. Winter. You know that I have nothing to do with whatever your complaint is today. I am a dermatologist. Please let us pass."

The man grabbed the handle of Shirley's baby carriage. "In the Name of Jesus, child, do not let these godless people lure you into mortal sin." He leaned over the girl. Sweat shone on his forehead and left huge wet circles under his arms. Shirley recoiled, her expression revealing both anger and disgust.

"The Lord says that a woman's role is to populate the Earth. Stopping a pregnancy, no matter how it is done, is a sin!"

Shirley's face, flushed from the heat, grew redder. "So, what is your problem? Can't get it up?. Get your hands off my stroller, or I'll file a complaint with the police!"

A couple of passing teenagers, observing the confrontation, laughed out loud, calling, "You go, girl!" The man let go of the stroller, but there was fury in his face, and hate in his eyes.

July held the clinic door open for the stroller. "Come on, Shirley. Mr. Winter is just not as smart as you are. Maybe you should pity him."

"Don't antagonize him, Doctor. He might be dangerous." The short, plump, gray-haired clinic manager peered out at Mr. Winter and his followers.

July snorted. "Oh, Milly! He's just a headline-grabbing old fool."

"You don't know him. You have only been coming here for a few months. He seems sort of normal on the surface, but I know his wife. He's a nasty piece of work who would probably shut us down entirely if he thought he could get away with it. And, dear, you really need to eat more, you know," she continued in her motherly, fussy way.

Again, July held her tongue. She knew Milly meant well. She should learn something about Mr. Winter. Maybe Milly was right. She also needed to find out about the last dermatologist volunteering at the clinic, a Doctor Garner. He left unexpectedly, and she wondered why. Had there been personal threats that drove him away? Maybe next weekend, if there were no emergencies at the hospital, she would find out more.

The waiting room was empty except for a girl engrossed in a magazine, sitting in the corner. "Hi, Roberta," Shirley called. Roberta gave a little wave, but did not look up.

July turned to the receptionist. "Rose, do I have the back office and exam room again?"

"Yes, and you might have to take some of the other doctor's patients. She is running late. I know just how much you love doing that." She peered over her steel-framed granny glasses, giving July a mischievous grin.

"You are a mean old lady, Rose Garcia. Deliberately torturing me." But, she smiled. "Go on back, Shirley. We may as well get started. Let me have Ralph and the stroller. You go splash some cold water on your face. Cool off for a minute after that hot walk. Okay?"

She bent down to the toddler, holding out her hands. "Gamma," he said, reaching for her with chubby arms.

"Not quite, but close enough," July smiled, ignoring for the thousandth time the tiny stab to her heart. She could have, should have, at least one child in school by now. Lifting him onto her hip, she dropped her briefcase and patient files on the seat of the stroller and strode down the hall to the last exam room. At the same time, she was kind of glad that she had no children with Randy. It was not too late to find a good man. Or was it? Maybe she should try one of those online dating sites someday. Maybe.

July sat Ralph down on the exam table and blew up a vinyl glove, forming an impromptu balloon. "Look, Ralph. What is this?" Ralph laughed, banging the balloon down on the table.

Roberta passed in the hall, eyes averted from the open exam room door. Hurrying around the corner, she pushed the back door open a few inches. Someone handed her a small box wrapped in duct tape. There was a whispered reminder. "As close to the doctor as you can get it. Drop it into a garbage can, a drawer, or anything. You have six minutes. Get it done or else!" There was a muted rumble as the large waste container was pushed up against the door, blocking that exit.

Roberta peeked around the corner, her heart hammering. Doctor Sullivan was reading something, her back to the hallway. And there, within easy reach, sat an open briefcase. She slipped the box in and hurried away, bumping the door in her haste. She was not supposed to, she knew. She had been told a hundred times, but dialed her phone and told them anyway. They still had three minutes to get out.

The exam room door made a clicking sound as it closed. July, reviewing the chart, assumed that her patient was entering. "It looks good, Shirley. I think that we got all the margins." She turned. No one was there.

"Shirley? Milly?" She paused, listening. "Huh!" She turned back to Ralphie and retrieved the toy before it drifted to the floor. Suddenly, there were loud voices in the hallway. She picked up little Ralph and opened the heavy door.

"Hurry, hurry!" Milly's voice was shrill with fear. "Get out, Doctor! Run! Bomb!"

"What?

"On the phone! Said there's a bomb! Hurry!" She gasped, tears starting down her powdered cheeks.

July thrust the baby into her arms. "Go! I'll get Shirley." She turned, ran back down the hall, and tried the door marked Ladies. Locked!

"Shirley!"

"Occupied." The voice came faintly through the heavy door.

"Come out now! Bomb scare! Hurry! We need to get out of here!"

Shirley's frightened face peered out from behind the door. "Bomb? Ralphie!"

"Milly took him out. Come on!" July grabbed the girl's hand. Pulling her toward the back door of the Clinic, she slammed into it elbow first and bounced back. "Yow!" Pain so sharp that she almost fainted shot all the way to her shoulder. She grabbed her arm but kept moving. "My God! Someone locked that door! Come on, run!"

Pushing Shirley ahead of her, she fled down the hallway, shoes slipping on the tile floor. They burst through a side door. Shirley jumped from the top of the steps, landing on her side, rolling down the grass slope to the sidewalk.

July's shirtsleeve caught on the latch plate. She jerked hard to get loose, tearing the chambray material, and tripped, falling down the steps. She landed on asphalt, sliding several feet on that same painful elbow and the right side of her face. There was a loud bang and a *whooshing* sound. Flaming debris rained down around her as she passed out.

July woke hours later to the soft, rhythmic whisper of an oxygen pump and the squeal of rubber shoe soles on polished tile. A window showed the clear, restful, orange light of an approaching desert sunset. Voices somewhere nearby discussed symptoms and diagnoses. For a minute, July thought she was back in med school. Opening one eye, she could see a nurse's station and monitors through the partial glass wall. *Recovery room. I am in a recovery room.*

"When can I talk to Dr. Sullivan, Bitsy?" The deep voice sounded far away, sort of echoing, as though she was in a barrel.

"When she is ready, Rick, we will move her to the third floor. Not until then. She has multiple burns, a concussion, and a badly damaged arm. It may be a while." The man snorted in impatience. "Listen, Bits. This is an important case. Will you call me when she wakes up enough to be coherent?"

July tried to call out, to say that she was awake, but her mouth was too dry to speak.

"Go away, Rick," the nurse said, "we are busy here."

"Come on, girl," he was saying, smiling a sexy, lop-sided smile.

"Enrique Mora, you go away! Now!"

He laughed. "Okay, okay. You wouldn't want to join me at Blue Bellies, I guess."

"You guessed right."

"Ah, well." He gave an exaggerated sigh. "Another rejection."

Bitsy picked up a clipboard, threatening to smack him with it. Chuckling, he raised a protective hand as he left.

"Wow," said a young nurse's aide. "I'd meet that guy at Blue Bellies in a heartbeat. He's cute. Dresses like he has money. I wonder how old he is?"

"Too old for you. Don't get your panties in a twist over Rick Mora. He can be charming. But there is a dangerous man under that classy suit. He didn't get those scars from being a nice guy."

"How do you know him?"

Bitsy's gaze followed the retreating form of Captain Mora. "We were young once." She smiled, and her voice trailed off.

Chapter 3

Rick Mora sat resting, half asleep, legs stretched in front of him, a small notebook in his hand. It had been a busy winter for Las Cruces PD, and he was so damn tired. His head jerked up. *Dozed off again. Somebody please shoot me so I can get some rest.* He stood to keep himself awake and leaned against the wall.

Lieutenant Kincannon and Detective Eisenstein thought they knew where the drive-by shooter, Charlie Wallace, was hiding. Eisenstein was new. Rick did not know how he would handle any direct conflict, and Rory Kincannon was better at information than action. *I should take the lead before one of my team gets hurt.*

Rick let his mind drift to the piece he was learning on his piano, Liszt's Sonata in B Minor. It was tricky. He visualized the keyboard, mentally playing the movement that gave him a bit of trouble. He didn't have the timing quite right in one place.

He sighed quietly. Not enough time to practice his music, get to the gym and still find an occasional hour to spend at his favorite hangout, Blue Bellies Bar. He thought briefly about Marietta of the big boobs. She would probably be there later, looking to get laid, like half a dozen other Badge Bunnies. She was a nice girl. Why did she want to waste her youth screwing around with old, cynical, boozing cops? It was a puzzle. He talked to her about it once, but she just smiled, unbuckled his belt, and like the philandering jerk he had become, he took what she offered so freely.

Rick glanced again at his sleeping suspect. It was hard to believe that this girl could be old enough to be an actual medical doctor. She looked like a child, except for where the hospital gown stretched tight across full breasts. Curled in the bed, she seemed so small and thin, not much bigger than his little niece, Grace. A pale, delicate wrist lay on the pillow by her youthful face. Resting on a smooth cheek, the long, curved lashes of one unbandaged eye were strawberry blonde. There was something familiar about the little doctor. He was sure they had met before, but he couldn't quite place it. He rolled a matchstick from one side of his mouth to the other and looked out the window.

Gradually, the patient began to move restlessly. She managed to pry open her left eye, the unbandaged one, against the too-bright light, blinking rapidly to bring things into focus. The only thing she could see was a pair of men's black jeans and a silver belt buckle with a turquoise and coral bear inlay. She grunted in pain as she tried turning her head to see more.

"Are you awake enough to talk to me?" The voice sounded the same as the earlier low rumble.

Well, duh, but her mouth was too dry to answer. She tried to lick her lips, which were stuck together.

Large, brown, blunt fingers appeared, holding a straw to her lips. A chipped thumbnail showed a black irregular spot about halfway down. She pondered whether there was some underlying pathology, maybe a melanoma or just a bruise. The hands were certainly outdoorsman's hands. Rough, with scarred and deeply furrowed knuckles, they reminded her of her great uncle Luke. Rancher's hand. Cowboy's hands.

She sucked the cup dry. The hand disappeared. There was a gurgling sound as the cup was refilled and offered to her again.

"Thanks. No. Not right now." It came out in a hoarse whisper.

Once again, she was gazing at the man's sharply creased jeans. He was wearing a light blue denim blazer with a crisp white shirt. After a few moments, she realized she was staring at his crotch.

Running her tongue around her mouth, she tried to form words more clearly. "Who're you?"

"Captain Rick Mora. I'm with the city police."

"Sit down. Tired of looking at your junk." Her eye closed again.

There was a grunt, a sound of amusement, or maybe disgust? She couldn't tell which. The scraping sound of chair legs on tile followed, and air whistled from plastic seat cushions. He settled in the chair facing her, his expression cold.

July opened her one good eye. Broad shoulders filled that blazer. The open-collar shirt showed a strong neck rising from his deep chest. Clear gray eyes considered her through gold, wire-rimmed bifocals. His face was a study in ethnic diversity. With medium brown skin, a high, slightly crooked nose, and prominent cheekbones, he could have been the model for a painting of some old-time warrior. But, with those pale eyes and dark, reddish-brown hair lightly laced with silver, he was clearly of mixed heritage.

The frame of his glasses partly hid a long scar on his cheekbone. July's medical opinion was that it was an excellent job of closing that wound. There was also a thickened keloid scar at the edge of his chin and one anchoring the corner of his mouth. Both could use revision. She immediately thought how she could correct those, making them less visible, less like someone drew them on with a tan crayon.

The man was watching her, intent but expressionless. He was intimidating, sort of predatory, like a hawk. July swallowed, uncomfortable with this man sitting so close. Cold discomfort turned to rising anger. *Another of those arrogant, marginalizing jerks, perfectly dressed in business casual like an ad in GQ.* July fought all her life against men like that. She was instantly on the defensive.

"Whaddaya want, Richard, Ricardo, whatever."

"You can call me Captain Mora, Doctor. I am supervising the officers investigating the incident at the Women's Clinic. I understand that you were in the back office?"

"What incident? I fell and hurt myself. I didn't see any incident. I was in the exam room. Go away."

"You don't remember running out the side door?" His ballpoint pen clicked. "Why didn't you go out the back door?"

She stared at him for a moment. "Oh, there was something Milly said." She raised her unbandaged hand to her head. "Locked. I remember. The back door was usually unlocked, but it wasn't."

"You sure?"

"Yes, I'm sure." *Entitled ass thinks I'm stupid.* "I slammed into it at full speed, and it didn't open. Hurt my elbow. Locked! Ask Shirley. She was with me."

"I see a Shirley Gambino on the list of patients, but we haven't found her yet. Any idea where she would be?"

"I am her dermatologist, not her pal. The only thing I know is that she recently moved to Las Cruces. Her address should be in the chart with my briefcase, in the exam room. What do you mean you couldn't find her? She was there."

"We could not find any of those documents, and the clinic hasn't computerized their records yet."

"The paper records were in Ralphie's stroller with my briefcase. That much I do remember. Ask Rose. She might know where Shirley lives. She seems to keep track of everyone."

"What kind of accelerant did you have in that briefcase?"

"What?" Her eyes widened and her mouth dropped open. The man's voice was as cold as those silvery eyes. A chill stopped her usual harsh, sarcastic responses for a minute. She caught her breath and pulled up some bluster. "Accelerant? Me? Why? Wait a second, Bubba! Are you accusing me of something?"

"Not quite yet."

July's eyes narrowed at that, and her cheeks reddened. "How dare you! Who do you think you are?"

"My name is Rick Mora, and I am a policeman. My enemies usually call me Captain Mora." He spoke slowly, as though July was mentally deficient.

"Your enemies. What do your friends call you? Or don't you have any?"

"Doesn't pay to have many friends in my business. Would you answer my question, please?" He cleared his throat, his face expressionless. "Do you know why you are here in the hospital?"

Her green-eye squinted at him, and her cheeks flushed. She wanted to hit him. "I fell down the steps, got some gravel burns or something, and hurt my arm."

"More or less. You have a broken arm, a concussion, and some burns. Yes, you did fall. You don't remember the explosion? A witness says you covered your head as though you were expecting something."

"I did? Explosion? Oh. My. God! There *was* a bomb! Was anyone hurt?'

"Just you and Mrs. Garcia, the last one out."

"Is Rose okay?"

"No."

"Is she here in the hospital?"

"No. She didn't make it out."

"What? Oh!" Tears sprang to her eyes.

"Yes." He paused for a moment as the seriousness, the tragedy, of the event sank in. "Given the few facts that we have, the starting point was your location, in the exam room. And, with the chemical residue on the remains of your briefcase, you are clearly a suspect."

"Did I have an explosive? Why are you saying that? Why are you here? How dare you! I struggled for years to be good at helping people, and now you accuse me of hurting people? No way! I am a doctor. I don't hurt people. I repair people who are injured. I would never hurt Rose. Your information can't be factual. What motivation would I have?" July was almost shouting with indignation, fury, and maybe fear.

"Why did you cover your head just before the blast?"

"I don't know. Did I? To protect it from my fall?"

"Maybe so. Or maybe you were expecting a blast? Were you involved in an anti-abortion demonstration five years ago?"

"No!" July spat out the word.

"May I show you this photograph?" He held a copy of an old newspaper photo up for her to see. July's face showed clearly in the back of a crowd, some holding up placards with anti-abortion statements. Her expression was angry.

"Oh, for God's sake! I was trying to get to the door to see my patients. I was not demonstrating!"

He shifted the match stick from one corner of his mouth to the other, watching her calmly with his cold, pale eyes. It made her nervous, and angry. She was so heart sick and furious that she was in danger of crying in front of this jerk. July blinked back the tears.

"You damned idiot! This is the desert. The clinic is for poor women. I volunteer there. I treat them with samples provided by drug companies. That is what was in my briefcase, not explosives. Butt out!"

"My, my! Such language. Thank you, Doctor Sullivan. I will be back when you have had time to think about your situation."

"My situation is that I had nothing to do with any of this." Her voice rose an octave. "Leave me alone, you arrogant, egotistical, lowlife, scum-sucking, frigging... toad!"

He rolled the matchstick to the other side of his mouth and flicked imaginary dust from his immaculate lapels. "Egotistical is certainly true. Arrogant?" He nodded his head. "Idiot? Mm, sometimes. But toad? I don't know. I prefer to think of myself as a big frog in this small pond."

"Now you're making fun of me!"

"Possibly."

"How dare you!"

He continued gazing calmly at her with slightly pursed lips, hands folded across his waist, and legs crossed at the ankle. It was very quiet. So quiet that she could hear his slow breathing. His phone gave a single beep, and he glanced at the message. July lay back, exhausted, trying not to doze off in the presence of the policeman. She barely noticed the sound of chair legs scraping on tile as he rose.

Rick walked away, one eyebrow raised in question. The silent treatment sometimes elicited information from a suspect if there was any information to give. It hadn't worked on her. She was a tough little thing. He smiled.

The fire department investigator was in the hall, waiting to interview July as soon as Rick left. He stopped her. "Leave her alone, Amanda. Dr. Sullivan is not involved." He knew he was condescending, but didn't care. New to the job and hard to work with, Amanda was a trial. He wished Ernie Patel could replace her, but the Fire Captain was under pressure to conform to diversity rules, just as he was in the Las Cruces Police Department.

Amanda snapped back. "And you know that how, exactly? Some special Apache medicine man insight or something? Woo, woo, woo?"

He gave her a half-smile, refusing to rise to the bait, the racist insults this woman handed out every time they met. "That doesn't work with me. I spent my childhood dealing with small-minded insults. My folks raised me like any American boy. When the Army handed me a rifle, it didn't matter if I was half Apache or half Martian. They only cared that I could fight for my country, like other American boys. Save your insults for someone who cares."

He paused. "I do know something about Dad's ancestors. It was the Zuni people that called my forefathers Apache. It means *enemy.*" He put heavy emphasis on the word. "And that is about all I know, except this. I am not a Native American cop, or a Mexican American cop, or whatever your insult is today. I am just a policeman, and I am a good one. Get over it. I know it's a struggle for you, Amanda, but try thinking for a change. Doctor Sullivan intended to run out the back door. She thought the door was unlocked as usual, and slammed into it so hard that she broke her arm. If she had known, she would not have tried to go out that door, and would have been safely outside when the bomb went off. And, she would hardly have left the bomb in her briefcase, would she?"

Amanda didn't have a reply. Wanting to annoy her, he grinned and whispered, "Besides, I know my women."

"I doubt that you actually know any women, other than in the biblical sense. You say that you are an apple, red on the outside and white on the inside? What you really are, Captain Mora, is a *rotten* apple!" Amanda stormed away down the hall.

"Bitch," he muttered, tamping down a flare of resentment. But there was more truth to what she said than he wanted to admit. Amanda was trying to make it in what was still a male-dominated world. He should be more understanding. That is what his mother would say. "Don't be so judgmental, Enrique." Sure. Some day. Right now, there was work to do.

"Where are you, Rory," he said into his phone. "He's cornered? Don't push it. Wallace is going to come out firing, and Eisenstein will probably freeze. Wait for me. I'll come in from the side door. Yeah. The usual. If necessary, I'll draw his fire, so you can take him down."

Chapter 4

"Dr. Sullivan, can you hear me? Dr. Moussa here."

July, opened her eye to see a white coat beside the bed. The light from the hallway was almost too bright. She squinted uncomfortably. The doctor adjusted the bed curtain so that it was half-drawn, and the room was comfortable enough for her one-eyed gaze.

She turned her head slightly. "Please sit down, Doctor, so that I can see your face."

"Here. Take this chair, Mo." That same deep voice. *What the hell is he doing here?* Again, she heard the chair being dragged over beside her bed, and a *whoosh* of air from plastic chair cushions as a pleasant, dark-skinned face came into view. For an instant, July suppressed a giggle at the pencil mustache. Dr. Moussa reminded her of a Peter Sellers character, like Inspector Clouseau from those old movies.

The doctor leaned toward July, his expression compassionate. "I am going to remove this eye dressing now. You should be able to see a little, but not completely at this time. Your eye will continue to heal, but I want you to see an ophthalmologist after you are discharged. We did our best with your right elbow. Both radius and ulna shattered proximally. I made copies of the report for you to peruse at your convenience. It is not good. I am afraid you may always have significant limitations with fine motor control in that hand because the ulnar and radial nerves suffered damage in this accident."

He paused, waiting, but July did not answer immediately. "Do you understand, Doctor Sullivan? Did you hear me?"

Tears welled up. She had assumed it was just a simple fracture that they would quickly repair. This complication was unexpected. How much surgery would she be able to do? Could she make neat suture lines? Leave minimal scarring? Would she recover enough to keep her appointment to the Royal College in London? She sniffed and cleared her throat, needing to think about something else for a moment and give herself time to pull emotions together.

"Do you know if there is anything I can do for Rose Garcia's family? Funeral expenses or something?"

"She didn't have any family left. Captain Mora took care of final expenses and is having a marker made to go beside those of her parents." Doctor Moussa sighed. "We found something else. We did a scan, of course, because of your fall. Have you noticed any weakness in your legs recently?"

July nodded slightly.

"There is a growth. It is just lateral to the sacral plexus. We did a needle biopsy and, well." He cleared his throat. "We need more tests for staging, of course."

"Shit!"

"Yes." He paused. "Is there a particular oncologist with whom you want to work? Can I make arrangements for a consultation at one of the big cancer centers?"

July hesitated. "I will need to think about this, and please call me July."

He rose. "I will see you tomorrow then, July. It will be a few days before I want to release you. You know the drill."

"Of course. Thank you." She closed her good eye and listened to the squeak of rubber soles as the doctor left the room. It was very quiet for a minute, with only the sound of a cart rolling along the hall. What was happening to her? What was happening? She sat up and dangled her feet over the side of the bed, wanting to stand up on those aching legs, but she was too dizzy from the pain killing meds in her IV.

"Uh, oncologist? Bad news?" He stepped around the curtain. She had almost forgotten that the policeman was there. "Were you listening? You creep! You should have excused yourself. That was confidential information."

He ducked his head in what might have been a gesture of apology. A lock of hair fell over his forehead. It made him look less threatening, almost boyish for an instant. "Sorry. But Dr. Moussa knows I'm here on official business. We play basketball together."

"What? What about HIPPA? They can't just assume...."

"Yeah. Yadda, yadda. None of which matters in the end because I have a legal right to be here and to question you. So, get over it."

He came around the bed and sat in the chair in front of her. Leaning back, he stretched out his legs as though settling in for a friendly chat, except there was that icy cop stare, the strong jaw, the rough hands, the beak of a nose. He was still scary, arrogant, and just so damn male. Everything about him made her angry.

July regarded him with suspicion, feeling tense and hostile. He didn't look like any policeman she had ever met. His clothes were too perfect, too elegant, and they didn't match his battered features and working man's hands. She was more than a little afraid of him, but hid it under a mask of hostility. Offense is the best defense.

"You don't look like a cop. You look like a fancied-up cowboy. Smell like one, too. Cheap whiskey and leather," she said sourly. "What's your name again? Where is your ID?"

"I was a cowboy. I rode for your Uncle Luke when you were a baby. My mom even made me babysit you sometimes when you were a toddler." He flipped the ID open to show his gold badge. "Not cheap whiskey. Forty bucks a bottle. One of Kentucky's finest bourbons. And I bought my little niece, Gracie, a saddle this evening. I carried it over my arm, so I smell like leather. My name is Captain Mora. Rick Mora. What will you do about that anyway? About the staging and all?"

She continued staring at him, shifting around on the bed to face him squarely. "Why don't I remember you? Mora? The only Mora I remember is Buddy, and you don't look anything like him. You're too old. Besides, the subject was my health, and it is none of your business, you smug son-of-a-bitch! Are you drunk?"

"Is it ten o'clock yet?" he peered at the wall clock. "Must not be drunk yet. I like to stay just a bit sober until I go off duty." He looked at her with what July thought might be a glint of amusement.

"Oh!" he said in fake surprise. "I am off duty. Anyway, we professional drinkers never get drunk at work."

"You drink on duty?"

"Being a smug son-of-a-bitch, maybe I take liberties," he replied, and his eyes crinkled the tiniest bit at the corners. "You always were a stubborn little monster. Haven't changed much." He handed her a folded document. "Search warrant for your apartment."

"No."

"No what?"

"No, you cannot search my apartment!"

"Of course I can, and I will. This is more a courtesy notice than anything like a request."

"So, you get your jollies from going through ladies' underwear or something? I said, no!" She was horrified and suspicious. She really did not remember this man, this guy with his scary gray eyes, who had clearly been drinking.

"You don't get to refuse," he said.

"My personal things are none of your business, you frigging...." She glared at him. He was leaning toward her now, elbows on knees. She couldn't help herself. Full of frustrated rage and fear, she slapped him as hard as she could with her left hand.

He jerked back, the matchstick flying from his lips, eyebrows climbing up in astonishment. "July Marie Kozlowski, slapping an officer is a felony. You don't get to behave like a child anymore, with everyone in town forgiving your bratty behavior. I could arrest you for that!"

"What do you mean? Since when can't a big tough cop take being slapped by a girl." But her voice was a little shaky this time. "I don't believe you, anyway."

Rick started again. "My God, girl, are you ever going to grow up? There are consequences. I should arrest you. I require that my officers do so." He paused, watching her clear green eyes fill with tears. Rather than being angry, he was both ashamed of scaring her and amused by her juvenile response. Just like when she was a baby, she lashed out without thinking. But now, she was more than Luke's spoiled little brat. It was evident that anger and bluster just served to hide fear and lack of confidence. What was it about her? Really, here in the hospital, surrounded by medical staff, what was there to fear? Something was going on with her that he could not quite grasp.

"I deliberately antagonized you, so I got what I deserved. You have a heck of a left punch there, young lady. Anyhow, I am not going to arrest you. Not this time. Now, pretend you are grown up, please. This is a serious investigation into a serious crime. There are uncomfortable questions that I am obligated to ask, and you are obligated to answer.."

July gave him a hard stare. "Smartass, aren't you? What right did you have to watch me in my sleep?"

He sighed with impatience but smiled a little. "Yeah. Definitely a smartass."

She was staring at him like she was trying to see into his soul. "Captain Mora? As in the guy who took care of Rose's final...?"

"Right. Speaking of watching, I could find you a magnifying glass if you want to examine my pores or something," he said. "And, no, I did not stare at you in your sleep. I was reading my notes, half asleep, and just pretending I was working."

"Boozing old cops. Just what Las Cruces needs."

He chuckled. "Well, let's see. You were four, I think, when I went off to the Army, and now you are thirty two. So, see? I am not so old yet. The job ages us pretty quickly."

She was just flailing around, trying to avoid thinking about her problems, and he knew it, too. Dr. Sullivan had to be in a lot of pain and took her frustrations out on him. He could see that she was trying not to cry. Rick wished that he could offer some comfort, but despite a broad vocabulary, he had never been able to find words to express many of the things he felt so profoundly.

He made a sort of quiet humming sound as they regarded each other for a few minutes. Her freckles were standing out boldly, and her eyes were still not quite clear of tears. She really did look like a child still. Rick suppressed a smile.

"So, what was that stuff with Mo all about? You have cancer?"

He saw her struggling to come up with another insult to throw at him, but a sob came out instead. "It means that I might have cancer." July took a big breath. "Probably have cancer." She hesitated, looking away. "Do have cancer." She tried to hide her face, and the tears that spilled over, but her voice trembled, and her cheeks were wet.

Rick pulled an ironed handkerchief from his jacket's inner pocket, very gently pried open her resisting fingers, and placed the white cloth in her good hand. She clung briefly to his warm hands with her cool little fingers. It was as though she needed an anchor for a moment, any safe harbor in this storm of confusion.

"So, if this is cancer?" He made his voice softer.

"I won't know how treatable it is until I see the oncologist and have more tests. It depends on the type and how far it has gone. I should have thought about why I was so tired, losing weight. Why my legs hurt so much. I put it down to just working too hard." She sounded calm, reasoning, but her eyes told the truth. She was terrified.

"Doctors are terrible patients. I guess I will need an extended break from doctoring. And, for Pete's sake, why am I telling this to an arrogant ass like you?"

"Probably because I am here, and no one else is." He was silent for a minute. "I know this is all very hard for you. So much is happening to you in such a short time. Alexander Graham Bell said to concentrate all one's thoughts upon the work at hand because the sun's rays don't burn until they come to a focus. It has been useful advice for me."

She nodded. " I appreciate that you took the time and expense and all for Mrs. Garcia. Had you known her long?"

"No. Never met." He flashed her a quick smile, rose and was gone.

July was interesting. So angry and defiant at first, but at the same time kind of helpless. He had a momentary vision of pushing her in his mom's old porch swing, and singing her a funny song like he did years ago, and still did for his niece Gracie when she was hurt or sad. He laughed at himself. That would never happen now. The officers of LCPD didn't call him Old Stone Face for nothing. July was an adult. She didn't need his sympathy.

Chapter 5

July couldn't keep track of the time, dozing, waking, dozing again. Nurses came and went in the familiar rhythm of any hospital. Muffled voices in hallways and the quiet bustle of busy staff were all normal background noise, but she hated it. There were too many unpleasant memories. A day passed.

It was dark again when she finally came fully awake. She was slow to open her eyes, appreciating the dim light and the relative silence of late night. Gradually, she became aware of a soft humming, almost indiscernible. She smiled, thinking she was imagining things, but then the sound stopped abruptly.

July lifted her head slightly, and there was a pair of denim-clad legs crossed at the knee. She could see wear on the sole of the athletic shoe that faced her. This time, he wore a light green polo shirt with some irregular dark spots down the front. His hands were folded across his stomach. The skin on two knuckles was torn and bleeding.

Her eyes traveled up to that strong neck set on broad shoulders and the pale gray eyes. A cut, swollen lip was the obvious source of the blood spots on his shirt. He was smiling a charming, lopsided smile. There was blood on a few of his startlingly white teeth.

"What are you doing here?" She struggled to sit up, clutching the sheets to her chest.

"Hmmm?"

"Why are you here?"

"Lord Byron said, um, useless to inquire? Can't remember." His eyes danced around, not quite focusing. The words slurred a bit.

"I thought you said you don't really get drunk."

"I was prevacinating. Precavitating?" He chuckled. The grin widened, and a drop of blood ran down his chin. When he turned his head to look at a passerby in the hall, she saw blood in his hair and on the side of his neck.

"Prevaricating?"

"Yup. That word."

"You frigging idiot! Were you in a fight? What are you doing here?"

He looked around the room and back at her. He seemed puzzled. "Um." He paused. "I like this chair?" He patted the arm of the noisy chair. The words ran together, and he said share, not chair.

She tried to think of a good insult. She wanted to be mad. But there was something more to this guy than the usual 'I am better than you will ever be' attitude. He seemed to actually care. Or was that just wishful thinking? Of course it was. Why would anyone care about her?

"What are you doing here?" she said, enunciating slowly.

There was a long pause. He bobbed his head in time to some song only he was hearing. "I do not know. No, I do not. Nope." He spoke slowly, leaving a beat between each word, as she had. His eyes smiled.

"You seem to be injured."

He raised a hand to his head. "Yes." A slight slur to the word. Another lengthy pause. "Not too bad."

"You should be getting that cleaned up and examined."

"Oh." They stared at each other. His eyes cleared and focused a bit. "Oh," he said again, still speaking slowly. There was another long pause. "I guess I just came down here. Didn't I?"

"How would I know, numbskull."

He smiled a little. "Not really numb. Kind of hurts."

"Oh, for God's sake!" She was both amused and exasperated.

There were footsteps in the hall, and Dr. Moussa came in.

"Here you are! Honestly, Rick, you are a pain in the butt. You were supposed to be getting that cement head of yours examined."

"I'm alright, Mo." He touched the wound on his head and winced. "I just wanted, um, I wanted, uh. See, she doesn't have any fumbly," he laughed. "I mean *family* here, just her great uncle all the way up in Juniper Springs. I was just, um."

"You are drunk, and probably concussed. Get your skinny ass out of that chair and down to Radiology right now! I want to go home. I'm driving, remember? Did you say Juniper Springs? That's your hometown."

"Uh, huh. Hers, too. Sorry. I'll go now." He rose from the chair, slightly unsteady but not as confused as he had seemed a few minutes ago. "Good night, Dr. July Marie Kozlowski SSSullivan." He gave a little wave.

Dr. Moussa stood watching to ensure that he went on down the hall, then turned to July. "I'm sorry. He is a good man and a good friend, but sort of...," he shrugged.

"I knew his younger brother but don't really remember him. What happened to him?"

"Oh, too many drinks, as you observed. A couple of guys got into a fight, and Rick finished it for them, but one hit him with a heavy beer mug."

"A police captain involved in a brawl? That doesn't sound normal. What kind of policeman gets in fistfights?"

"A difficult one. Rick is a fighter by nature. I kid him that it's his Apache side coming out. Maybe he is using his fists as a version of counting coup like the Plains Indians did. But he's largely forgiven for it because he never starts it, so LCPD keeps him working."

"Is he going to be okay? I mean, hit with a beer mug?"

"Well, I have been patching Rick up for twenty-some years. I imagine that he will be fine. He has had much, much worse injuries." He paused.

"What?"

He shook his head.

"He drinks too much. I could smell it on him the other night, too. Self-medicating?"

Mo nodded. "Don't worry. I take good care of him. My wife used to be a nurse here. If he doesn't do what I say, she will bully him into it. Well, good night, Dr. Sullivan. I will see you tomorrow."

July lay quiet with her eyes closed, again trying not to cry, trying to figure out where all the tears came from in a woman who had almost never cried. What was happening to her? Even that terrible, scarring attack when she was in med school didn't make her cry very much. Men. It was always men that hurt her, wielding their power like a club. She tried not to hate alpha males like Rick Mora. It was hard, but much to her surprise, listening to Rick the Cop breathing was calming, kind of peaceful, and even reassuring. She snorted. It was probably some kind of psychological trap. Good cop-bad cop all in one person.

Chapter 6

It was noon of her fourth day in the hospital before he showed up again. July was playing games on her phone, struggling a little bit with one eye that was still healing. "Gaah," she said, frustrated.

"What's wrong?"

"Oh, this game. I swear there is no word that fits in these blanks. I have tried every combination. I think they are making up words."

"Let me see." He took her phone, and smiled. "G."

"What?"

"Starts with G."

"Gliber. Gilber. G what?"

"Ge. Cute and furry."

"Ge. Oh! Gerbil. I must be brain dead."

The skin around his eyes crinkled in what looked like amusement.

She was exasperated with herself and annoyed with him for seeing the answer so quickly. July gave him a cranky look. Above highly polished, black ostrich leather boots, Rick wore an immaculate, blue pin-striped suit that fit him perfectly. Heavy gold cuff links with a matching tie bar made him look more like a banker or a politician than a cop. Except for the still slightly swollen lip and the scars, he was the picture of powerful and oh so very entitled masculinity.

July sneered, covering her discomfort. "Pretty suit on a hot Spring day? Trying to impress the gangsters into surrendering?"

"I have a funeral to go to, to sing the *Ave Maria*."

She regarded him with suspicion. "Oh. Must be for some pretty highfalutin' person if a former cowboy from Juniper Springs gets out the gold jewelry."

"Are you always such a rude, thoughtless little monster? It's a funeral for a six-year-old friend who was very important to many people. I guess you could call that highfaluting, except you mean it to be insulting, diminishing. Shame on you. She was special."

July flushed pink, embarrassed. "I, I didn't think. Are you a good singer, then?""

"Obviously adequate to the task. Listen, girl. I may not be a regular guy. I specialize in being a mean son of a bitch. But that doesn't mean that I have no feelings. Don't be such an obnoxious little twit. Luke would be ashamed of you."

"I'm sorry. Really I am. It's just, you know, that elegant suit and all seems too nice for a policeman. I imagine big-time gangsters or Hollywood types dressing like that, not cops."

His lips twitched in a half-smile. "I have a good tailor. It's often wise not to look too much like a policeman. And for an ugly mug like me, good suits distract people from thinking I am just a thug, which of course, I am."

He cleared his throat. "Ah, I am sorry about the other night. It was inexcusable for me to disturb you like that." He looked at his feet, then up at her, his cheeks showing a reddish flush. For an instant, the arrogant, elegant cop looked sheepish.

"Well, at least it wasn't another boring night," she said.

He grinned a little. "I'm also sorry that all of this cancer stuff is happening, and I regret having to question you when you are under so much stress. It is my job, however, so if you think you can answer without too many four letter words?"

July nodded slightly. "I understand. I am sorry that I hit you. That was childish of me. What I don't understand is why you? Is questioning suspects normal activity for a captain?"

He sat in the noisy chair. "Well, no. Not necessarily. But this is a multi state investigation into clinic bombings, and, of course, this one was flat out murder. So, there is an element of political competition, especially because the FBI is involved. It falls in my lap because I want to protect my team from aggravation, and I don't want to expose a suspect who is ill to harassment, either. So, I kept you mostly to myself. Ready for some more questions?"

July nodded.

"It's about your husband."

"Ex husband."

"Yes. He is a miner?"

"No, he is an engineer. Works for a mining company."

"Engineer, mines, explosives?"

"Oh, for Pete's sake! He builds roads." She paused, annoyed. "I guess he would have access to explosives. But he is in South America, somewhere near Arequipa. I have not seen him in six years and hope I never do again."

"He doesn't come back to the States?"

"I don't know."

"Wouldn't he visit family or something? Friends from college? You both went to U of Texas?"

"Yes, we did. But his family is in Arequipa. Wife. Three kids. The family that he had before he married me. I suppose he still has them, but I wouldn't know."

"Oh." He looked away for a moment. Some husbands are jerks, and some wives are harlots. He knew all about that last one. Major infidelity is not all that unusual. Why was he so bothered by it?

But, he was protective toward this girl before. The last time was that day when he was home from Basic Training. She was still in pre-school. He had rescued her when she fell from her old horse. In return, she had bitten him and cussed him with every bad word she ever heard from the cowboys on her great uncle's ranch.

She noticed his hesitation. "Oh, it's okay. I realized pretty quickly that I was in love with the idea of family and not really in love with Randy." Rick understood all too well.

He shifted uncomfortably. The shallow wound in his shoulder was itching and burning. His head throbbed where the mug had struck. But both would heal up in a few days. If you get between two dudes in a fight, you get hit. And, it was entirely predictable that Charlie Wallace would target the kid, Eisenstein. Rick was glad that he was there in time to distract the jerk into shooting at him, ready for it and moving, instead of at his new detective. He focused back on what July was saying.

"It took me almost two years to catch on. I thought Randy was going there on business, and Clarise, his other wife, thought he was coming here on business. I should have figured it out. What a fool I am! Anyway, it doesn't make any sense for him to be involved. He would avoid me like the plague, I guarantee. Uncle Luke swore he would shoot Randy if he came near me again, and he meant it. I would rather have the asshole arrested for bigamy, except I divorced him. So, maybe he is not a bigamist anymore, unless he found another stupid woman to scam."

"So, what was your clue?"

"He finally admitted that he didn't want to have kids with me."

"Yeah," Rick said, mostly to himself. "I know about that problem." He cleared his throat, wondering why in the world he said that, not that it wasn't true. He noticed July staring at him. He stared back, counting those freckles scattered across her nose and cheeks.

"Well, you have been through a lot. I apologize for my annoying presence." He sighed very quietly. "I wish we could just leave you alone. Maybe we will, but you have to realize that circumstances mean you are on the list of persons of interest."

"Who is we?"

He looked out the window, but all he could see in this light was his own reflection. The deep lines in his face, and wrinkles around his eyes, were very evident. *I look like I am seventy-five, not forty-five. No wonder July called me an old cop.* "I don't know yet. I will probably assign Lieutenant Kincannon. He may want to talk to you, so please let him know where you will be. I will be unavailable for a few weeks, on vacation."

"Vacation. I have never been on a vacation," July said. "What would a fancy dressing cop from the sticks do on vacation? Take his trophy wife to New York for the Broadway shows? Maybe a week-end in St. Tropez with the yachting set? Meet the Queen for tea?"

He chuckled. "More like stocking shelves at the feed store, I'm afraid." He almost admitted that he needed to dry out, to get his drinking under control. It had gotten bad lately. He paused, unable at the moment to think what he needed to say, to ask. *Shit, I am exhausted. Somebody needs to hurry up and kill me before I do it myself.* He gathered his scattered thoughts.

"If it makes you feel more comfortable, we have a woman offi-cer who went through your personal effects. I only looked at books and your desk and computer stuff. We did not find anything incrimi-nating. I guess I won't see you again. I wish you would carefully consider what enemies you might have. It is possible that you were the actual target, not the clinic. There will continue to be security at your door here until you are ready to be discharged. Best of luck to you. I'll tell your Uncle Luke I saw you. Don't hit any more cops, okay?"

"Security? I don't need security."

"Really? There is a reason why you are in the hospital, the vic-tim of a crime, and as yet we do not know what that reason is."

He gave her a lopsided grin, hesitating a little, feeling that there was something else he should say, and wondering why he felt that way. There was nothing more. He was leaving, going home. She was leaving, going somewhere for treatment. What was the matter with him? He shrugged mentally and quietly left the room.

She listened to the uneven sound of his boots as he strode away down the hall. *I wonder why he limps like that.* Suddenly, the room seemed cold and empty. She realized that she had not returned his handkerchief. Crumpling it, July started to pitch it in the trash-can by her bed, but then smoothed its folds and looked at it more carefully. There was a white-on-white monogram in one corner, *M*, enclosed in a wreath of tiny, satin–stitched leaves. Some little wife must love him very much. She clutched the tear-dampened fabric, crying for what she never had, and probably never would.

Chapter 7

Then there was the funeral. Rick and his mother sat on either side of Sylvia Tapia, each holding one of her hands. Rick's niece, Grace, who called him Papa, sat on his other side with her grandfather. Rick tried to listen to the service, and accept. But he never truly understood faith, never truly believed that there was a purpose to a child's death. He rose on cue, as he had for so many funerals over the years, and stepped to the lectern.

The organist began, and Rick sang the *Ave Maria* in his beautiful baritone. When he reached the phrase *Dominus tecum,* it kicked him in the gut. He found himself trying to pray for the first time since he was a good little boy so long ago. He prayed that Claudia was with the God in which his parents and Sylvia believed so profoundly.

As Rick stepped down from the lectern, his little niece Grace piped up, "Papa, is Claudia an angel now?" The audience stirred with a few quiet titters.

"Yes she is, baby. Tonight we'll sit and look at the stars and wave at her."

"And sing her the rainbow song?"

"And sing her the rainbow song."

After the funeral, attended by many policemen who had worked with Carlos, Claudia's dad, Rick talked to his long-time friend, Chief of Police Eric Andersen, about maybe retiring, whether he was getting burned out. Should he just quit and get away from the streets? Eric tried to persuade him to apply for the Chief position.

"I don't like the politics, Eric. You know that. I'm a street cop. Besides, I am uneducated, and you have those college boys to pick from. Nah! I don't want a promotion."

Eric persisted. "You think about it, Rick. You're just tired. And now that you have little Gracie to worry about, you need to protect yourself, maybe step away from the grunt work. That was a close call when you took the bullet from Charlie Wallace. I know you were trying to protect Eisenstein, but you take so many risks, Rick. There are way too many people who would like to dump your body in the Rio. I am not going to forget about it. You may not have a degree, but you are way smarter and more knowledgeable than me. I will submit your name because it's only a few months until I retire. You are our local hero, and we want to promote from within. You know that is an important policy in Las Cruces."

Rick just smiled, "Local hero? More like the poster boy for Jerk of the Year." He made the gag me with a spoon gesture they had shared when Eric was his sergeant twenty years ago.

Rick signed off on necessary paperwork and left the rest to Kincannon. Charlie Wallace had lived, so there was only a cursory investigation. He took the stairs down. Before he even reached the back door, he could feel the heat radiating through the west-facing metal door and knew the brass handle would be hot. It had sure heated up early this year. He reached into his pocket for a handkerchief to protect his hand, thinking of the one he had left with July, then smiled to himself. She amused him.

Little Doctor Sullivan seemed too young to be practicing medicine, even though she must be, what was it? Thirty two? Rick liked her defiant behavior. After so many years as a policeman, his instincts about whether someone was lying to him were good. She was not lying.

He kind of wished that he could stick with her case. Rick had a niggling feeling that she was the target, and she was still his friend Luke's precious little girl, grown now or not. He turned over what he had learned about the case, looking for a clue, for what was missing or out of place. He would let it simmer and call Rory if something important popped up. Someone had put that bomb in her briefcase. Why July Sullivan? Why that particular clinic?

He remembered telling her that he had few friends, and it bothered him. That had always been true. He learned not to mind too much, but he realized how it might look to her. Here he was, a healthy, successful, middle-aged man with what? No wife, no girlfriend, few friends at all, some terrible habits, and lots of enemies. It seemed more like the description of a serial killer than a policeman.

Oh, there was Mo Moussa. Mo had patched Rick up for so long that they were now friends. And Lieutenant Quintana, whom everyone just called Q, was another. He and Q were stationed together, teenage soldiers in the Middle East. There was also Sharon Reynolds. She was a music teacher at Madison High.

Rick and Q were amateur musicians. They played together pretty well, eventually forming a trio with Sharon, performing for charity events and their own amusement. But other than that he really wasn't very close to anyone, just his folks, their neighbor, old Luke Kozlowski, and Grace, back home in Juniper Springs.

Rick never made friends easily. His mixed heritage, leading to insults like Half-breed or Crazy Horse, had hurt, limiting his options when he was young. Now, it was his own behavior that limited those same options. These days, his partial native heritage would be an advantage in some social circles. But raised white, as his father was, he knew next to nothing about the Apache side of their family, nor did he care. What did it matter now, in his middle years? Too late. Too late for lots of things.

He remembered a few stories from Grandmother Mora when he was small. And he had read old newspaper clippings about his grandfather, Iron Horse, a much decorated hero of World War I. That was all. There was no tribal tradition, no clan brothers to fall back on. Except for the few hours a week spent with his folks and little Grace, or a music session with Sharon and Q, it was a solitary life.

Still, what he had told July was true. In his position, it didn't pay to have many friends. The law must be enforced as equally as possible, not influenced by personal concerns or friendships.

Suddenly, inexplicably, he didn't want little July Kozlowski Sullivan to see him in such a negative light. He wanted something else, but he wasn't sure what. Was it to seem like a nice guy, which he was not? He dropped the thought. "Getting old and maudlin," he muttered. "Old before my time."

Rick slipped on his aviator-style sunglasses and used the folded handkerchief to push the lever handle on the door before stepping out into the oven heat of the parking lot. He drew a breath of asphalt scented air and strode quickly to his truck, a glob of hot tar sticking to the sole of his boot.

Even protected from direct sunlight by the solar panels forming the parking area roof, the forty-five-year-old Ford pickup was meltingly hot inside. He reached in and started the motor, giving the air conditioning a minute to blow the worst of the heat out. He gazed idly at the tan brick police headquarters building, wondering if he would return. It was battered, streaked with gray where the rain gutters had leaked. He chuckled a little. He was battered and worn and gray streaked, just like it was.

He uncapped the pint of bourbon he illegally kept in the truck, taking a sip. Twenty six long years a cop, if you counted the three as an Army MP. Too long? There were times when it seemed that he had lost his soul in the pursuit of a justice that too often was not just. The mindless work of loading hay bales and stacking feed sacks at the family farm store would do him good. He took a couple of long pulls on his flask.

The old truck slipped smoothly into gear as he merged with traffic, validating his skill as an amateur mechanic. Accelerating onto the freeway, he quickly reached the speed limit and was sorely tempted to put the pedal to the metal. A glance in the rear-view mirror showed a sedan with the heavy black grill guard characterizing local patrol cars.

Rick smiled to himself, remembering the youthful temptation of trying to outrun the deputies. He had managed to do it once. But he was also caught twice, jailed, and the last time his classic and precious, '32 Chevy coupe was confiscated. That, and more than six rough months in the county jail with some very dangerous adult cellmates, mostly cured him. He knew very well what might happen to Gordo Tapia in lockup because it had all happened to him.

He started to signal a turn toward the hospital and quickly corrected himself. There was nothing much he could do for little Doctor Sullivan. He clicked his Bluetooth on. "Mo, about Dr. Sullivan. She still there? I am a little uncomfortable with her situation. She might have been the target of that bomb. She's leaving Tuesday? Would you let Kincannon know when? Just to be sure no one follows her, you know? And on your rounds tonight, will you ask her, in your subtle way, whether there have been any calls or visitors that alarmed her? Yeah, I knew her a little bit when she was small. She doesn't remember me, though. She was a pesky little brat. Still is!" They both laughed.

Blazing heat followed him all the way to the river. Even the prickly pear cactus shriveled during prolonged droughts like this one. But today, clouds showed above the rim of the mesa. He crossed the bridge, tires rumbling over concrete seams, and smoothly maneuvered the winding road to the top. The air grew dramatically cooler as he climbed higher.

Topping out on the long, level surface of the high desert mesa, Rick could see that the clouds were working up to a thunderstorm. White tops billowed upward as each cloud's flat base grew darker and darker, moisture seeming to suck in the afternoon light.

Rick rolled down the window, shutting off the air conditioner. Fresh air scented by tiny yellow blossoms of creosote bushes washed him clean of worries for the moment. He straightened his shoulders, singing a loud baritone version of an old song about tumbleweeds tumbling down a trail.

A few hours later, Rick wheeled into the parking lot of the family store. Rain had come and gone. The air smelled of damp pines.

Puddles in the graveled lot reflected the blue of a clearing sky. He couldn't help but track a little mud onto the worn wooden floor of the covered porch.

"Mom? Dad?"

The cash register, his mother's usual haunt, was unmanned. He walked toward the rear, finding a customer examining labels on dog food sacks.

"Hey, Rique! *Como le va,* man?'"

"Good. Taking a break to help out here, Joe. How about you?"

"Gotta find something with no corn. My little pooch throws up anything with corn."

"Mom will know. Have you seen her?"

"I heard her yelling at your dad out back," Joe grinned. Everyone knew that Rick's mom often yelled at his dad, or at Rick for that matter.

"Let me get her in here to help you, Joe."

"Glad you are back, man. I mean, even though you're, you know, kind of a rough guy, you are a lot better man than your brother. And that bitch Cindy told my mom that she would get you back, now that her Hollywood whatever left her, because you want your house back."

Rick blinked in surprise. "Geez! Well, that's not happening! The whole idea of my house is ruined by her living in it all this time. Contaminated!" Rick grinned, but decided it was not the time to discuss his ex. He gave Joe a friendly punch on the shoulder, and went out the back door.

Gisele, Rick's gray haired fireplug of a mother stood, hands on hips, criticizing the way his dad was folding the tarps used to protect hay bales from the recent rain. "Rafael, leave that for the employees to do. You'll strain your back."

"I'll do that, Dad."

His mother wheeled around, starting to smile, but then caught herself, and scowling, said, "Not in those good clothes, you won't." She looked more closely. "Enrique, you are bleeding on that nice shirt."

"Yes, ma'am. I bumped it, and it's bleeding through the bandage. I'll change. Hop down, Dad. You guys have customers waiting."

He winked at his father and walked out through the hay yard's chain link gates to his truck. In a few minutes, he had changed to faded jeans, tee shirt and work boots. His dad was waiting for him, sitting on a bale.

"You sure about this, son? How do these long vacations affect your job?"

Rick plopped down beside him, stretching out his legs with a sigh. "Well, I'm as high in the line as I can go. I just need to make it through two more years. Then I'll have my twenty-five in with the city, and Gracie's future will be secure. Don't worry about it. I don't."

Rafael regarded his son with a wrinkled brow and sad eyes. "But that is your retirement money you are talking about, son. Won't you need it?"

Rick shrugged. "You know, I probably used up my nine lives long ago. You need to accept that I might not make it to retirement. It's okay, Dad. I chose this career knowing the risks I would face. It's not the common criminals. It's doing battle with corruption and the Old Guard that is such a risky business. I feel like they are closing in on me. They may win the war someday, but I am winning the battles for now."

"Enrique, why don't you quit? You have so many talents. You could build houses or be a cabinetmaker, or run the store. We have all that great grazing land, and you were always a good cowboy as a youngster. You could raise a pretty good herd on that land. Your mom and I can afford Grace's education, at least some of it. After all, if we have to sell the store someday, what else would we use the money for, eh? It doesn't all need to be on your shoulders. You deserve a better life."

"Dad, we've talked about this before. I am good at what I do. Very good. What more can any man ask of life? Remember when we used to read *Horatius at the Bridge* together? That poem sums it up. It doesn't matter if my death 'cometh soon or late' because

I am making a difference. It's just how things are. I have survived four attempts to kill me, so let's just be happy about that, okay?" He put a hand on his father's bony shoulder. "One day, Dad, they will succeed, and you will need to explain to our Gracie why her Papa Rick doesn't come home anymore. Besides, if I were building houses or herding cattle, I'd die of boredom." He grinned. "Come on. I need some exercise. You know, it might be better to roll these tarps."

Rafael gave his oldest boy a trace of a smile. "Good idea, son. I have been leaving a lot of the outdoor work to the young kids, the stuff that your brother used to do. I am glad that he is in Bahrain or wherever. I wish he were away from here permanently. I haven't wanted to say anything to you about him on your days off, but it is too small a town for his behavior not to affect our business." He shook his head sadly. "Don't tell your mother that I said that. She knows, of course, but we avoid the subject."

"That bad?"

His dad nodded his head.

Rick blew out a breath. "Well, is Buddy planning on staying in the Army? Did he re-enlist?"

"Seems so. We don't really know. He doesn't communicate with us anymore. Haven't heard from him in six months, maybe more."

"And I never ask about him either. I'm not much as a big brother, am I? Not so good at being a son, either. Buddy needs to stay away from here, for his sake and Gracie's, too. I'm sorry that I don't spend more time up here. I will change that if I can."

"Hey, I can still lift a bale! You worry about yourself. I can manage quite well. Really, Enrique, I can."

"I am sure you can, Dad, but after all, you are running toward seventy now. Maybe we will have you with us longer if you can get a break now and then, eh? What would Mom do without you? For that matter, she should take a break, too. We will work on that, okay? Come on. Let's roll these tarps."

"It will make your shoulder bleed more. What did you do?"

"Grazed by a shot a few days ago, just after Claudia...," he paused, sighing heavily. "It bleeds every time it gets a little bump. Bad location. But I got the guy, Claudia's killer. It's okay. Shallow wound is all."

Dinner that night was the same as ever at the Mora house. Gisele had never taken much time to learn how to cook, preferring to spend any free time with her needlework. Rick's appetite was not up to par, given the selection.

"Eat up, son. You are going to need your strength."

"I'm kind of tired, Mom. I need to figure out where to stay this time, get some more jeans and work shirts, and stuff like that."

"Why won't you ever stay here?"

"I'm used to being alone. Don't think I can sleep with anyone else in the house anymore."

"Not even a girlfriend?" Of course, everyone in this small town knew about his reputation for hard-living, and even as a kid, he attracted the girls.

"No, ma'am. Not even a girlfriend."

Rick's mother sighed. "Then, I guess we won't have any grand-kids from you. Such a shame. You would be a great father. You are so good with little Gracie, and she loves you so much."

Rick had taken on the financial, and much of the emotional, role of father to little Graciela, and he loved her as though she were his own daughter. He was glad Buddy deployed to the Middle East. If he had known, at the time, that his younger brother got fifteen year old Maureen pregnant, Rick would have made sure that Buddy was arrested and prosecuted for statutory rape.

"He got another girl pregnant when he was home on leave last time. We didn't even get a chance at keeping the baby. Two potential grandkids right here in town, and none for us. We didn't want to tell you."

Instantaneous rage boiled up, the anger he still struggled to control after all these years of trying. He leaped from his chair, fists clenched, eyes burning. "That fucking...."

Rafael slapped the table with a calloused hand. "Enough! Watch your language, boy."

"Yes, sir. Sorry, Mom. Geez! What happened to the baby?" He was so angry that he almost choked on the words. There was a burning in his stomach, like a worm eating at his guts. Why did his good, honest, hard-working parents end up with a couple of worthless sons like Buddy and himself?

"Buddy said that Roberta aborted the baby. He said she decided she couldn't raise it alone. I would have taken it, but Buddy told her we didn't want the poor little thing because of some medicine she was taking. He said the baby would not be normal." Tears shone in his mother's eyes.

Rafael took his wife's hand, squeezing it gently. "Gisele, honey, you know we are too old. We are too *old*. When the baby enters high school, I will be in my eighties. What kind of father could I be at that age? It wouldn't be right, *mi alma*. You know that."

"Why would he do such a horrible thing?" Rick asked. "Let his baby die without even discussing it with you? You mean Armando's sister, right? Roberta Tafoya? I didn't know she was sick."

"It was some medicine for her acne. Remember how red and swollen her face was all the time? It's what Buddy told us, and she left town real fast, so we were never sure. I hear she took a job at a resort down in Tucson or somewhere."

"Acne medicine causes birth defects?"

"That's what Buddy said."

"That little...." He drew back a fist, ready to punch the door, the wall, anything, but stopped, not wanting to remind his mother of his failings. She knew what a terrible, savage man he could be. She knew about all the times he faced discipline by his own police force, was required to take the anger management course or undergo psychological evaluations. He didn't want to remind her that her angry, difficult little boy had grown up to be a trickster, a shape-shifter, one moment the elegantly dressed, talented man appearing to be reasonable and cultured, and the next a rabid, fighting, killing coyote.

"Enrique, you are my hard-working, wonderful son. But, your temper! You have become so cold. For a long time, I have been afraid that you would hurt someone too badly. What would happen to you then, *mijo*? What would happen? You wouldn't live more than a few hours in jail. There are too many people who would pay a lot of money to have Captain Mora killed."

Rick took a few minutes to swallow his anger. He felt like there was a great black rock in his chest, its enormous weight pulling him down. "Sorry, Mom. You know that I would like to have kids. But I'd be an absentee parent a lot of the time. It's one reason why I can't have Gracie down in the city with me." He carefully didn't mention that he was afraid one or more of the people who had targeted him might hurt Grace instead.

"And, you would have to cut down on the drinking," she scolded.

"Yes. I would, Mom. I will try to cut down one of these days."

He rose from the table. "I'll do the dishes tonight. You all go on and watch *Antiques Road Show*. Is that still your favorite? I think I'll just sleep at the store tonight. Is the cot still in the storeroom?"

"Are you sure, Rick?"

"Yup. Go on now. I am used to doing dishes."

Rick slowly cleared the table, pondering his options. Six years ago, he came close to eating his gun, seeing no future that he wanted. Then, the birth of Gracie had given him purpose again. But some days, he wondered if it was worth it. He was so soul sick. It was harder and harder to put on the good son and kind Papa face when he knew that inside, he was just a crazy coyote, deserving to be shot on sight. Rick sighed. He loved his folks and Gracie, but every moment of every day, he knew he was unworthy of the love they returned so freely.

He couldn't think ahead very far. He and his dad had spent much of their money buying land in tax sales. Grace would have a decent inheritance, but college meant cash, not grass and timber. He didn't want to think about it, not any of it.

He ran hot water in the battered tin basin. It was years past time that he installed some more modern plumbing in this old kitchen. Washing the dishes, his thoughts strayed far away. He knew a dermatologist. Should he call July Sullivan? Ask about birth defects and acne medicines? In the end, he decided that it was too late to matter. Drying the dishes and putting them away kept his hands busy, but his mind went back to his marriage twenty-three years ago.

She was just a casual date for a few weekends. He had never meant for it to be more than that. But, when she told him she was pregnant, despite what he thought was careful use of protection, he quickly married Cindy out of respect for both of their families. Four months later, he learned that she lied about being pregnant. She laughed, unconcerned about her dishonesty.

Rick was furious that his life meant so little to her. He struggled with the madman inside of him to keep from hurting her in response. He could easily have killed her. That was when he started down the long, long road to becoming the hard, often intoxicated, philandering jerk that he was now. But quite a few women were happy to just screw with the tough cop. That was enough.

Down at the store, he put a handful of coffee in the basket of the old percolator, filling it with water, and set it on the hot plate to boil. From the porch, he would hear the *burp-burp* of the pot when the coffee was brewing.

Rick sat in the ladder-back chair on the covered porch, absent-mindedly playing a tune on his guitar. He tipped the chair back to hook his heels in the railing. The air was damp and fresh, almost too cool for the tee-shirt he was wearing. *Burp, burp. Burp, burp, burp.* It was sort of a musical sound. He slowly rose, meandering through the store to pour a mug of caffeine, lacing it with a dollop of bourbon for a nightcap. He stopped at the bulletin board next to the front door, idly perusing ads handwritten on cards, scraps of notebook paper, and pieces of napkin. There was one in pencil.

Small furnished cabin 3 miles N of town.
Pets okay. Contact Luke Kozlowski.

Rick pulled out his cell phone. "Luke? It's me, the cowboy who can't rope worth a damn." He laughed at Luke's profane reply. "Hey, is that old wreck of a cabin still standing?".... "How about letting me live in it and do some repairs for you? I am up here for a few weeks, maybe longer, to at the store. May I look at it tomorrow morning?

Sure, 7 a.m. is fine. Thanks."

Rick settled back on the porch, watching the shadows crawl slowly up the face of the mountain across the narrow valley, listening to birds settling into the big juniper tree as darkness took over. He relished the relative silence of the night. It was hard to imagine his future. Could he return to life here in his hometown? He loved the woods, the canyons, and all that beautiful land he and his dad had purchased. But he could not see himself as anything but a hard-working, efficient cop. Rick sighed. He had to admit that the power of his position, and the chance for a violent confrontation, were big parts of what kept him risking his life every day. It was not an admirable picture.

Gradually, the sky lightened again. A three-quarter moon rose, spilling silver light into the yard. Two coyotes trotted toward the dumpster, yacking and whispering to each other.

"Hey, you two! Go find your dinner someplace else!" He waved his coffee mug at them. They paused briefly, looking toward him, then turned back to the dumpster. Rick laughed and stood up. "Hey! Move it!" They trotted off, looking over their shoulders at him, tails held level with their well-fed bodies.

The encounter improved Rick's mood. He went to bed in the dusty storeroom, sleeping heavily until dawn woke the birds, and the birds woke him.

Chapter 8

It was terribly hard to sleep in the hospital. July never really appreciated what patients had to endure. The last time she was hospitalized, while she was in med school, she had been too traumatized to notice. But now she got it. If it wasn't the lights, it was the noise or the doctors bringing students and residents on rounds. It was pain, too. Pain from her fractured arm. Pain from her burned spots.

Worse was the fear. July felt an almost physical fear of the cancer eating away at her body and the lifestyle changes that she would have to endure, at least for the short run, if it was really a cancerous tumor. In her heart, she knew it was.

There was money, thank God. She had plenty of bucks socked away, so there would be no shortage. It would be hard to stay upbeat though. July didn't have any close friends anymore. The doctors and nurses she worked with had families that took up their spare time, so she had never socialized very much with the people from work. To be honest, she hesitated to get close to anyone. It was fear of emotional pain, rejection, humiliation that she had often experienced as the little red-haired runt from the backwoods. She hid that fear, even from herself, by working harder than her colleagues, always staying busy. Loose ends and idle time scared her.

"Gaah!" she said out loud, annoyed with herself.

There was the click of high heels in the hall, and blonde,

gorgeous, efficient Bebe Gauthier swept into the room, followed by the lady cop on duty. July smiled at the officer. "It's okay. She's my partner."

"*Bonjour, Cheri!* How are you?" The perfect smile behind perfectly carmined lips almost reached her eyes, but not quite. She looked over her shoulder at the retreating security before saying any more. Something about that hesitation bothered July, but she shrugged it off. *Getting paranoid. How silly is that?*

Bebe was a gem when it came to running the practice. All four dermatologists had about a teaspoonful of business knowledge between them. Bebe had managed her husband's elegant spa in New York, she said, until he became ill a couple of years ago, and they moved here to the desert for his health. She had stepped in and improved purchasing, hiring, patient flow, and pretty much everything else for the practice, leaving the doctors to doctor.

The only drawback was that she also pretty much disliked them all. July had not wanted to get involved with Bebe. There was something odd about her. But despite July's objections, the others had allowed her to put up one-fifth of the bucks when they incorporated, so Bebe was not only the manager but also a partner.

"I'm not so good, Bebe. It is going to be a while before I can practice again."

"Yes. I assumed so. The police sent some little...," she made a dismissive gesture. "The stupid girl was most bothersome, questioning all of us, questioning some of your patients, wanting to review our accounts to be sure there was no radical political group contributing funds to us."

"What?" July sat all the way up, burns, cast arm, and gasped with pain that silenced her momentarily.. "How dare they!" A cold lump of apprehension lay like a stone in her guts.

"Oh, yes, July. They are most persistent and most difficult to deal with, even for me." Her voice was sympathetic, but it could not disguise the contempt, maybe even hate, that July knew she had for her partners.

"Is there a detective named Mora involved?" July almost growled.

"Just the one detective, a girl."

July lay back down carefully, very conscious of the pain her sudden movement had caused.

"So, darling July, we had a corporate meeting. The little worm told us what she should not have. In addition to your wounds, you have cancer, too?"

July shrugged and nodded, exasperated and angry about the invasion of her privacy, confidential information bandied about without her permission. Could she sue the insurance company, she wondered? How had they found out about the cancer?

Bebe almost smiled, a cold, joyless grimace. "Anyway, you will have many big bills and not be working. So, we have bought out your share of the corporation. Here is the check. A big one, no?" Again, the almost smile. "Of course, *Cheri*, you understand that the practice cannot include a doctor who is investigated for a felony, eh? I brought a copy of the by-laws for you, just in case you do not remember the agreement."

It was as though July was enfolded in dense fog, and the things she valued, the things she had worked for, were slowly disappearing into the cold, gray mist.

Chapter 9

Luke Kozlowski remembered when the oldest Mora boy was an exceptional athlete and darned good horseman, helping out at the ranch from the time he was about ten. But he was also wild and hot-tempered. Every time he saw news stories about successful detective Enrique Mora down in the big city, it surprised him. These days, those silvery eyes in the brown face were even more startling than when Rick was young. Maybe because his face was leaner, bonier, sculptured by deep down, world-weary fatigue. He was still athletic, though. His chest and shoulders were broad and deep. Thick biceps stretched the fabric of shirt sleeves.

"Good morning, Luke." Rick extended a firm hand. "I saw your little niece, July, down in the city." He smiled at the older man, who never seemed to age much. He was a little more stooped than the time Rick had seen him a few months ago. Maybe his eyes were kind of rheumy, but he could still pass for a weathered sixty-five, even though eighty-something was probably closer to the truth.

"Rick, every time I see you, I wonder where that smart-ass, rough-neck kid has gone?"

"Worn down to a mere shadow of my former self, I guess."

"Heh, heh," Luke chuckled. "Always thought you would come around eventually. Too smart to let that temper control your opportunities. Did you catch that killer of the little girl? And how was July?"

"Oh, July is as full of vinegar as ever," Rick replied, not sure how much she had told her great uncle. "She didn't remember me, but she is still a pistol. Slapped me this time instead of biting me like she did when she was four. And we did catch the drive-by shooter. You remember that Wallace family from over in San Manuel? It was their oldest son, Charlie."

"Wallace? Man, that is sad! So, why did she slap you?"

"Because she is July Kozlowski and doesn't suffer fools lightly? Because she has a female version of a Napoleon Complex?"

Luke chuckled. "Well, come on in. You remember, I always meant to fix the place up, add a bedroom, and use it for an income producer, but I just haven't gotten around to it. So, it's kind of a mess." He pulled out an old skeleton key and fitted it into the rusty lock. It took some jiggling and fussing, but after a few minutes, the door swung open with a squeal of tired hinges.

The first thing Rick noticed was the smell of mice. Old country houses were always full of mice. There was probably a missing chink in the adobe mix that sealed gaps between the hand-hewn logs. He would find it and fix it. A lovely old propane cookstove proved to have a large packrat nest in the oven. They laughed at the startled and defiant expression of the nest's inhabitant when they opened the door. Tiny rat voices squeaked as momma hunkered down defensively.

"Don't worry, momma. I will move you and the babies to a safer place." Rick gently closed the oven. "I see there are a bunch of things to work on, Luke. Do you have any preferences for what I do first?"

"Hell, I don't care, son. I remember that beautiful house you remodeled before you married Cindy. You do whatever makes you comfortable. It will be better than it is now, no matter what you do. But, do you think you might have time to help me with my little gelding, Topper? I just got him, but I am moving a lot slower, and he is so smart and quick that he almost spooks me sometimes. You were always better with horses than I am."

"Okay. I am happy to do anything you need. Just point me in the right direction." They walked through ankle-high grass down to the barn.

"Geez, man! He is gorgeous." Rick approached the corral slowly. The two-year-old gelding, dun-colored hide gleaming in the sunshine, ran to the fence, sliding to a stop just before he would have smashed into it. His ears pointed toward Rick. Nostrils flared to pick up the scent of this unknown human. He circled the fence line, hooves throwing up divots of grass, and ran back through the gate, pulling up in front of Rick with a wet snort.

Rick laughed, wiping the horse snot from his arms and shirt. "We will get along fine, Topper. We'll be pals. Okay?"

"I got him for me, but I think he needs a younger hand. I'll give him to July. I sure wish she was still around. You, too. Kept me young. But everyone grows up sometime." He sighed a little.

"I think I've been gone too long," Rick said. "Maybe I need to stay, at least for a while. It seems like there are a lot of things I need to work on, and not just the cabin."

"But what about your job, boy?"

"Ah, you and my dad! I don't know, Luke. I am good at my job, but...," he shrugged and smiled. "Just a little case of burnout, I guess."

Chapter 10

Shirley Gambino tucked her long, wavy hair under the cap and put on the gray work shirt with 'Juan' stitched on the pocket, the tails hanging out. It was loose on her slender frame, hiding breasts and hips. She hoped she looked like a teenage boy taking his little brother to the park or something. It was important that no one recognize her. Someone was willing to kill her Ralph for some unimaginable reason. Could it be the clinic they hated so much, or was little Doctor Sullivan the target? Maybe it was one of the no-good members of her own family. She knew a few hated her and her brother, Abe.

There were all of those possibilities, but Shirley doubted most of them. She thought she knew who planted the bomb, and she was afraid the guilty one knew that she knew. As Shirley rolled across the lawn, escaping the fire, she saw a movement out of the corner of her eye. A tall lady with gray hair was hurrying from the back of the building, her black orthopedic shoes glaringly obvious and out of place on that hot Spring day. When the bomb went off, the lady did not flinch or look around as everyone else did, and she had looked right at Shirley.

"I know Mrs. Winter saw me at the clinic before," Shirley told her brother. "Will she come after us? She put that explosive in the room with Ralphie and Dr. Sullivan. She is not afraid to kill us!"

"Are you sure it is the same lady? You didn't see much of her face from that angle," Abe questioned. "And what would be her motive?"

"I humiliated her husband, and people laughed at him. I know her face was kind of a blur there in the shade of the trees, but I was in the sun, and she looked straight at me! And, where was Mr. Winter? A few minutes before, he was right there by the front door. But when the bomb went off, he was gone. Was he driving the get-away car?"

"You might be right. She could be dangerous. Why not talk to the police? I know this detective, a good guy. He looks mean, but he is fair. He is the one who proved I was not involved in that robbery the cousins pulled. Here's his card. You call him. I got you one of those throw-away phones. Okay?"

"Okay." She took the card. In black print on a cream background, it said *Enrique 'Rick' Mora,* and gave a phone number with an extension. She would call the detective. Really, she would. But not today. Abe's girlfriend, Sheena, had promised to share babysitting with her. So today, she had to find a new job. The carwash down the street was always hiring.

The baby stroller was gone, of course, burned up in the fire. She traded her old cell phone for a rusty red wagon. Even though it was unlikely anyone would recognize her, her heart pounded in fear as she and Ralphie left their new apartment, the one Abe found for her.

She walked up to the window at the car wash and tapped on the glass. "Hey, mister. Got any openings? I am a real hard worker, and I have a reference from my previous employer. I have a regular babysitter, too. I won't have to miss any shifts."

The man stared at her for a minute. "Can you lift that garbage can over there?"

Shirley stepped up to the can, and keeping her back straight, bent her knees to lift the heavy can, just like they show you to do in those workplace safety videos.

The man grunted. "You almost fooled me, kid. Here, take the application and bring it back tomorrow. Come dressed for work, with your own shirt tucked in, and jeans or shorts just above the knee. None of that hot pants stuff, okay? You don't have to dress like a boy. No one here will bother you. Got it?"

Shirley nodded eagerly and turned away, clutching the paper tightly.

"Hey, girl! Don't you want to know what we pay?"

"No, sir. I know it's minimum wage, but I can walk to work and don't need a fancy wardrobe, so it is good for me. I just have to work really hard and get promoted to Crew Leader. You'll see. I'll do it!"

He laughed. "Hey, Bobby, get your crew in gear. Your customer is raring to go." Under his breath, he said, "I think I am just about to hire your replacement."

Chapter 11

A hard lump in July's throat seemed to be cutting off her breath. She knew that it was an esophageal spasm brought on by her anxiety over being cut out of the partnership. But it still felt like she had swallowed a volleyball.

The loss of her practice left July so devastated that she could barely think. Step-by-step, she told herself. Step-by-step. Concentrate my energy, just like the detective said. First, work on the tumor. Make appointments? No. First, call home to the ranch.

"Uncle Luke? It's July. How are you? Well, I am not real good. Yeah, I got hurt in an accident. It's kind of bad. But it looks like I might have a little cancer, too. Can I use the ranch as my base for a few months? I am not sure what therapy protocol we will follow. Might need surgery and radiation or chemotherapy or all three, and kind of sick in between. I will be glad to have fresh air, but I want to get out with the cattle, too, if I can. Will you bring my horses down from the pasture? And, of course, I want to experiment with some new cookie recipes."

"Cookies! I have missed those cookies. When are you coming up, honey?"

"I think I need to get my first treatments out of the way, so maybe the end of June. I will keep you posted. I love you, Uncle Luke!"

About lunchtime, Dr. Moussa appeared. "Sorry to keep you waiting. It was a busy morning." He removed the temporary cast and examined his handiwork. Everything was as good as could be expected. He built a new cast around the arm.

"Have you lived here in Cruces long, Dr. Moussa?"

"Thirty years, almost. What do you need?"

"My old Volvo is probably a goner. Can't drive it with my right arm in this cast anyway since it's a stick shift. Do you know a reliable person who could find me a good used car?"

He smiled. "Of course!" He punched in a number. "Yousef, I want you to find the perfect car for this lady. She needs...," he relayed July's preferences.

"Yes? Let me ask her. A Honda Element? Is that the boxy one that looks like the offspring of two Land Rovers? And it gets good mileage? Ah, she is nodding. Can you bring it over here tomorrow for her approval? I am releasing her at 10 a.m. Okay." He ended with a rattle of words in some other language.

"Sorry. Yousef is my eldest son. We speak Arabic at home. That is one of the things that drew Captain Mora and me together. Yousef will give you a bargain price. If you don't like this car, he will find what you do like, and give you a loaner while he looks. He is a wealthy entrepreneur, that boy. He could buy and sell his old doctor dad. Only in America!"

"Captain Mora speaks Arabic?"

"Oh yes, almost as well as I do. Rick is a brilliant man." He patted her good shoulder and was gone.

Brilliant? Rick the Cop must have some good points to be so admired by a nice guy like Dr. Moussa. He sure hadn't shown many admirable qualities as far as she could see..

July gently touched the gravel burn around her right eye. The skin was rough and scabby but not too painful now. Most importantly, she could see out of it quite clearly. The burns were uncomfortable, but not too bad. The main pain came from her arm, and pills were helping with that. She would have to skip the morning dose in order to be able to drive her new car all the way to the big city. That might be a real challenge.

Chapter 12

Rick was there to help his dad open the store. How surprised his grandmother would have been to see all these new products in the building she and her husband built so long ago. They even had pre-fab chicken coops now. The work was good for him, taking care of customers or doing things with Grace during the day. His little niece didn't know anything about her biological father. As far as she was concerned, her papa was Rick.

Once he settled in Luke's cabin, Rick had Gracie, his parents, and Luke for dinner every night. After a few days, Luke suggested that they all just eat in his big kitchen. Rick loved it. Dreading the day when his vacation would be over, and he would return to being himself, he reveled in being Papa and son for a while.

Rick and Grace played with Topper, teaching him to wear the halter he should have learned about as a baby and how to follow Rick's lead. They played games in Luke's big old house, Rick pretending to be Spiderman, springing on and off porch rails, and swinging from the open beams for Gracie's amusement. Sometimes, he swept her up and ran to the top of the stairs. Holding her on his lap, they slid down the long banister, Grace laughing madly all the way. After dark, they sat on the porch, rocking and visiting, Rick and Grace in the big old porch swing until she fell asleep, and the grandparents took her home to bed.

Luke watched how his friend held the child close, cherishing and protective, but not smothering her with attention. "You either need a woman or a cat, boy. Something to cuddle."

Rick just snorted. "No woman in my life, and no cats. I spend my evenings working or working out or drinking. No place for a woman or cats. I wish I could be a real father to Grace, but my dad and her other grandpa are doing a good job, and my life is too dangerous to have her live with me. I know Sylvia Tapia would help care for her when I'm at work, but after what happened to Claudia, I can't risk it. Besides, I am really not a nice guy. When I'm up here, I try to be the man my folks would want me to be, but the rest of the time? Hell, man, I kill people."

His hands rubbed together in an unconscious washing motion. It was quiet for a few minutes. Then Rick grinned at the older man. "Nice try at domesticating me."

But he sometimes wished that he were a different kind of man. If he were not such a damned crazy coyote, if he had another job, if there were someone... *Aaah, if, if, if! I am getting to be an old fool!* And, in the back of his mind floated an image of strawberry blonde eyelashes .

As he walked back to the cabin, hopping from stone to stone across the stream, Rick called Dr. Moussa. "Hey, Mo, you know that little Doctor Sullivan? Where did she go for treatments?"

"Albuquerque. I have her cell number if you need to talk to her, Rick."

"Good. She should be safer there. I, uh, just wanted to be sure she was out of Cruces. We still don't know if she was the target of that bombing, and, uh. Never mind. Just checking."

Mo chuckled. "Imagine Rick Mora wanting to know what that pretty little doctor is doing. You are so darn pitiful, man! I wish you would get a life. Or, a wife."

"Oh, shut up, Mo."

Chapter 13

Shirley's friend Sheena did her best to cut Shirley's long brown hair. "Oh, my God, Shirl! It looks awful! I am so sorry," Sheena moaned. But Shirley's brother, Abe, was laughing. Shirley peeked in the mirror. It was perfect. Kind of a raggedy pixie cut. It reminded her of an old Audrey Hepburn movie. No one would recognize her.

"Gotta go, guys. Can't be late for work!"

It took exactly five minutes for her to get to the car wash. Shirley loved the work. She took great pride in making things look nice. By week three, Shirley was the Crew Leader. Clyde was delighted that the crew members were working more quickly and efficiently with her cheerful encouragement.

"Hey, Shirl! See that car coming in the driveway? They are a real problem. The old guy is always threatening lawsuits and stuff. Be extra attentive to them, okay?"

Shirley nodded, hurrying to greet the driver as he stepped out of the car. But, as he unfolded from the driver's seat, she froze in terror. It was Mr. Winter and his wife. Fortunately, they barely looked at her as they got out of the car, reaching back in for her purse and his briefcase. Thinking fast, Shirley pulled her cap down over her forehead and jammed her sunglasses onto her face.

"Good morning, sir," she squeaked in as high a voice as she could manage. "Will you want the Executive Package today?"

Mr. Winter looked at her suspiciously. "No. I don't want any of that foofaraw. It's a rip-off! Are you new here?" Shirley nodded. "I am watching you, girl. Set no vain hopes on robbery. No thieves will inherit the Kingdom of God!"

"Yes, sir." One of the verses her father had made her memorize popped into her mind. "Treasures gained by wickedness do not profit," Shirley squeaked.

"What?"

"Proverbs 10:2, sir."

Mrs. Winter laughed. "Just give her the keys before she shows you up for the fool you are." But Mrs. Winter tipped her head, examining Shirley intently.

The crew gave the car the Professional Package quickly, with Shirley surreptitiously watching the Winters the whole time. As she approached the office, keys in hand, she heard Mr. Winter saying, "I am sure I have seen her before."

Clyde replied, trying to rein in his sarcasm, "Well, we only have a few million people here in the valley. So, you may have seen her somewhere. But I imagine that you are mistaken. She looks kind of like Audrey Hepburn. Maybe you saw some old movie, and that is what you are remembering." He smiled.

"What did they ask, Clyde?"

"Asked your name." He saw the fear in her eyes. "You got a record?" She shook her head. "Cops after you?" She shook her head again. "Don't worry. I think the old fart is scary, too. I told him that you are my niece, Sophia Zobel. Okay?"

"Thanks. It's just that he threatened my son and me when all we were doing was going to the clinic for a regular doctor's visit." She did not mention that she believed Mrs. Winter had tried to kill her son.

"Don't worry. I won't let him hurt you while you are here."

"Thanks, Clyde." She said no more. Shirley didn't want Clyde to know that it was Mrs. Winter she feared. She decided that she had better take a long, winding route home, just in case. Maybe it was time to call her brother's cop friend, but what real evidence did she have? None. Yet.

Chapter 14

After that long drive, July was tired and in pain. Albuquerque was even hotter on this early summer day than she remembered. Her hotel was immediately across from the parking garage. She pulled up to the valet park and noticed that the young man standing patiently waiting by the driver's door was wearing white cotton gloves.

She smiled at the fellow. "Burned your fingers?"

"Yes, ma'am. Too many times. Are you for the Cancer Center or the hotel?"

"Hotel first." She wilted against the side of the car for a moment, watching the bell girl trotting toward her. In a moment, she was checked in and resting.

Waking after dark, July slowly made her way downstairs. Dinner was a good one in the hotel dining room, and there was a mildly interesting TV movie to distract her from her pain and fear. When her wake-up call came, she was already up and dressed.

The oncologist was competent enough, but July instantly disliked him. Maybe it was the slightly condescending tone. Perhaps it was his hundred dollar haircut and the immaculate, never rumpled, 'I am a doctor' lab coat. She had expected some collegiality between doctors. After all, they had most of the same training, and she was near the top in her field. But no. Again, it was a man addressing her as though she was mentally incapacitated, less than he was, inferior. Nevertheless, he seemed very much on top of what needed doing.

There would be plenty of time to think during the next couple of weeks while they waited to see how well the protocol worked, time to think about the future. Would she find another practice to join? Should she stay to help Uncle Luke with the ranch and forget being a doctor? Who could have bombed the clinic? Was it even possible that someone was actually trying to kill her? Could there be someone out there who hated her enough that they were willing to treat little Ralphie as collateral damage?

July woke several times during the night. At one a.m., sitting looking out at the night, she found herself wishing that the annoying detective was around. The silence and loneliness of an unknown future were beginning to get to her already. It was so much easier to do verbal battle with the boozing, brawling cop than to deal with the sneaky cancer cells hiding deep in her body. She remembered the feel of those warm brown hands and realized, not for the first time, how alone she had always been. Alone and often afraid, although she worked hard not to show it. *Oh, for God's sake. I don't need a man, and that cop is a drunk. What's the matter with me?* She snapped on the TV, looking for a distraction.

At the treatment center, the patients already waiting made her feel a little uneasy. They looked so pale and drawn. She sat near a gray-faced woman wearing a colorful turban on her bald head. In a few minutes, the woman turned to July and struck up a conversation. "I am Lupita. Now, tell me about yourself."

July hardly knew how to begin, but under the kind questioning, she began to relax. It seemed like just a few minutes until she was called back to undergo her first round of testing. The technicians were quick and competent, passing her from one testing unit to the next with minimal waiting. It would be a day or two before they had all the results for the doctor to review.

July had a light lunch of melon and seared scallops in the garden cafe on the hotel's top floor. From there, she could look out into the shimmering heat and the distant range of mountains where she grew up. She wondered what Uncle Luke was doing today on the far side of the peaks. And, she wondered if Captain Mora was there doing what? Scaring customers away from his parent's store? July snorted in amusement.

At loose ends for the afternoon, she walked over to Trader Joe's for some organic snacks, but the heat and the pain in her arm were exhausting. By the time she got back to the hotel, she was in pretty bad shape. Gloria, the bell girl, rescued her, taking her bag, turning down the bed, making sure she had a carafe of ice water.

July smiled her thanks and was soon asleep. She woke as the sun was setting and sat looking at the city beneath her window. What Captain Mora said about her being the intended victim of the bomb stuck in the back of her mind. The extended hotel visit would be the ideal time for a little research. She opened her laptop and searched for the Las Cruces Police Department's phone number. There was a robot directory. She punched in mora.

"Major Crimes."

"I'm sorry. I was calling for Detective Mora."

"Captain Mora is on leave. How can I help you? Do you have a crime to report?"

"No, it's a personal issue. I just really need to talk to him soon. Do you have his number?"

"I cannot give that out." He paused for a moment. She heard fading voices in the background and a door closing.

He came back on the line. "You are the third Badge Bunny this week to call the Captain on 'personal business.' I don't know what you ladies see in that ill-tempered cold fish. You know, he never gives you gals the time of day until he gets a buzz on, and then all sudden, you all think he's some great conquest. If you ever saw what a mean, dangerous, son-of-a-bitch he really is, you would be running like, umm, bunnies!" He chuckled at his wit.

Badge Bunny? She didn't know whether she should be offended or amused, but decided on the latter.

"Badge Bunny?" She said, wanting to hear his explanation.

"Oh. Sorry. That is what we call you ladies who hang out at Blue

Bellies. You know, like Marietta."

"Marietta?"

"Yeah. The gal with the huge bazooms and the long brown hair? Always has her law books with her? You know."

Bazooms? Does he mean bosoms? She tried not to laugh. "Uh, sure. Marietta," July replied, having no idea whom he meant. "Having a boring night, officer?"

"Oh, babe, totally dead out there tonight. You know I am younger, better looking, and not such a tightwad as Rick Mora. I know how to entertain a lady. Could I interest you in dinner, drinks, some dancing, maybe?"

"Not tonight, thank you. So, Detective Mora is a mean, dangerous, philandering tightwad? I got the impression that he is married."

"Well, he was, but his wife kicked him out years ago. No big surprise. I can't imagine any woman wanting to live with him. It's hard enough to just work for him. I, on the other hand, am single and as mild and kind as your mother's Labrador Retriever."

July couldn't help giggling. What a line! "I'm sure you are. It sounds like the Captain doesn't have much going for him."

"Well, he's a great cop. Can't deny that. I swear he just scares people into surrendering. And he's an outstanding musician. He and Lieutenant Q and Mrs. Reynolds have a band. A good one, too. They play for charity stuff. They call themselves, *Your Worst Nightmare.*" He laughed. "Cap is different when he is playing his music. He even smiles or cracks a joke sometimes. And he can really sing. He'd win *American Idol,* hands down."

There were other voices in the background now. One said, "Hey, Bo, stop entertaining the ladies on department time. Get that report finished, and do it now."

"Yes, sir! Uh, honey, I have to get back to work now."

She hung up the phone, trying to imagine what the fellow looked like, and laughed. It did her a world of good.

July decided to do her own research. It required a subscription to access the back files of the Las Cruces Gazette. She shuffled through her purse for a little-used credit card she kept just for small purchases, and became a member of the Gazette's public.

Richard Mora was a City Councilman with lots and lots of attention from the press. Ricardo Mora was either the owner of a local furniture store, a minor league baseball player, a major league thief, or the winner of an outstanding scholarship to Stanford. There was no reference to a policeman named Rick Mora.

She thought about other options. If not Richard or Ricardo? Oh, of course, Enrique. And, there he was. Detective Sergeant Enrique Mora making a major drug bust. Lieutenant Mora testifying before a Congressional Subcommittee on border security, wounded in the line of duty, suspended for some rough stuff with a suspect. An editorial listed his "uncivilized" personal qualities, "inappropriate to a city officer, and scandalous for a police captain." And another called him "Our local hero, Enrique Mora, walks in the boot steps of Elfego Baca, who stood for law and order in the early days of New Mexico."

There was a photo of Detective Lieutenant Mora receiving his second Governor's Award for apparently being an obstinate, dangerous, married but kicked out, mean son of a bitch, who was also quite courageous. She found an article about Captain Mora being the keynote speaker at a law enforcement conference. Finally, there was a photo of three people on a stage and a caption identifying *Your Worst Nightmare* playing at a fundraiser for Boys and Girls Club, with E. R. Mora on lead guitar.

He did look cold and hard in some of the photos, with those gray eyes, but somehow, she could not entirely believe it. There was the feeling of calmness that she experienced listening to him breathe. The apology for intruding on her life and his questions about her health were not necessary. They were just kind.

It was all confusing. Mora was just the sort of man she should fear, wasn't he? Arrogant, powerful men like him were not to be trusted. Yet, some called him a hero, and his tolerance of her aggressive behavior was not what she expected from men. He seemed amused rather than offended by her efforts to keep him at bay. She remembered the battered hands that were so gentle. He was a puzzle. It was not what she had learned to expect..

In the meantime, what had she been trained to do? Analyze! It was time to use her head. What was the differential diagnosis here? Who were the players? What could be the possible motivations? Was the bomber after her? She had never had a complaint from any of her patients. Other than the people at the clinic and her practice, she hardly knew anyone in Las Cruces.

What about Shirley as the intended victim? July knew very little about the girl. She seemed like a fairly typical young single mother. Was there an angry ex in the mix? Was she involved with that criminal element in her family?

The clinic was the most likely target. Could Mr. Winter be involved? Was there someone who had a grudge about a past abortion? But then, why put the explosive in her briefcase?

July was beginning to feel a little sick. She lay down on the soft bed, trying not to vomit.

Chapter 15

Luke sat on the deep front porch of his rambling old house, watching the coming night slowly changing pastures from green to gray. Surrounding pines began to show black against the twilight sky. He sipped a whiskey and worried about little July.

She had been such an odd girl▯short, skinny, very tough and stubborn, determined to show the world that she was not just some little orphan kid from the country. She covered her weak spots with bluster and anger. What on earth would July do here in the mountains, on this rundown old cattle ranch? She must be terribly ill to want to come back here. Would he be able to care for her? Honestly, he could barely care for himself some days.

There was the sound of approaching footfalls, and Rick stepped up on the porch with a grocery bag in his hand. He smiled, pulling a little side table over next to Luke.

"Ready for some more of my guacamole and chips, Luke?"

"Sounds good, son. I will get fat with you feeding me all this good stuff. Let me get a bowl or something."

"Got it all ready. I could use some of that whiskey, though."

Luke started to rise, but a grinding sound from his knee sat him back down with a grunt. "These damned old joints. Gotta wait a second before I can stand sometimes."

"I know what you mean. I'll just get a glass and help myself."

Luke smiled, nodding. Wild Rick had turned into a thoughtful adult. It was real nice having him as a neighbor for a while. Too bad it couldn't be permanent. The old man spat over the porch rail. "You said you don't have time for a woman, Rick? Why not?"

"No women. Once burned, twice shy. Once in a while, if I have had a few too many drinks, I hook up with one of the Badge Bunnies. But I have never gotten close, emotionally that is, to any of them." Luke chuckled at the joke.

"Hell, I don't even remember their names half of the time. No, no girlfriend." Rick shook his head, disgusted with himself. He wasn't raised that way. They sat in silence for a long time, sipping and snacking, listening to the sounds of the night.

Rick was suddenly alert. He rose and leaned over the porch rail. "Listen, Luke," he whispered. A single coyote yapped close by. A great-horned owl hooted from the barn rafters. Luke sat in silence, then whispered, "What am I supposed to hear? There are always coyotes and owls about."

"Is that shotgun on the mantle loaded?" Luke nodded. In a second, Rick had reached in and grabbed it. "Hey! Get away from there!" he yelled, running toward the barn, just as Luke's little gelding, Topper, started squealing in alarm. "Get! Get!" The boom of the scattergun echoed from the hills. There was another boom, then the sound of something large crashing through brush along the creek. Rick's voice, talking to Topper, carried up the hill to Luke.

"Geez, he was a big one!" Rick chuckled as he stepped back up on the porch. "Scared the piss out of little Topper. You would think he would have smelled that bear before it got so close. I locked Topper in for the rest of the night. I should have done it earlier."

"How did you know there was a bear there, Rick? I never saw anything! There is barely any moonlight at all."

"Remember Shakespeare? How the Earth has music for those who listen? You know that I spent a lot of my childhood nights out there." He gestured with his chin. "Out there listening. I didn't see the bear, Luke. The coyote did. Then I noticed the sound of something moving through the creek. It had to be something heavy because it rolled some rocks when it climbed up the bank. Then that coyote gave an alarm yap."

"Huh. Thanks, boy. You know, that is something old Iron Horse would have noticed. You are a lot like him."

"I am? I don't know much about him. I only know that my grandmother was determined to raise my dad and me outside of the tribal traditions so that we would fit in better here. She didn't like me running the woods, either. One time, she said I would never be a lawyer if I didn't settle down. I have no idea why she wanted me to be a lawyer. I know I always disappointed her. I didn't understand at the time."

"I think it was difficult for her, especially at first. Remember how light-skinned she was, despite that Yaqui blood, and kind of elegant in her dress and all? Even though Iron Horse was much admired, there was still this thing about inter-marriage. It was okay, of course, for a white man to take an Apache woman, but for an Apache man to take a woman who appeared white? Not so much, especially among the women of the town."

Rick nodded, and changed the subject. He knew all too well about attitudes in the town. "What's up with that bratty little niece of yours?"

"My little July is pretty sick, I think. She was always so independent. It's hard to imagine her wanting to be here. I was so proud of her for getting her M.D. I had a special license plate made for her car. It said DOCSLVN, for Doctor Sullivan."

Rick chuckled. "She will hate having me for a neighbor." He took out his phone, scrolling through the contacts. "Wally? Rick Mora here. How is it coming with restoring your old Chevy? Good, good. Listen, I want to do a favor for someone, and I wonder if you would see if there is a vanity license plate on that old Volvo? The one from the bombing at that clinic? It reads DOCSLVN. If it is still there, can you FedEx it to Mountain Feed and Seed here in Juniper Springs? Thanks, man. I owe you one."

They sipped and crunched in companionable silence for a few minutes, but Rick could tell that the old man was hesitant about something. "Can I help, Luke?"

"I don't know how to take care of her, Rick. She must be very sick to leave her home and come here."

Rick was surprised to realize how much he was worried about the little doctor, too. "Listen, Luke, I don't want to be a pain in the ass, but I can help take care of her. You would not believe how much time I have spent in hospitals. How about if we start by getting a room ready for her? Is her old bedroom close to a bathroom?"

Luke smiled in relief. "We need to shift things around some. We can put her in my bedroom, and I will use her old room."

"Show me." Luke's room was spacious, but needed painting, and the window didn't open but an inch or two because of the warped casement.

"What if I put in a new window, Luke. And, maybe some new paint?"

"She has always liked lilacs. Maybe we can find a lilac color?" They spent an hour planning to remodel the room for July. Rick was enthusiastic about fixing the old house.

"When do you expect her? Is she doing her radiation or chemo or whatever?"

"She said end of June. So, we have at least a week."

"Good. We start Sunday. Oh, wait. I'm hosting a barbeque dinner on Sunday."

"Why not have it here? We have that huge back deck, and if it rains, there is plenty of room indoors, compared to your folk's house."

"Good idea, Luke. We'll do it here."

Rick walked to the cabin with a bit of bounce in his step. He found July's hostility toward him sort of amusing, even exciting. "Now I am being weird," he muttered to himself, but it didn't feel weird. It felt right. He snickered, wishing once again that there was not an insane coyote living in his mind.

Chapter 16

It was too warm in the rebuilt El Rio Women's Clinic. Milly left the doors and windows open and fans running for as long as she could, attempting to eliminate as much of the odor of fresh paint as possible before the Grand Re-Opening.

The girl sitting at the reception desk filling out an employment application was sweating a little. "Were you ever a patient here, Roberta?"

"Yes, ma'am. I saw a doctor for my acne."

"Oh. Well, it seems to have cleared up nicely."

"Yes."

"Now, I know I am not supposed to ask, dear, but just so I can plan for backups in case of illness. Do you or any of your children have health problems? It doesn't matter for hiring, just for my planning."

"I understand why you asked. It gets busy around here, and you need to have several people able to cover each job. I...I don't have any children."

"Well, that's too bad, dear. You are such a pretty girl. I am sure you will have beautiful babies one of these days."

"Thank you." She ducked her head. "Shall I show you my typing speed, or filing skills or something? I am really good with most office machines, and I stay updated on new technologies."

"No. I find that anyone who can fill out that form on the

computer as fast as you did has more than adequate skills for what we need here. Would you be able to start on Monday?"

"Yes, Monday will be fine." She dialed a number as she walked to her car. "This time the smoke bomb will work the right way, for sure?"

"It was a terrible accident, Roberta. The bomb wasn't supposed to start a fire. They must have had something flammable stored where it wasn't supposed to be. They were lucky that whatever it was didn't catch fire when the clinic was full. Just keep your mouth shut about this and tell me when the next dermatologist is scheduled. Remember that you were the one who placed the bomb, and I am the one taking care of your baby and all those surgeries he needs. Just remember!"

Chapter 17

Luke teased Rick that he was not acting like the rough, crime beating cop they all read about in the Las Cruces papers. Rick laughed, pleased that Luke treated him almost like a son. Sharing the old man's company made him happy. They had so many interests in common. He wished that he could just stay here forever, fixing the cabin, upgrading the house, working with the horses and cattle, and eventually taking over the store. It would be good for Gracie to have him around more, relaxed and mostly sober for a change. Rick snorted, amused at his daydream. He was a lawman and a very good one. Better stick with what he knew.

They were busy cutting up melons, dressing them with a lime-mint mixture, when he heard, "Papa! Papa!" as Gracie raced in ahead of the rest of the family.

He swept her up. "What have you been doing since yesterday, Princess?" He listened while she related her adventures with Josephina, the new American Girl doll he had brought, and what Grandpa Lonny's dog had done.

"And, I love, love, love the new Felicity bonnet, Papa!"

Luke asked, "What is a Felicity bonnet, honey?"

"For my doll, Uncle Luke. I have this doll named Felicity Harriman. She is from the olden days when girls wore bonnets sometimes. Papa knows all of their names and the clothes they wear and stuff." She was so proud of her Papa and his knowledge of little girl things.

None of her friends had such well-informed fathers. "And, my papa is the only papa who knows how to make little cakes with blue frosting roses for tea parties!"

"I am very popular with the pre-school set," Rick bragged with a grin.

"I guess you still want to adopt Gracie," Maureen, Grace's biological mother, said to Rick as she arranged the table, "but Dad says the courts won't let you."

"True."

"Why not?"

"Well, it's a long list. What it boils down to is that I'm not a nice guy. I have a terrible reputation as a drunk and a philandering jerk. No family court would ever give me custody of a child."

"But you aren't like that."

"Yes. I am. It's all true."

Maureen stared at him. "No, Uncle Rick, that isn't like you at all. You don't mind if I call you Uncle do you?""

"No. It seems appropriate somehow. It's that when I am here, I try to be the man my folks wanted me to be. But there is that other side of me."

"Is that why Cindy divorced you?"

"Is that what she says?" He snorted in disgust. "When I was married to Cindy, for all of four months, I behaved better. I divorced her because she lied to me about important things that changed my life. I wanted my house back but couldn't afford to buy out her share. Have you ever been to the place?"

"No. We were invited to a couple of her fancy parties, probably because she wanted Dad to give her a cheaper price on some cement work he did for her. But none of us like her. She wants to get back together with you, though. She told my mom. Had a big fight with that actor that was living with her, and he left."

"Well, that's not happening! I put so much work into that house, and she just betrayed my trust like it was nothing."

"You must be really angry."

"I was, but it doesn't do any good. Anger just eats you up inside."

He paused. "You must be really angry at Buddy."

"No. It was my fault as much as his. I don't know how I could have been so stupid."

"You were only fifteen, too young to have good judgment, but he had no excuse. Your dad thinks Buddy didn't know how old you were, but I know that he did. He committed a crime. A serious crime. Still, at least you have the support of family and friends, so it was not such a terrible mistake on your part, was it?

"I am twenty-five years older than you are, and still make stupid, dangerous mistakes pretty often," he added. "Don't be too hard on yourself. I have plenty of money to support Grace, and with all of us, she has a great extended family. You have no reason to feel guilty or to worry about Gracie. Just follow your dream. You will be a great designer. And speaking of design, Mom! Maria! Come in here for a minute, please."

The whole group followed as he led them up to July's new room. "Luke and I are fixing this up for his niece, July, and we are looking for ideas."

"Oh, little July is coming home? How wonderful for you, Luke!"

"We don't know how long she will stay. But we want everything to be pretty and feminine and nice while she is here. So, we thought maybe lilac colors, and new linens and a nice chair and such."

Maureen looked around the room, pacing it off, humming to herself. "Let me do it. Let me design a room for her." Her eyes were sparkling. "It could be a part of my portfolio. May I, please? Look." She described a lovely room with new paint and wainscoting, artwork on the walls, and a revised bathroom.

Maria interrupted. "What she is really going to need is something from her childhood. If you men are going to be treating her like a little girl, then give her something to cling to, from when she was a little girl."

Rick was puzzled. "Like what?"

Luke held up a hand, and hurried down the hall. He came back with a dirty gray, stuffed rabbit, one ear torn partly off and missing its nose.

"This is Captain Bob. She dragged this thing with her every-where when she was little, and as a teenager, she would hug it when she was upset."

Rick took it. "Can you repair it, Mom? If you sew it up real nice, I will try to get it clean. Shampoo?"

"I can sew it up nice, but you should probably try one of those detergents for delicate fabrics."

Maureen almost danced around the room, peppering them with ideas.

Rick said, "Don't get too excited yet, but I understand that they have an advanced study program at the Design Institute that lets you intern with some big names. Is that right?"

She nodded. "But you have to pay your own way. You know, living expenses and all, so only rich kids can do it."

"It sure seems like it would be a good thing for you to do if we can pull it off. Get me the details, okay? Maybe next semester, if we plan ahead."

"Okay! Oh, Uncle Rick! Okay! But you don't need to do all of this for me, for us."

"Rick," Maureen's mother spoke up, "it's too much. It will be very expensive, and you have your own life to live, with that new girlfriend and all."

"I don't have a girlfriend, Maria. What made you think that?"

"Well, she was in town looking for July because she had a surprise present for her. She asked about you and then July, so I just assumed. I mean, she knew that July would be up here recovering, and...." She paused. "I was too busy to pay attention, but now that I think about it, it doesn't make any sense. How did she know if you didn't tell her, and if you had, she would know how to get hold of you."

"What did she look like? Did she leave her name or anything?"

"Just a lady. Wore one of those big straw hats. Sunglasses. I really didn't pay attention. We were swamped. I wondered why she had a rental car if she was just coming from Cruces. It had a number on the back, like a fleet car."

Rick didn't want to alarm Maria and his mom, so he said nothing, but Lieutenant Kincannon would get a call later tonight. Someone had done some very thorough research. How did she know that he was here, that July was returning to her hometown, that he was living on her uncle's ranch? Was he being surveilled? Was his truck carrying a tracking device? And if so, why? There had to be a pro involved. He covered his concern with a smile.

"I don't really have much of a life, Maria. Work and bars and work and Grace, and that is about it. I am not going to have my own family, and this gives me a little happiness in a not very happy life. So, don't worry about it. I want to do this for Maureen if I can pull it off."

He did not mention that he didn't expect to live much longer. Maybe helping Maureen accomplish her goals would compensate a little for all the terrible things he had done in his life.

He snorted in silent contempt at that idea. It was something Father Don, down at St. Mark's, would say. *Maybe if I could honestly repent, but I can't. The truth is that the evil that men do does live after them.*

Maria studied him for a moment. "Everyone from Juniper Springs hears the news stories about you. They make you seem so dangerous, reckless, even cruel, not at all like this generous man we know." Rick blushed at the undeserved compliment.

It was a very successful dinner. Eventually, Luke pushed back from the table and said,

"Rick, I wonder if you could ride out with Tomás one day soon. He is worried about the condition of the pastures, and I just don't have the energy to argue with him."

"Sure. I'd like that. Maybe you will come, Dad? It will be interesting to see what Luke's young foreman is accomplishing. Maybe we will have to steal him to manage all that land we bought." Luke threw a carrot at him, as Rick laughed.

It was late when Rick phoned Rory Kincannon about the mysterious woman. July was relatively safe at the hotel. According to Gloria, the bell girl, she wasn't leaving her room much, and all of the staff knew to report anyone trying to learn her room number either in person or by phone. Hotel Security had been alerted. There was nothing much that could be added, but Rick had trouble getting to sleep that night.

Chapter 18

As requested, Luke's foreman, Tomás, brought down two extra horses, leaving them in a pasture close to the house. "The sorrel hasn't been ridden in several years, so he may be a little rank. I hope you don't mind. I can top him out for you."

Rick smiled. "No, that's okay, Tom. I can manage."

"But, Captain, I mean, he usually bucks pretty hard."

"That's fine, Tomás. I am okay with it. You warm up the bay a little for my dad if you don't mind?"

It had been a long time since Rick had pitted his strength and skill against a bucking horse. The bay came readily to the halter, but the sorrel didn't want to be caught. Rick had to rope him to get him up to the corral by the barn. It took a few minutes. He had never been a good roper.

The horse humped up for the saddle, so Rick put him on a long line and chased him around for a few minutes before tightening the cinch. Without giving the horse time to resist, he pulled the cinch, grabbed the bridle close to the bit, turning the horse's head into him, and swung fast into the saddle.

There was a moment's hesitation, and then the sorrel exploded into a squealing, twisting, pitching, hurricane of tail and mane and hooves. Rick rode the first few jumps easily enough but lost a stirrup and sailed into the dirt. He landed on his back with an explosive grunt, taking a few seconds to roll out of the way of the flying hooves.

"You are slowing down, son," his dad laughed.

Rick stepped to the middle of the corral, watching the horse run around and around, timing his next move. After a moment, he stepped toward the oncoming horse, which skidded to a stop and started to whirl the other way. Rick grabbed the reins, once again mounting quickly. He stuck with the jumps and bucks and spins this time until the horse agreed to be ridden.

"Hey," young Tomás said, "you are good for an old...." He paused, and his face flushed.

"An old man," Rick finished for him. "Well, when you were in diapers, I was the State High School Champion. I wanted to make the pro rodeo circuit but got shot in the shoulder in Iraq, so that joint is not as strong as it needs to be. Let's look at this range problem that concerns you."

The three rode north at a trot for most of the morning, checking the cattle and water resources, the sparse grass growth, and the fences. They saw as many elk as cattle, herd after herd. Where the hills turned steep, climbing up the face of a mesa, they paused. Tomás pointed across the fence to the adjoining property.

"Look at the quality and quantity of the grazing over there. Even though the slopes are steep, there is a fine stand of grass. I'll bet it's great up on the top of the mesa. Down here, we might be able to feed the stock into early August, but that will be about it."

"What about the south pastures?" Rick asked.

"Same. We need to do something, or Luke will have to sell off at least half of the stock. He should use this end of the place as a hunting reserve or something. He could keep maybe a hundred fifty head on the south pastures, not enough to make a living as he is marketing now, but if he tried to get into the grass-fed beef market, he would make a lot more."

Rick regarded the sincere young man speculatively. "Let's check the grass up on the mesa."

"That belongs to someone else, the M slash M. A real mean outfit, I hear. They bought it some years back. Never met any of them, or saw anyone up there, though. We had better stay on this side of the fence."

Rafael laughed out loud, and Rick chuckled. "That outfit would be Dad and me. I promise not to shoot you. There is a gate down here a way, as I recall."

Before they were through, Rick had arranged for Tomás and his crew to check the fencing on the M/M acreage, all sixty-five thousand acres of it, bought in a series of tax sales over the previous twenty years. It wasn't the biggest ranch around, but pretty good-sized. Tomás would move Luke's herd up there for the remainder of the summer. Rick was surprised at how happy he was about solving this problem for his friend Luke. It had been a good day.

Chapter 19

The unrelenting heat dragged July down physically and emotionally. She was used to spending at least a little time out of doors, but it was pretty hot even at night. The first few days, she took early morning strolls on trails in the Bosque, the woodlands along the river, or took in an afternoon movie. But nausea had begun to take a toll.

Worse, the burning pain in her feet and legs from the treatments was miserable, and the broken elbow itched and ached. She was so terribly tired. She had looked forward to the surgery, which was quickly over. Now it was the chemotherapy, chemical killers wandering around in her body, seeking out cancer cells.

Nothing helped much. July tried to distract herself by learning everything about fire bombs and accelerants, and searched for Shirley using social media resources. She ordered her meals in from room service but seldom ate them.

A day after her latest treatment, Gloria confronted her. "Dr. Sullivan, you need to get away from here, at least for a few days. Maybe you should go home for a while. Wouldn't you feel better if you were around family? Since it isn't clear whether you will need more treatments, why not wait at home?"

"There is just my great uncle. I am afraid that I will be too much trouble for him."

"Well, maybe you should go see? Even if you just go for a day or so, you might feel better. Staying in the room like this is too depressing."

"I guess it is. But, right now, I am not even sure that I can drive as far as Juniper Springs."

"Of course, you can't." Gloria unplugged July's cell phone from the charger, and handed it to her, standing there scowling, hands on hips.

July smiled a little. "Okay, okay." She scrolled to Kozlowski, pressing the icon.

"Uncle Luke? I don't know. I am not feeling very good, " and she began to cry. Great sobs made her incoherent. Gloria gently took the phone from her shaking hand.

"Sir? I work here at the hotel. Dr. Sullivan isn't eating well, and she is in a lot of pain. It is so hot here that she isn't getting out of her room much. Oh, can you? I'll be sure that she is ready. My name is Gloria. Tuesday morning, about ten. Wonderful. Thank you."

"He and a neighbor are coming to get you and take you home until your next treatment, if there is one. He sounded excited that you are going home for a little bit. He said, 'We two old bachelors will take care of my little girl.' Isn't that cute?"

She patted July gently, pouring her a glass of water. "Take a few sips. You aren't getting enough fluids."

July nodded, trying to stop crying, and obediently took a sip. She needed to do better, or her kidneys would shut down. She had to get better. Who else was there to take care of Uncle Luke in his old age? And what about her career? Was there really someone out there who wanted to kill her? Unable to decide what to do about her future, she felt like she was tangled in a black web that was holding her down. She sat there, numb, staring out the window at nothing.

Chapter 20

Luke was worried, but not about the ranch or the cattle.

"My little July called. She is mighty sick, Rick. We need to get her tomorrow. Can you take off from work again? I told her we old bachelors would take good care of her."

Rick looked at his dad, who nodded. "No problem, Luke. You guys go get her."

"Thanks. We need the two of us to go so that we can bring her car. She hates being dependent on others."

Rick smiled to himself as he walked back to the cabin. How would she react when she saw him and realized that the other old bachelor was the annoying cop? He hoped she wouldn't hold it against him. Either that, or maybe he could win her over. He sure didn't want to make Luke uncomfortable. They were getting to be almost like family. He sighed. Taking care of Luke's place was fun. Too bad that it was a temporary thing. It wasn't often that his goal was doing something nice for someone, but Luke had done so much for that difficult boy Rick had been. Here was another opportunity to pay him back.

Rick slept soundly, waking a little after 5 a.m. The sky was already light, and in a few minutes, began turning from pearly gray to pale yellow to sunrise orange. He hummed as he cleaned dried mud, leaves, bits of hay, and a few twigs from the floor of the truck. One of his mother's old soft quilts he rolled and placed behind the seat, and put a fresh pillowcase on a bed pillow. He carefully wrapped the restored bunny, Captain Bob, in an old tee-shirt.

Luke appeared behind him. "Mornin', Rick. It's early, but I'm ready to go. Maybe we can stop at that cafe in Hooper?"

The heat came up to meet them as they wound down the switchbacks toward the river. The Hooper Cafe sat in the shade of some ancient cottonwoods, its false front a relic of the Great Depression. On the covered porch, warped floorboards hid under a bank of rocking chairs, placed there for the enjoyment of customers who liked the Old West feel of things. And the place was famous for their huevos rancheros, Rick's preferred breakfast.

They were both happy and joking, looking forward to taking July home with them. Rick sang along with the radio, changing lyrics to nonsense or political commentary for Luke's amusement. As they turned into the drive between hospital and hotel, they could see a small figure hunched over in a wheelchair, an attendant standing behind her. Even in the deep shade of the portal, that distinctive red hair stood out.

"Oh, my little July! She looks so sick and weak. We had better change plans, Rick. I'll drive her car home, and you take her in the truck. She might need help in and out of the car, or up the stairs or something, and I won't be able to carry her."

Rick nodded in silence. She looked so pitiful, not at all like the defiant lady from the hospital. "I'll get her, Luke. She can curl up here on the seat of the truck like we planned. I hope she won't mind that I am driving it instead of you." He pulled up in front of the hotel, Luke jumping out almost before he stopped the truck.

"July, honey, here we are. We will get you home quick as a wink. I'll drive your car, and my friend will take you in the truck so you can lie down on the seat if you want to."

Gloria handed the car keys to Luke. "That is Dr. Sullivan's car there, the beige one. I had the valet bring it down for you."

July held a slip of paper out to her great uncle. "Guess who is living right over there in the retirement apartments? Your old friend, Katrina. I had lunch with her a few times before I got so sick. She would love to see you."

Luke's eyes lit up. "Kate here? Oh, I'll have to come see her."

"Do it now. Take her to dinner. You can use my car, and your friend can drive me home. Go on now. Call her." She squeezed his gnarled hand.

Rick spread the quilt on the truck seat, then stood to the side, holding the bundle wrapped in the old tee-shirt. July turned her head to see Uncle Luke's friend, but the bright sun blinded her. "Who are you?"

"It's me. The slimy toad."

She recognized the deep voice right away. "Not that creep! What are you doing with my uncle?"

"We've been friends for thirty-five years. I've known him a lot longer than you have. I'm on vacation, remodeling Luke's old cabin and working at my folk's feed store."

She gave Rick an angry, cranky look. It reminded him of that little redhead he had rescued so long ago.

"Hey, you looked just like that the day you told me you were an angwy wabbit. I am glad you finally learned to pronounce Rs. Medical school might have been tough if you had to wepeat evewything fow evewybody." He grinned at her.

"What?" She stared at him for a minute, suddenly remembering. "How could I not have recognized you? Those pale eyes!"

"Yup. I was that annoying teenager you kicked and hit and bit when you fell off your pony. And now, I am the irritating cop you slapped. Must be fate." He smiled at her.

"I did not fall off my pony. I jumped off. And he was a real horse, not a pony."

"Uh, huh. Sure you did, and he was barely tall enough to qualify for horse status."

"Well, maybe I sort of jump-fell, and he was 14.1 hands tall. That makes him a horse."

He just grinned at her. "Let's get you in the truck and go home."

"Don't tell me what to do, toad!"

Rick unwrapped his bundle. "Captain Bob says he wants to go

home." He placed the little rabbit in her lap.

She snatched up her old toy, hugging it to her cheek. "Uncle Luke? You fixed Bob?" So many memories resided in that little cotton body. July felt a confused rush of emotions.

"No. I didn't do it, July. Rick did."

She gave Rick a questioning look. "You?"

"Mom sewed him up for you. I hope you don't mind, but she likes to embroider." He turned the rabbit so that July was looking at its face. She tried to suppress that childish giggle, but Bob was so cute. Beneath the new pink yarn nose, there were now two big white teeth, carefully satin-stitched.

"July, honey, I'll call Kate another day. I'll drive you home."

"No, Uncle Luke, Kate is hoping you will call today. You are already here. You may as well stay. My room is reserved for you for the next two nights. This asshole can drive me home." She pulled herself together, giving orders like the authoritative doctor she was, suppressing the little girl's tears that threatened to flow again.

Luke looked at Rick, shrugging his shoulders in apology. "But you can't be in that big old house alone, honey. What if you fall?"

"I'll stay, Luke. I'll keep your little girl safe."

"I am not a little girl!"

"Excuse me. What should I say? I mean, you aren't very big, so ...? Geez, Luke, you must have had a heck of a time raising this one."

"Damn right, he did."

"And you are proud of that?"

She fumed in silence for a minute, stung by the deserved criticism. "How does he know I will be safe with the nasty, scary cop? The guy with the terrible reputation and all those muscles?"

"Okay, you two. Squabbling like children. Behave, or I'll whip your butts," Luke admonished.

Rick laughed. "Come on. I'll take good care of you. I promise." He lifted her from the wheelchair. *My God, she doesn't weigh anything.* He felt a surge of pity. Rick spent weeks and weeks in the hospital after being shot in the gut. It was a dark, depressing time. He knew how hard all the treatments and long, lonely nights must have been for this girl. Woman. Lady. Whatever.

Luke hurried to open the truck door as Rick carried her the few yards through the searing sunshine to the truck with its air conditioning running. "Your chariot, mademoiselle."

Placing her gently on the seat, he buckled the seat belt around her. Luke leaned in and patted the pillow on the bench seat between July and the driver's spot. "You can curl up and sleep, July. Rick really will take good care of you. He's a good man. He spent hours trying to get Captain Bob white again, and he and Maureen fixed up a room for you real pretty. You go on now. I'll be along after I see Kate."

He turned to Rick. "Is this all okay with you?"

Rick nodded, thanked Gloria with a generous tip, then noticing July watching him, he hopped around to the driver's side.

"Was that a bunny hop?" July asked.

"Yup. How did I do?"

"Not as good as Captain Bob, but fair, I guess. Actually, you looked pretty funny, hopping along in your clunky old boots." She sounded cranky, but she was smiling a little. "I still have your hanky. I'll wash and return it."

"Don't bother. Mom made me dozens of them."

"Oh. No devoted little wife?"

"Nope. Far, far from it."

"This Maureen Uncle Luke mentioned. She isn't your wife?"

"Nope. A young friend. The mother of my niece, Gracie."

"Your brother's wife?"

"Nope. Thankfully, she didn't marry that rotten little prick."

"Oh!" She paused, "I imagined you with a wife and kids. Maybe a white cottage with a climbing rose, a picket fence, and all that kind of stuff."

He smiled a little. "I wish that were the case. But, no. Nothing like that." He was irrationally pleased that she had thought about him at all. White cottage with roses. He almost laughed. Where did this girl get such a silly idea about him? It sounded like someone else entirely. Like the kind of guy that sometimes, in the lonely dark, he wished he could be.

She hugged Bob. "How did you get him sort of white?"

"He took showers with me, bravely suffering many indignities with shampoos and white vinegar and anything my mom could dream up."

July, weak and sick as she was, burst out in those juvenile giggles again.

"What's so funny?"

"Well. Bob never was white. He was a gray bunny!"

Rick whipped around to look at her. "You are kidding!"

"Nope." She tried to imitate his deep voice, and he gave her a grin in return.

"Damn!" He began to laugh, too. Spending a few days babysitting this girl would be good for him.

Chapter 21

July lay down on the seat, her head on the pillow by his knee, her bunny hugged to her chest, thinking that when he was not being a jerk, he was kind of charming, this cop friend of Uncle Luke. She imagined some sweet old lady mother fixing the battered bunny, and Rick in the shower. *Whoa! I'd better not think that way about Mister Muscles.* She fell asleep before they were out of town.

By the time they reached the highway junction, she was awake again, overcome by nausea. She gagged audibly. Rick pulled off on the shoulder and got out, hurrying around to open the door for her.

"Here, girl, let's get you some fresh air." He lifted her out, carrying her into the shade of a roadside tree. "Lean on me." He kept a steadying arm around her waist as she bent to vomit.

"I'm sorry. I'm sorry."

"It's okay. I've got you." He held her as she gagged and spat, but almost nothing came up. "You are too dehydrated, July. Let's get some fluids in you. I'm worried about your kidneys shutting down." He lifted her back in the truck.

Disgusted with her weakness, and seeing no joy ahead, she replied, "It doesn't matter. Everything I planned for, worked for, is gone. No job, or husband, or babies. Why bother?"

"Geez, what a selfish attitude. Luke needs you to get well. Don't you dare let him down! That old man gave up a lot of his life for you, and now you are going to chicken out on him? What a whiny little brat you turned out to be. Where are your guts, besides being barfed out?"

"Don't you dare judge me! You know nothing about me or my problems."

"Bullshit. I know that you have an education, a home to go to, and family. You're spoiled. Think of all the women at that clinic where you were injured. How many of them don't have the things you have?" He was deliberately harsh.

July shrank away from him, and Rick saw the pain in her face. He softened his tone. "Do you know that old saying about sorrows coming in battalions? Kind of describes your situation now."

"I actually know that one. Hamlet, isn't it?" He nodded. "Do you have a frigging quote for everything?"

He grinned. "Pretty much."

She shook her head. "Being around you could be seriously annoying. So, you are the bad boy older brother? The trouble maker? The one who was in jail?"

"Right. Buddy is the dumb oaf, and I am the bottom-feeding toad."

She examined him critically. "That time when I bit you, I didn't make the connection that you were the Mora's older son. I just dimly remember some guy in combat boots making me go home when I didn't want to, and calling me a little tiger. Take off your sunglasses again."

One eyebrow raised in question, he pulled off the dark aviators and regarded her calmly. "You were just starting pre-school when I went off to the Army. I am not surprised that you didn't know who I was."

She stared at those pale gray eyes. "Every Juniper Springs teenager knew about that brother of Buddy's, the one who outran the cops. And now, you are a policeman."

"Yup. Twenty-three years with the city. I guess I do need to give you a magnifying glass, Doctor. Is it my acne scar?'

"No, it's the little dot of discoloration here on your cheek." She touched it with her finger. "How long have you had that?"

"Since Buddy stabbed me with a pen when he was about ten. He never did like me much."

"Let me see your hands."

He held them out to her. The black mark on his thumbnail had moved to the nail's outer margin.

"Okay. I guess it was just a bruise. I thought it could be a melanoma when I saw it in the hospital."

"And you remembered it?"

"My job."

"Huh," he said. But he was amazed that she had remembered, and pleased, too. "Time for some ice chips."

"I don't want any." She brushed his hand away.

"Okay. Well, then we will sit here in the heat until you do."

"Really? You are going to treat me like a child?" Her voice rose a little.

"Really. At least until you start acting like an adult." He held up a spoonful of chips.

She gave him a hostile look, but took the spoon from his hand and shoveled the ice into her dry mouth.

"Now, tell me that doesn't feel good."

"That doesn't feel good."

"Liar."

She almost smiled, and his mouth twisted up a little at the corner in recognition. "One more, and then we can go."

"Oookaay." She drew out the word in a pretense of exasperation but clearly felt a bit more energy, sitting up straighter and looking around.

As they climbed higher toward the mountains, July did begin to feel a slight interest in her surroundings, and even more in her chauffeur. He seemed so different than he had in Las Cruces. For one thing, he looked years younger. She examined him with all the interest and curiosity of her enquiring medical mind. Was this very visible change due to the different environment? Reduced stress? More exercise? Less alcohol? He didn't smell like booze now.

"So, where is Buddy these days?"

"Don't know. Don't care. Deployed to the Middle East or somewhere."

"Don't care?"

"Nope. And, I hope he is not coming back to Juniper Springs. I will probably have to hire someone to help Dad when I go back to work. If I go back to work."

"If?"

"Oh, just wishful thinking." He paused. "I don't know. I have been a policeman for a long, long time."

"Are you a good cop?"

"Matter of opinion."

"One of your staff thinks you are a cold, hard, mean, dangerous, tightwad who gets drunk and apparently screws the ladies that he would like to have for himself."

"What?" He was so startled that he almost ran off the road. "Where did you hear all of that? When did you talk to my office?"

"Is it true?"

"Shit!"

"Tsk, tsk. Naughty boy! Is it true?"

He fumed in silence for a few miles, and punched the steering wheel. She regarded him with amusement.

"Yes. I guess. Kind of. Someone said all of that?"

"Oh, and more. He clearly thinks it is unfair that the ladies like the tough guy instead of him, because he is as mild-mannered as a Labrador Retriever. So, is it true?"

"Crap! Must have been that little twerp, Bo." He hesitated, not wanting to talk about himself.

She waited.

Eventually, he gave in a little. "Maybe there is a little truth to it. I don't understand it. What do they see in old guys like me? It's embarrassing, but, ah...."

"But you take advantage of the opportunity."

He flushed red. He wanted to lie, deny, deflect, and at the same time, he felt a strong push toward being honest with Luke's girl. The latter impulse won. "Yes. I do. I am a low-life, bottom-feeding toad, just like you said that day in the hospital. I don't know why those young girls are interested in an old boozehound like me. It's inexplicable."

"Huh. Well, when I consider all the stories and suffering and joy I hear from my female patients, it is explicable. Has it occurred to you that they wouldn't be interested in you if you didn't satisfy some of their needs, too? I don't mean just sex. A woman can get that almost anywhere. I mean, there must be some other factor. Like, maybe they admire your strength, your status, your power in the community? Gaining strength or status from you? Or, maybe you make them feel safe, so they can express their sexuality without being afraid?"

He looked mortified. "I never thought of any of that."

"Do you know, that night when you came to my room drunk, you were very charming, in a weird way, and kind of boyish. Maybe they want to mother you by seeing to your needs?"

"Oh, geez. That's creepy!"

July laughed at his discomfort. "I called to talk to you, but you were already on leave, and that guy thought I was a Badge Bunny. Made me a great offer of dinner, dancing, romance. I thought it was funny." July chuckled. " I asked him to tell you I had called, but I guess he never did."

"So, you gave him your name?"

"Sure. I said that maybe you were up in Juniper Springs, you would go check on Uncle Luke, not just call him. I do worry about him."

Rick paused. So, had someone leaked that information somewhere along the line? Was July at more risk than he had thought? Even in Juniper Springs?

"Why did you want to talk to me?"

"I was trying to figure out who was the target of the fire bomb, and if they had ever found Shirley, or interviewed Mr. Winter. But then I got so sick that I couldn't focus on anything for very long, so I dropped it temporarily."

"I had that problem when I was in the hospital the last time. If it hadn't been for Graciela, I might have just curled up and died of self-pity, kind of like some redhead I know." He grinned at her.

"Graciela?"

"My little princess. My niece. Buddy's daughter. Smartest kid on the planet. I am so happy that we have her."

"We?"

"Extended family. Her grandparents on both sides, and me. We all are raising her. I am Papa Rick. I only get up to Juniper Springs for a few hours some weeks, or maybe for dinner. But I try to make it special, and we talk on the phone almost every night."

"Doesn't sound like the same guy your officer described to me."

"Yeah, well." He paused, "I am a nasty bastard in most ways, and it works for my job. Maybe you could call me a split personality. A jerk with a strong paternal instinct." He gave her a wink.

July lay back down on the seat with her rabbit, not asleep, but just resting this time, feeling safe. That was a puzzle in itself. She had almost never thought she was safe. She wondered why, with this admittedly rough womanizer, why didn't she feel uncomfortable, threatened, in danger?

As they approached the little town of Hooper, Rick asked, "Need a bathroom break? Ready for some more ice chips? Hungry?"

She nodded, "Maybe some ice chips. Not hungry."

Suddenly, that tension between them faded into the background. It was more like just taking a drive with a neighbor or an old schoolmate. Rick suppressed a sigh. Why was he such a damned, whatever he was? Why couldn't he have found a girl like this when he was young? Someone intelligent and pretty and fun to argue with?

He knew why, of course. He could still hear the snap of jaws, and feel its breath on his leg. He could still see the insanity in the eyes of that infected brain, hear the crack of the rifle and his dad's horrified voice, "Did it bite you, son?"

He didn't know how to say it, how to explain it to his parents. And now, thirty-five years later, he still could not put into words what had happened when the coyote's body died. But he felt it.

He felt that poor rabid brain that invaded his soul, and now lived in him.

Jesus, I am a pitiful mess! He didn't know if it was a prayer or a curse. He needed a drink.

At the gas station, July wanted to pee, but she was afraid that she couldn't get up from the toilet as weak as her legs were. "I...I need to pee, but...." She stammered, cheeks flushing pink.

"I am going to carry you into the bathroom, and then I will turn my back, and you can use my belt to steady yourself getting down and up."

"But...."

"July, I have spent a lot of time in hospitals. For now, I am just your nursing assistant. Okay? Call me Mary or something. I may not be as good as Gloria, but I am strong and reliable, and I'm a good cook, too."

And, that is what they did, with Rick talking to her the whole time. He told her about the last time he was in the hospital, and how long it was before he could eat anything after being gut shot. He told her about the mean nurse who always ripped the bandages off so as to cause him maximum pain, and then one night drew a ragged pattern around the hole in him and labeled it *Kapow*, like something from a comic book. And, he told her more about Gracie.

After a few minutes, she relaxed enough to empty her bladder, then pulled herself up, using his belt for leverage. She leaned against his back, trying to hold on to him and pull up her pants with her good arm, but her legs were so shaky, her feet so painful.

"Here, girl." He turned slowly around. Leaning her against his chest, he pulled her pants the rest of the way up and zipped them for her. It surprised her that she felt neither embarrassed nor threatened.

"You are a very good nursing assistant, Mary." She got a big grin out of him with that.

"Better?" he asked. She nodded.

This time, when he picked her up, she relaxed against him, feeling cared for and special in a way that she never had since her parents died so many years ago. Rick felt that change in her and rested his cheek on the top of her head just for an instant.

July slept fitfully as the old Ford moved smoothly up the mountain. Rick, watching her carefully, noticed her curling tighter on the seat, and pulled a corner of the quilt over her shoulders. It seemed strangely intimate. He enjoyed being protective and gentle for a change. He always was with Gracie, but this was different.

July woke as they crossed the cattle guard at the entrance to the ranch, sitting up a little. He looked down at her and adjusted the quilt again. It was still a half-mile to the house.

"How are you feeling? Nausea?"

She nodded. "I can't seem to get past the nausea, the cramping, and pain. Eating, drinking, even just standing, are all so hard to do now."

Rick parked at the steps to the ranch house and turned to look at her. "I know. I remember after I was gut shot. The days were so long. The nights even longer. The pain so unrelenting."

"Did you cry a lot?"

"No. Didn't fit my self-image, you know. I am one of those guys who cries over lost puppies or something. Hallmark movies. But not much otherwise. " He shifted around in his seat to face July. "When Gracie was born, I couldn't stop crying. Right there in the hospital, Mr. Tough Stuff just poured tears all over that poor little baby." He laughed at himself.

July stared at him, sort of amused. "So, Captain Jerk with the strong paternal instinct, how do you cope?"

He looked away, out across the meadows to the forest where he had spent so much of his lonely childhood. "I'm not sure that I do."

Chapter 22

Rick carried July up the steep steps, shallow dips worn in them by decades of booted feet. He settled her in a padded wooden chair at the scrubbed pine table, and squatted on his heels in front of her for a moment.

"You okay here for a bit?"

She nodded. Rick mixed up a tonic of cherries and gelatin, then sat down beside July.

"Do you want to sip, or shall I spoon it for you?"

"Do I have to? I'm real tired. Can't I just lie down?"

"Not yet. And, that is an excuse anyway, isn't it?"

"Maybe."

"You may pout and whine, but you need nutrition, and you know it, Doctor."

"I am not pouting and whining, Detective! I am whining and pouting."

"Oh, my deepest apologies."

She punched him in the chest.

"Ah, hah!" he laughed. "Something else we need to work on. That was the worst kind of feeble."

There was a book on the table, *La Mort heureuse,* by Camus. She picked it up. "Is this yours?"

"Re-reading it. His first book, you know."

"But, it's in French."

"Surprise! French people often write their books in French." He smiled, amused.

"You speak French?"

He shrugged. "*Je le parle mal.*"

"And, I suppose you speak Spanish."

"Adequately."

"My, my, an educated cop!"

"Nope. Not even a high school education. My mother's father was French-Canadian. Her mother is part Spanish, and my dad's side is a mix, too. So, I spoke three languages growing up."

"Not even high school? I thought you had to have at least that to be a policeman."

"I got in by the back door. I was turning seventeen and in jail again. The judge said that I could either enlist or go off to prison for two years. So, I enlisted. They used to allow that back in the old days. Then after a few years of combat and some more as an MP, I joined Las Cruces PD. And, here I am. Sip, or it's the spoon."

"Oh, okay. How many times have you been hospitalized?" she asked, stalling. He picked up the spoon.

"Okay, okay. No spoon-feeding. I will sip. How many times?"

"Three major wounds, and a few minor ones. First time, I got shot through the shoulder while I was in the Army. Tore up every-thing and angled down into my chest. I was a mess. That ended my dream career as a bronc rider because that shoulder is not strong enough for competition-level riding. About twelve years ago, this son-of-a-bitch shot me in the leg. Right here, above the knee. Broke my leg, the same one that I broke riding broncs. Never healed quite right. Then the gut shot thing."

"So, the knee is why you limp a little. Did you catch him? Did he go to jail?"

Rick looked at her for a minute, again not wanting to tell the truth, but for some crazy reason, he wanted her to like him, the real him, warts and all.

"No. He didn't go to jail. I, uh...I killed him, right then."

"Oh!" July recoiled a little. and stared into those pale eyes. "I guess that was, umm." She wasn't sure what to say. "I mean, did you get in trouble?"

"Kind of. Whenever we use deadly force, we get in trouble, a little or a lot. That time it was just a little since he shot me first."

"Have you ever gotten in a lot of trouble?"

"More than once. Sip!"

She obediently took a sip of the warm, slightly sweet drink. "Mm, that is good. How did you know how to make this?" It was soothing.

"When I got gut shot four years ago, I had to find things I could keep down."

She paused, sipping some more. "Did you kill that guy, too?"

"I wanted to, but it was a bad injury. Couldn't manage it, and he got away, probably to Mexico."

"How many people have you, um, you know, done in?"

He chuckled at her term. "Done in? Heh. Cute. Sounds like a two-bit detective novel. I don't really know. I was in active combat and didn't count, but it was way too many. As a policeman? Six."

"When I first saw you, I thought you were scary, but not that scary."

"It is a professional advantage to look a little scary sometimes. Comes natural to me."

The corner of his mouth quirked up a little. "I don't want to scare you. I want to make you feel better and be better. I know how depressing it is to be all alone in some soulless hospital. If I do scare you, just say so, and I will retreat to the cabin unless Luke needs me to help with something, like carrying you up the stairs."

"I'm not really afraid of you anymore. It's just, I don't know. You are really kind of odd. Why did you tell me about killing people? I think most men would have lied."

He looked at the table for a minute, running a thumbnail along the edge of the pine plank. A lock of hair hung over his forehead, nearly touching the gold frames of his glasses. July suppressed a desire to brush it back.

"I don't know exactly. Luke and I have been friends for a long time, ever since I was a kid. I worked here until I got sent to jail. I guess I want you to be comfortable with me while I am here. I can't ask that if I am dishonest. I tell my Gracie not to lie, so I had better not lie either."

July stared into those silvery eyes, only a foot or two from her own. The dark ring around the outside of the iris was deep blue, and there was a tiny fleck of blue marring the pale gray perfection of the left iris, too. They weren't cold or hard now, but warm and fascinating.

"You know, when I had the energy to try to figure out something, anything, about the bombing, I did a little research on Detective Rick Mora. I know that you are an intelligent, tough, and courageous officer. You may be a philandering jerk, and mean and dangerous to criminals, but you are also kind of handsome, and strangely charming. It's weird, but somehow you make me feel safe. I haven't felt like that since...never, I guess."

"You are absolutely safe with me. But, handsome? Crooked nose, acne scar, fight scars, Buddy scar? Hah! That is nice of you to say. And, I am not as much of a philanderer as I am made out to be. I just occasionally, uh. It's just that I am not sneaky about it, like a lot of guys are."

"Banging the Badge Bunnies," she said, and saw the blush coming up from the open neck of his shirt, spreading across his cheeks. "Do Bunnies earn notches on their bedposts?"

"Yeah, sort of."

"I think you are ashamed of your behavior."

"Not really. Well, maybe a little." He was quiet for a moment. "My folks didn't raise me that way. No intimacy." He paused. "You know, that old saying about how the evil men do, lives after them? I am going to leave a world of black marks behind when I finally bite the dust." He looked down again.

"More Hamlet?"

"Julius Caesar. My folks don't deserve to have two such terrible sons."

Then he smiled and said, "I am just not accustomed to talking about what a louse I turned out to be."

"You mean, you guys don't brag about your conquests?"

"We are more conquered than the conquerors most of the time. It's not like we need to pursue the bunnies. They pursue us pretty hard. And if any young fools get out of line with the ladies, I have a word or two with them."

"Even when they are off duty?"

"Well, I'm off duty, too, or I wouldn't be there."

"But you can't tell people what to do when…."

"I can't? Huh. That's funny. I've been doing it all these years."

"You're making fun of me again."

"Who, me?" He was smiling at her. "They could challenge me if they think I don't have the right to tell them what to do."

"Has anyone done that?"

"Sure. They tend to regret it. Ladies are safe in our bar, and it is their choice if they want to drink or not, hook up or not. And I enforce that rule. For the ladies at our bar, the male libido is not their problem to solve."

"How do you enforce that?"

"Forcefully." Rick waggled an admonishing finger. "You keep sipping. I want you hydrated before. I carry you up to bed."

He gave her a startled look. "No, I mean, before I help you up to your bedroom, so you can get some more rest." He wiped his forehead with his palm. "Geez!"

"Okay," she replied mildly, but couldn't suppress a grin. "What do you do when you aren't working or banging bunnies?"

"Are you always so crude?"

"Yup. I guess so. Why beat around the bush? May as well say what I mean."

That grunt again. He rolled his eyes. "There are some things better left unsaid." It sounded like he was lecturing her. He went on in a milder tone. "I have to work hard to keep in shape. Most of the creeps I am after are half my age, and many of my team members are, too. So, I play basketball, or run, or lift weights. Maybe a little sparring or tennis. Yousef, Mo's son, beats the socks off me at tennis. A lot of my work is desk stuff, so I invest quite a lot of effort in staying strong. And I play my piano or guitar. I have two musically inclined friends, and we play together as often as we can. I even played with the symphony once, and am invited to the Santa Fe Music Festival this Fall. Some nights I watch TV, but not very often. I need to be active. And I read a lot."

"Don't you have a girlfriend?"

"Why are you so nosy?"

"For doctors, being nosy is a professional advantage sometimes. Comes natural to me."

He laughed. "*Touché*!"

Just then, there was a clatter of small, booted heels on the wood floors, and a little dynamo flung herself through the kitchen door, dressed in jeans and a red paisley shirt with matching red cowboy boots.

"Papa, can we get my pony today?" She came to an abrupt halt, staring at the woman with her Papa. She put a hushing finger to her lips. "Shh! We have to be very quiet because you are July, and you have been very sick, and you are Luke's special little girl, and you need to rest so you will get better, and my Papa is going to make you all well, and when you are better, you can go on our dates with us." She paused to catch her breath.

"And, you must be Grace."

"Yes, I am. My name is Graciela Mariposa Mora. And, my Papa is Enrique Rodrigo Bu... what is it again, Papa?"

"Beaupré."

"Enrique Rodrigo Bowpay Mora, and I am his niece. How do you do? I mean, *comment allez-vous?*"

"As well as I can, thank you. How are you?"

"*Muy ben, gracias*! That means very well, thank you."

"You say it very well, too."

"Grandpa Rafael is teaching me Spanish. And Grandma Gisele is teaching me French. Papa thinks I need to know how to talk it."

"Speak. How to speak it, Gracie. We talk to each other, but we speak a language."

The little girl leaned into him and put her arms around his neck. "Okay, Papa, how to speak it. Are we getting my pony today?"

"When can you have your pony?"

"I know. When I am six," She sighed loudly.

"That's my girl."

She turned back to face July. "I have a real crown, like a real princess. Can I show it to you? It's at the cabin."

"I am too tired to walk over there today. Can you show it to me tomorrow?"

"Yes. Oh! You probably need to go up to your bedroom now. It is beautiful! Papa and Uncle Luke and Maureen and the boys made it for you. I can show you my crown when we have our tea party. I always wear it then. They aren't really tea parties because Papa doesn't like tea very much. We have lemonade or cocoa ".

"Wonderful. I will look forward to that. Maybe Papa is more used to coffee."

"No, he is more used to whiskey, but Mama Gisele gets mad at him when he drinks whiskey, so we have lemonade or cocoa."

Rick cleared his throat. "Grace, will you run up to July's room and make sure that I have the towels hung nicely in the bathroom?"

She shot off his lap and tore out the door. They could hear her little boots clattering up the stairs.

July gave Rick an amused look. "Out of the mouths of babes?"

He spread his hands, shrugging in apparent surrender, and stood, pulling July's chair back from the table. He called into the living room. "Mom? You there?"

"Coming!" A stout, gray-haired woman was just entering the house from the porch, carrying a large bucket overflowing with yellow-pink fruit. She plunked it down on the kitchen table with a sigh of relief. "Gracie and I picked some early apricots from Maria's garden for you, son. You can make July an apricot pie, and maybe some apricot jam for me, eh?"

"Sure, Mom."

"I am glad that you are home, July. Your Uncle Luke has missed you so. These two foolish men can dote on you and make you well, eh?"

"Thank you, Mrs. Mora. It is nice to be home. I'm delighted to meet Gracie." Her voice was sort of fading with fatigue.

"Come on. Time for a rest." Rick picked July up and climbed the stairs to the second floor, turning left at the landing.

"But, my room is the other way," July commented.

"Not for now," Mrs. Mora puffed, trying to keep up with them. "Enrique said you would need to have a bathroom close, so they changed things around." She scurried ahead of them into the re-modeled room, turning down the covers on the bed. Rick placed July in the armchair.

"Now, what do you need to be comfortable?"

"Gosh!" She looked around the room. "This is beautiful. I love the colors, and the little desk, and this armchair. I can sit here and read." Noticing something special on the wall, she turned back to Rick. "My license plate?"

"I have connections. Now, pajamas? Nightgown?"

"I don't remember where Gloria packed them. I'll just lie down for a few minutes like this. But first, I need to look at what Gracie is so anxious to show me, if I can just use you as a crutch for a minute."

Rick took July's hands, helping her rise, then walked behind her, his arms on either side of her as she took the six steps to the door, bracing against his forearms to take some of the weight off her painful feet. Gracie was jumping up and down in the bathroom doorway, barely able to contain herself.

"Look, July," she whispered loudly. "See how pretty?"

July looked at what she remembered as an old bachelor's worn brown bathroom, now lovely and bright and feminine. Tears slipped down her cheeks.

Gracie leaped forward, hugging her around the waist. "Don't cry, July! Papa can change it. Really, really, he can."

"I love it, Gracie! It is the nicest thing anyone has ever done for me. I don't mean to cry. I hardly ever cry."

"Mom, can you get my old blue sweats off the clothesline? We just need to tuck July into bed for a little while, and they are nice and soft." He folded his arms around her and walked her back to the bed.

"This is kind of old-fashioned, but we found this cowbell for you to ring. Either Luke or Dad or I will be here at the house all the time for the next week. You just ring it. And, for a few nights, I will be right next door. You are not to try walking alone yet. Okay? Grace's other grandmother, Maria, is bringing you a wheelchair."

"This is so embarrassing. I am not used to taking orders, you know. I'm the doctor. I give orders."

"Yup, and I know your patients choose whether to follow them. I, on the other hand, am the police captain who expects his orders to be promptly obeyed, even by doctors."

"July," Gracie said in her stage whisper, "when Papa talks in that voice, you had better do what he says, or he will put you on time out." She looked so solemn that July could not help laughing through her tears.

"Let me help you change, July," Mrs. Mora insisted. "You and Gracie go on, son. I have to get back to the store before long, but Maria will come to get Gracie after a while."

Rick's old sweat pants and tee-shirt smelled of pine-scented mountain air. Big enough for two of her, they were indeed soft with age. July rolled over in the bed, with its pretty new sheets, and was almost instantly asleep.

Rick and Gracie fussed about the kitchen, making a special chicken soup for July, and baked an apricot pie. Just at dark, Gracie's other grandma, Maria, came to pick her up. As he carried her to Maria's truck, he sang in his fine baritone, asking why there were so many songs about rainbows. Upstairs, July heard the beautiful rendition of Kermit's song and smiled.

Gracie kissed Rick goodnight and whispered, "Not too much whiskey tonight, Papa. Remember, you have to behave so that we can take care of July tomorrow."

He felt a sudden prick of tears and held her tight for a moment. "Okay, baby. I won't forget."

Chapter 23

Some slight noise warned Rick that July was awake and moving around. He took the stairs two at a time and peeked through the open door. She was sitting on the edge of the bed.

"What do you need, July? How can I help you?"

"You are going to spoil me."

"That's the intent. I think Luke always spoiled you, didn't he?" He helped her to her feet. "Bathroom?"

"Not yet. Can I sit on the front porch for a while?"

"I'll carry you down. Okay?"

"Let me try the first few steps." She stood on the top step, reaching a foot toward the next one down, but her knee gave out, and she fell forward.

Rick's strong arms curled around her, pulling her back against his chest. "Let's not try that. Not yet." He could feel her trembling a little, her soft breasts pressing against his forearm.

He felt a quick surge of desire and chastised himself immediately. He had never thought of himself as a cradle robber. She seemed like such a little waif, truly child-like. But the thought stuck in his mind that some, maybe most, of the Bunnies he hooked up with were younger than July. He was a little surprised to find just how deeply he was ashamed.

"Let me carry you for a couple of days. You can be a little girl this week, and we will work toward teenager. Okay?"

"Okay. It's just that being carried is so awkward and embarrassing."

"Well, how about, as soon as you feel just a little better, we try dancing to get some strength in those legs. Would that feel more natural? You can still lean on me and let me keep my arms where they can steady you. That way, we can exercise your legs backward, forward, and sideways. The rest of the time, the wheelchair will be downstairs for you."

She nodded, pleased with the idea. As he picked her up, she noticed how good he smelled. She sniffed him audibly.

"Uh, oh. Do I stink?"

"You stink good. Kind of sweet or something." It was a warm, homey smell, not at all what she expected from him. Not whiskey, shaving cream, soap, or anything she could place. It was vaguely reminiscent of when she was a tiny girl, before her parents died. Funny how although she had very few visual memories, smells brought back the feeling of family.

"Gracie and I baked a pie, so I probably smell like apricots. Maybe with a touch of the chicken soup we made for supper?"

"I might be able to sip a little of that tonight. I am almost, kind of, a little bit hungry."

"That's why we made it. Let me get you established on the porch swing, and I'll bring you a mug. Mom took one of her old quilts and made it into cushions for the swing. She thought you might want to spend time there."

"That was so thoughtful of her. I don't deserve this wonderful treatment."

"Of course you do. You are still Luke's special little girl, and Luke was a lifesaver for my folks. He did his best to keep me busy and out of trouble when they were about ready to give up on me. He succeeded a lot of the time, too. If it weren't for Luke, I doubt I would have lived to adulthood. And Mom had such a good time with her sewing machine, making chair pads for the kitchen and curtains for your bedroom. Maureen picked out the material, but Mom sewed them."

The night was cool, the air damp and fresh. It was such a change from the city. She took a deep breath. It raised gooseflesh on her arms. She rubbed them a little.

"You're chilly. Let me wrap this around you. It's warm. I'll run over to the cabin and find you a jacket."

He took off his denim shirt, wrapping it around her. In the moonlight, she noticed again how powerful his arms and chest appeared, revealed by his thin undershirt. He looked strong, masculine, and very sexy. She looked away. That was not how she should think of this guy. She should think of him as Uncle Luke's cop friend, just another old bachelor. All those muscles! She usually was antagonistic toward men who looked like that.

"This is fine if you aren't cold. I am warm enough now," she said.

"Okay. I'll get you some soup."

July's cell phone buzzed, and she lifted it, but his strong hand wrapped around hers, taking the phone from her grasp. "Dr. Sullivan's office," he said. "How can I help you?" There was the sound of breathing, and then the caller disconnected. He hit the callback icon but no one answered. Taking his phone out of his pocket, he called his office. "Find out whose phone number this is, Rory."

July was staring at him in surprise. "Sorry," he said, "but we still don't know who was responsible for the bombing, or why. So, the fewer people know that you are here, the better."

She looked flustered, confused. He tried to keep his eyes on her face, but the old blue tee-shirt clung revealingly to her full breasts and prominent nipples. He pulled the denim shirt around to cover her better, and looked away. *I need to think of her as just a girl. She is so much younger than I am. Gracie is our little girl, and July is our little big girl.*

.She heard the blender running. In a moment, he appeared with two mugs in his hands, and sat down beside her.

"That heated up fast."

"My five-hundred-dollar blender. It heats or cools or combs your hair. I'll make us some ice cream in it one afternoon."

"I'm impressed. You must be quite a cook."

"Saving money is all. Eating out costs a lot, you know, and I am saving for Gracie's education. Plus, Dad and I bought a lot of land in tax sales. That drained my savings a whole hell of a lot. So, I learned to cook to save money, and I'm a good cook. It's a reaction to the fact that Mom is famous around the county for her bad cooking. Do you remember?"

She shook her head.

His phone buzzed. "It's a burner phone, Cap."

"Let's hope it was just a wrong number, Rory. Thanks."

"So, really," July said. "why don't you have a girlfriend? Don't you want someone to warm your soup, and bed, and the cockles of your heart?"

"Cockles of my heart?" He laughed. "What are those, exactly, Doctor? Never heard them mentioned by the coroner."

She poked him with an elbow. "Can't answer a simple question?"

"I'm a busy guy. My work week is usually well over sixty hours. Most of the women I am around are either criminals, or witnesses, or colleagues, none of which would be appropriate girlfriend material. And, when I have any time off, I come up here to spend time with Gracie." He shrugged.

"No prospects here?"

"Haven't looked. A lot of the women here, in my age group, are friends with my ex-wife. She has become quite popular since she started sleeping with some Hollywood hero or other. Hayward or Howard or something like that."

"Who was your wife?"

"Cynthia Sanchez."

"Really? I remember her. She is a total bitch. I didn't know you were the wicked husband who was trying to take her house away from her."

"Yup. But that would be my house. It never was hers. She got half of it in the divorce. Dad and his cousins and I remodeled it. It came out pretty nice."

"She doesn't seem like your type."

"She is just the type for a horny young fellow to get mixed up with. I got her pregnant, supposedly, when I was still a crass youth. Back in ancient history, in this small town, they expected men to marry a girl if they were so careless as to get her pregnant."

"How can someone be supposedly pregnant? You are, or you are not."

"Or, you lie about it to a naive fool who believes you."

She gave him a sympathetic look. "Oh. I'm sorry."

"Me, too. But it was a long time ago now."

"Did you know my folks?"

"Just your mother. She was a gorgeous girl. Short like you, but blonde. A senior when I was a freshman. I was the envy of the ninth-grade boys when I got to kiss her in the school play. Your dad was quite a bit older than I am, maybe ten or twelve years. Also short. Good-looking guy. I knew who he was, is all. "

"What was the play?"

"The Music Man. She was Marian, and I was the Professor."

"You seem more like a high school athlete than the lead in a play."

"Or both. Broke my leg just before school started that year, so Coach made me try out for the play to keep me busy. Or, out of trouble was more like it. And my voice had changed, so I could sing a little bit."

"I remember hearing that you were a trouble maker. There were lots of stories about you. How did you go from your folks' precious son to town bad boy?"

There was a lengthy pause. "Well, I don't quite understand it myself. Something happened to me when I was ten. Dad shot this rabid coyote, and somehow...ah! Chalk it up to my being kind of crazy, okay? All before your time anyway. The annoying kid who put you back on your old horse and led you home was the somewhat revised me, revised by Army basic training."

July paused, wanting to change the subject to one less painful. She remembered the beautiful baritone. "Was that you singing Kermit's song?"

"Did I wake you?"

"No, I was listening to the night sounds. It was so peaceful, and your song was so perfect." She leaned back. Rick put a supportive arm around her, and they rocked in silence, like a big brother and little sister. Coyotes yapped in the distance. A mockingbird began its complicated serenade from somewhere along the creek.

July nodded off, the mug drooping dangerously. Rick slowly removed it from her hand, surprised to find that it was empty.

"Bedtime," he whispered, rising and picking her up. Upstairs, he started to slip the denim shirt off her shoulders, but she clutched it against her, sleepily. He smiled. *So like Grace.* Next door, he fell asleep dreaming of dancing with a red-haired waif.

The moon was setting when he woke to the creaking of July's bed springs. He rolled out of bed, padding barefoot around into the bedroom next door.

"July? How can I help?"

She tried to rise, but wobbly knees gave out before she was on her feet. "I need to go to the bathroom. I'm feeling sick."

"Come on." He held out a hand. She clutched it with her good hand, but nausea overtook her again, and she began gagging. Rick grabbed the wastebasket by the desk and sat beside her, steadying her as she spit and choked until nothing more came up.

Rick cleaned out the trash can, wiped her face with a warm, damp rag, and had her sip a little water. She hunched over, curled almost into a ball, tears dripping from her chin. "I am so sorry. I'm such a mess! I just keep crying and crying. I was never like that. Never! What has happened to me? Six weeks ago, I was successful Dr. Sullivan. Now who am I? What am I?"

Rick picked her up and put her back in the center of the bed, arranging her pillows and blankets, then sat beside her.

"Maybe you have never been this sick before. It takes time to heal. You know that."

She had been terribly sick before. Well, injured really. But she never talked about that time. She had fought it out alone in an Austin hospital, bringing charges against Dougie Gilman from her hospital bed. She hadn't even told Uncle Luke, although he found out about it later.

July leaned against Rick, and her hand dropped to his side. "Oh!" She sat up and looked at where that hand had touched. The scar was large, star-shaped, thick. She put her hand over it. Her palm barely covered the edges. "My God, Rick!"

"Exit wound. Hollow point round. It was very nasty. Gracie was just a baby, and I didn't want my folks to know. I couldn't let them see me like that. I told them I was on a special assignment so that I couldn't come home for a while. I thought it would be easier on them, when I died, if they didn't remember me as an invalid. Of course, it never occurred to me that the entire story was on Las Cruces TV. I'm a numbskull sometimes. But they understood and honored my wishes."

"Look closely." He pointed to an area above the scar.

"Oh, my God! When you aren't being a toad, you are an idiot!"

He flopped back on the bed, laughing. In bold red and black lettering, there was a tattoo. *Kapow!* it read, in an arc over the scar.

"I told you. Mo had a fit."

She peered into his silvery eyes. "Why are you so nice to me?"

"When you aren't being an odious little pest, you are entertaining. And you're Luke's precious girl. I owe him so much. I can never repay him. Anyhow, my folks would whip my butt if I wasn't nice to you."

"Well, there's that, I guess."

"Shut up and go to sleep. Sleep is the best medicine of all."

"Okay, Mary." She gave him a poke in the ribs.

He stretched a protective arm around her, and in a few minutes, began to snore lightly. She quietly turned off the light, pulled the covers over them, and soon was asleep again herself. Curled against his side, she dreamed of muscular arms, silvery eyes, and laughter.

Chapter 24

"I have to get down to the city for my follow-up appointment, Uncle Luke. If you and Kate are going to that Arts Festival in Albuquerque, can I ride down with you? I can get my appointment out of the way while you two visit or lunch or whatever."

"Let me take you, July." Rick turned from the sink where he was washing breakfast dishes. "That way, Luke won't have to wait for you. We can just go down and straight back. Or, we can stay the night if the trip is too tiring." Rick was not comfortable with July being on her own. Someone hated her enough to put a bomb in her briefcase. There were several possible places where information about July could leak, intentionally or not, including the cancer center. He wanted to get a feel for their security procedures. Could someone from there be involved?

"Oh, Rick! You do so much for me with all this cooking, cleaning, toting me around. I hate to take more of your time, keeping you away from Gracie and your folks."

He grinned. "Just wait until you are well. I'll take it out of your hide one way or another. I'll get you to bake me those croissants, or the chocolate almond torte Luke tells me about. Besides, if your appointment is the same day that Luke has a date with Kate, maybe we can all go out to a nice dinner together. What do you think?"

"Kate and I would like that, son."

July's appointment wasn't until three in the afternoon, so Rick took the slow, scenic route to the city, stretching out the time spent alone with July. He wanted to say something special to her, or do something special for her, but didn't know what or how. It was like there was something in his chest, a pressure or a flutter or ... he couldn't describe it even to himself. But it was all about being close to July, just the two of them. He told himself that it was because he had never had a little sister, and almost believed himself.

They drove down through the foothills into the valley, stopping along the river road to buy early cherries at farm stands. At the cancer center, he left the truck with the valet and asked for a wheelchair.

"I don't want it, Rick. It embarrasses me."

"Think of it as a royal coach. Queen July, elegant in her green gown, approaches the castle. Her public awaits her arrival with bated breath. Struck dumb by her beauty, they gaze on her in silent admiration as her faithful man-at-arms...."

"Who is a total idiot," July said, giggling.

"And you are a silly wabbit," Rick said in his best imitation of Elmer Fudd.

She laughed. "Okay. One more time."

They sat in the waiting room, side-by-side. After a moment, Rick took her hand as though it was the most natural thing for him to do. July's chemo friend, Lupita, was wheeled in, and July waved to her.

"July, you are gaining weight." Lupita was almost skeletal but still smiling. "Is this your husband, dear?"

Rick sprang to his feet. He had almost said *yes* in answer to the question. "Enrique Mora, *a sus ordenes, Señora*. July has spoken of you."

She offered a hand, which he took gently in his own. Lupita smiled at July. "Such a well mannered young man, too." July grinned at his quick response, deflecting an actual answer.

The two women had almost a half hour to talk. Rick listened carefully to the phone traffic, the conversations at the reception desk, the interactions behind the glass partition. Nothing raised a red flag. Names of patients were not left in the public eye. There was no gossip among the office staff. No personal data was exchanged other than insurance sources, and one person asking to have records forwarded had ID and permissions checked.

When July was called, Rick rose with her. "I'm going with you." He didn't ask.

The doctor was abrupt, almost rude. He said that they would not plan additional treatments yet. He asked very briefly about symptoms. July explained that the burning pain in her feet and legs was a severe problem, but she was mostly over the nausea.

"Well, if you would have taken the medication I gave you as directed, and exercised as I directed, maybe you would be having fewer problems." His tone was condescending, insulting. Another man trying to exercise his power over a woman. He smirked and rose, heading for the door.

Rick blocked the way. "Do you have any questions, July?" He could see the angry flush on her cheeks and a glitter of tears in her eyes. She shook her head.

"So, Doctor, you are just going to walk out without offering anything but snide criticism to your patient?"

"Step aside, please. I am a busy man."

Rick stepped closer to him. "What you are is an arrogant little prick. Dr. Sullivan will be seeing another specialist in the future. We will have her records picked up tomorrow. You will see to it that your staff has them ready. Do you understand?"

The doctor stepped back, indignant and nervous. "Are you threatening me? I will call the police!"

Rick smiled and opened his ID wallet, his fingers covering the lower part of the gold badge, so that Las Cruces was not visible.

"Go ahead, you little shit. Tell them you are talking to Captain Mora. Let's go, July."

They stopped to sign paperwork releasing July's records to her uncle tomorrow and went on to meet Luke and Kate for dinner. Rick thought about Lupita's question, and how he had very nearly said he was July's husband. How embarrassing was that? He also resolved to learn more about that doctor. Was he just an arrogant prick, as Rick said, or was there another reason for his hostility toward July?

Kate had made a reservation for the four of them at a restaurant where Luke was comfortable in his usual jeans and cowboy boots. Rick dressed in chinos, polo shirt, and loafers. July wore a sundress that emphasized her hourglass figure. It was as green as her eyes.

To Rick, it all was like a wonderful escape from reality, a dream, maybe. He was proud to have beautiful, smart, funny July on his arm. He hadn't done anything like this for years, and his expression mirrored that thought as they wove their way through the restaurant, Rick supporting July.

Kate said, "Look, Luke. They are perfect together, aren't they? The way he looks at her? That's not your bad boy. Something's brewing there."

"Yup. He hovers over her, and she is eating it up. That's not like her at all. Not like him, either."

On the way home, July moved to the center of the bench seat, close against his side. She was used to put-downs or propositions or banter from men, not this protectiveness. She didn't understand it. "Rick, had you thought about asking me if I was ready to change doctors? I am, but had you thought about asking?"

He was startled by the question. "No, I didn't. I'm used to being in charge, and I just reacted. I'm sorry, July. But he didn't care about you, and I wanted to smash a fist into the nasty little bastard's face. He can't treat my...my friend that way." *Shit! I almost said my girl. What the hell?*

July felt the tension in his muscles, noticed the doubled fist resting on the steering wheel, and was oddly grateful. Usually, she would have insisted that she didn't need a man's help, but he was trying to protect her, and for once she didn't mind. She liked it. "I understand." She paused, searching for a distraction. "You know what? This was like a date. Thank you."

He took her hand and held it for a minute. "I haven't been on a date in so many years that I had forgotten they were fun. And about that doctor, I guess I expected him to apologize or something. I'm sorry." She just smiled at him, resting her head on his shoulder for a moment.

It felt good. Maybe he was turning into a wimp. He chuckled under his breath. Wimpy Captain Mora, tagging around after some girl two-thirds his age. Ridiculous!

But she was tagging around after him, too. A couple of days later, Rick needed to check in at his office, and July went along. They started at her old practice, supposedly to just greet her former colleagues. But, in reality, she wanted to get a feel for whether, now that there was no felony charge against her, there would be a chance for her to buy her way back in.

Bebe greeted her with a plastic smile. "How nice to meet your friend, July. I have heard of you, of course, Captain. So, July is no longer a suspect? How nice. But, my dear, we have already brought in another team member. So sorry!" Her smile widened, and as usual, her eyes did not smile at all.

As they drove away, Rick commented, "That lady doesn't like you one bit! What's the problem? She looked at you like you are a fat worm, and she's a hungry robin."

"I know. She has always hated all of us, and I have no idea why. It's just weird."

"Maybe you will find something better." Bebe stuck in his mind. Why would she hate July and her colleagues?

They stopped briefly at the El Rio Clinic to admire the renovations after the explosion. Rick noticed a young lady who looked familiar. He started to speak to her, but she turned quickly away, so he never got a good look at her face. He wondered at the reaction. Someone he had arrested in the past? No, there was another connection, but he couldn't place it.

Milly saw the girl's reaction. "Are you okay, Roberta, dear?"

"Oh, yes, ma'am. I'm fine. Just a little upset stomach." She smiled and hurried down the hall to the ladies' room. Enrique Mora was the last person she wanted to see. Not knowing what Buddy told his parents about the baby, she feared that Rick would ask too many questions if he recognized her.

Rick felt a familiar ripple of caution. Bebe. The girl at the clinic. There was nothing specific, but he knew not to ignore his instincts. Why did he feel like there was a connection there? While July dozed in the truck, Rick talked to Rory Kincannon. "What progress on the bombing, Rory?"

"Not much, Cap. I tracked down that Winter guy and thought I had something there. He's a chemist, and has worked on a few military projects that involved testing explosive materials. But he never approached the clinic building the whole time he was there.

"And his wife?"

"She wasn't with him."

"Why? She usually was among the protesters. Get on it. And see what you can find out about a woman named Bebe Gauthier," Rick said.

Chapter 25

"You are singing a lot, *mijo*. You seem to be happy playing nursemaid," Gisele commented.

"I am enjoying myself, Mom. July is a funny little brat. You know, with all that has happened to her in the last couple of months, she never complains. Pretty amazing. Very strong."

"Uh, huh. Son, she is a grown woman, not a little brat. Give her the respect you are saying she deserves. So, when are you going back to work? Surely, your vacation hours have been used up by now?"

"No. Remember, I didn't take any vacation last year, so I had six weeks saved up, and I can afford some leave without pay, too. We still don't know whether that bomb was directed at July, the clinic itself, or what. I know she is relatively safe up here, but...." He paused, not entirely understanding his motivation, and not wanting to explain.

"Anyway, I do go in some days. Tomorrow, I am going down for a few hours. I think I'll see if July wants to ride along again. And Grace. We could go to the American Girl store."

"Be careful, Enrique. The whole family can see how wound up you are in July."

"It's just payback to Luke, Mom. Helping him take care of his girl. That's all."

Gisele just smiled at her brilliant, observant, analytical son who was so blind to himself.

Rick didn't want any of this new life to end. Late nights, he was in Luke's kitchen working on his laptop, checking on reports by his team so that he minimized the time he needed to go to the office in person. He felt guilty about not being there and rationed his vacation days by interspersing them with workdays. Luke's shotgun remained on the mantle by the door, loaded. If Luke and Rick were gone, Rafael or Tom was there.

When Rick had been away for the day, he gloried in that moment when he pulled up to the house and heard the creak of the old porch swing as July swung slowly. Or, caught a whiff of Luke's pipe smoke as he relaxed in his lounge chair. He told them not to bother, but there they were, waiting for him.

On a day that Rick and his girls went to Las Cruces together, July stayed in the truck, enjoying the slight breeze off the river, while Grace went upstairs with her Papa.

"Hi, Grace!"

"Hi, Uncle Q!" Grace greeted Lieutenant Quintana. "I know a new song."

"You do? Will you sing it for me?"

"Okay. You have to help me, Papa."

So, there was hard-nosed old Captain Mora with a lively little girl who called him Papa, singing *Wheels on the Bus*, complete with hand gestures and body language. They made windshield wipers go back and forth, wheels go around, and passengers bounce up and down. The room full of detectives could hardly believe their eyes.

"Very nice, Gracie. I never heard your Papa sing that song before."

"Oh, Papa knows lots of kid's songs, like the one about bunnies, and one about baby elephants. He sings them with us at our tea parties."

"Does he drink tea at your parties?"

"Papa doesn't like tea, and Grandma Gisele won't let him drink whiskey around us kids, so we have lemonade. But he bakes us real fancy cakes for our parties, huh, Papa."

"Yup. With marzipan frosting and little roses for decoration."

"Yes! They are beautiful!"

"Very cool, Grace." Q punched his friend and boss on the shoulder, then turned to the room at large. "Okay, you all. Back to work."

Rick took Grace by the hand, and they trotted downstairs to the parking lot. The group in the room, mainly ignoring Q's order, watched from the windows.

"I didn't know Cap had a kid."

"What a cute little girl! How old is she?"

"Marzipan? Really? Little roses? Cap does that?"

Then, someone spotted July as she slipped out of Rick's truck and stretched for a moment. "Hey, Lieutenant, who's the babe? She's with our Captain?"

"That little girl is Grace, his niece. She just calls him Papa because he takes care of her. And the redhead is Dr. Sullivan, his friend."

"Dr. Sullivan? As in the bombing at that clinic?"

"Yes. No comments from the peanut gallery."

No comments, but there were lots of raised eyebrows and grins.

"Hey, young lady," Rick asked July, as he buckled Grace into her booster seat, "are you too tired to shop after all?"

"No. I feel like I really need to get out doing stuff. It's just that I tire so easily now. I feel like a prisoner in my own body."

"I know, babe." He thought for a minute. "So, how about if we do something else? Let's go see the dinosaur tracks out there in the Robledo Hills. Maybe something different like that will spark some energy."

July smiled, and Grace was delighted. "Really. Papa? Real dinosaur tracks?"

It was a nice drive along the west side of town, heading north through grove after grove of pecan trees. Turning west on a dirt road into the hills, they hadn't gone far before they came on an older sedan. It had pulled off the road into the creosote brush. One door hung open.

"Stop, Rique. Someone might need medical help."

Rick pulled ahead a little way and stopped. "I'll check. Scoot over here in the driver's seat, July, and keep the doors locked. You know how to use this old radio?" She nodded. "Remember that you have to push the button to talk, then release it. I'll see if there is someone needing help."

He called central dispatch, reporting that he was investigating an abandoned vehicle, but when he gave the license number, it turned out that the car was reported stolen. Rick was torn between doing his duty as an officer, and protecting his girls. There was no visible threat, but he felt some discomfort about this scene.

"Don't unlock the doors for anyone. I'm going to check around while we wait for a deputy. Hang onto this. Do you know how to use it?" He handed July the pistol from his shoulder holster. She nodded. He pulled his old service revolver from under the seat, checked the loads, and chambered a round. In the distance, he could see the flashing light bar of a county Sheriff's Department SUV. It pulled up behind the gray car, and Rick walked back to meet the familiar bulk of Sheriff Gus Peralta.

"What's the story, Gus?"

"We think the asshole that stole this wreck shot up the Circle K on Allen late last night. Wounded a bystander, and the poor girl died this morning. I've called for backup, and...."

Rick had raised a silencing hand, his head cocked to the side, listening. Gus gave him a questioning look. Rick pointed to the trunk of the car, and as silently as his boots allowed, stepped up to take the keys dangling from the ignition. Gus started speaking again, as though in casual conversation, as he stepped back and aimed his side arm at the trunk, nodding to Rick to open it.

As the lid swung up, there was a frightened squeal. The lady inside covered her head protectively. "Don't shoot! Please, I won't tell anyone!"

"I won't shoot you, Caroline," Rick said. "Can you climb out of there?"

"Oh, Captain Mora! Thank God, it's you!" She struggled a little, her knees bruised and one wrist swollen and red. She was gasping for air. Gus helped her to stand. "I could have died!"

"Yup. Could have. You still at the Palomino Club?" Rick asked.

"I'm surprised that you remember me."

"Hell, yes. That little outfit you wear? Kind of hard to forget. Haven't arrested you lately, though. What were you doing with this asshole, besides the obvious?"

"I only met him a few days ago. He was going to take me to dinner because his usual girlfriend didn't show up. Then we heard on the radio that the girl who got shot at the Circle K died, and he got all panicky. He must have had something to do with it. He has someplace to hide out here, I think. All of a sudden, he attacked me. I begged him to just leave me, but he said I would go for help. I'm lucky he didn't shoot me."

"The sound would have carried to that last farm. Probably why he didn't. Why don't you find some nice old fucker, and stick with him? It would be a lot safer."

"He bought Sheree a really nice bracelet last week. They had a date for today, but she never showed up to work, so he invited me. Then when he heard, he locked me in the trunk. He left me to die, didn't he?"

"Looks like it. So who is Sheree? Why didn't she show up?"

"She's a dancer, too. I am worried about her. It's not like her to miss a date. She has a sick kid to support. Really needs the money." Caroline was white, shaking, and beginning to cry.

Grace was straining to see why the lady was crying. "What happened, July? I can't see what happened."

"Wait, Gracie. Papa will tell us."

Rick said, "Gus, when your guys get here, they will mess up the scene. I'm going to track him. You get my girls covered. July and Grace. Surround my truck with your guys. Keep them safe."

It only took him a few minutes to pick up the faint trace of a boot track, a rock that had rolled, another track. Soon he was trotting, following a trail that circled back toward the pecan groves. "Gus, he's headed back toward the farms. I'll stay behind him. Get your guys in front of him."

He was running fast now, knowing about where the man was headed. There was an old pecan warehouse just over the hill. He reached the top of the hill above the pecan grove, caught a glimpse of a blue shirt, and dove head first into the dirt. A round passed so close that it stirred his hair. The shooter's shirt stood out against brown and green background colors. Rick pulled the trigger twice, rolled to his left, and fired again. The blue shirt turned red as the body collapsed into a ditch at the base of the hill.

A patrol car pulled up in seconds, and a deputy ran up the hill. "You hit, Captain?"

"I'm fine. Let's check out that old warehouse." He limped down the hill, the young deputy trying to help. "I'm okay. Really. I always limp a little. Worse on slopes. Wait for backup. We don't know if there are others in that barn."

It was only a few minutes before the Sheriff himself came tearing up the road. He pulled a rifle out of his car, tossed Rick a shotgun, and motioned to deploy the three of them to cover all exits from the dilapidated building. Gus entered first and quickly called to the other two.

The odor of corruption mixed with the slightly acrid smell of old dust. It was probably Sheree. At least the body wore a pretty bracelet with shiny silver bangles. Gus called in his forensics team. "Take Captain Mora back to his truck, Deputy. Never ends," he sighed. Rick nodded.

Caroline was sitting in the back of the other cop car. "Did you find him?"

"Yup. What does Sheree look like?

"Long black hair in cornrows, and thin."

"I guess we found her, too. You aren't stupid, Caroline. Find a safer job."

"Was she okay? Is she...?"

"Just find a safer job."

Caroline burst into tears. "Oh my God! Oh my God!"

Rick got in his truck and slammed the door. He drove in silence, despite Grace's questions. At the beginning of the Dinosaur Trail, he lifted her out of the truck, and hugged her tight for a moment. "What is a dinosaur, Gracie?"

"A big, big thing like a lizard that lived a long time ago."

"They are all gone now, aren't they? But they left something of themselves behind for us. So, we get to remember them and enjoy them, don't we? We don't have to be afraid, or worried or anything just because they are dead, do we?"

"No, Papa."

"So, they lived, and they died. And we live and die, too, and it is not anything to be afraid of when someone dies. We can still have them with us in our minds and our hearts. Remember when we had the wake for Lucy's grandmother, and everyone told their happy stories about her so we all could remember what a fun person she was?" Grace nodded.

"And we wave at Claudia when the stars are out, too. When I die, maybe you will hear my voice when coyotes howl and elk bugle, or see me in a cloud. You can laugh at all the silly things we did together, and somewhere, I will be laughing with you."

"I know, Papa. Grandpa Rafael has told me about a million times, 'cuz he worries about you." Eyes sparkling with humor, she joked, "When it thunders, maybe you will be putting me on time out!"

Rick laughed. "Maybe so, baby. Listen, what happened back there is a lady died. That is sad, and that is why her friend was crying."

"Oh. Did the bad man kill her?"

"I don't know, honey. We are out in the county, so it's not my job. The sheriff will have to figure that out."

Grace looked away for a minute. "But Papa, what if that man shot you? We heard it. Popopop."

"Then you and July would have driven away and gotten help. The important thing is that he didn't. You know I have been shot before, and here I am, still being your Papa. But if he did shoot me, and I died, you would still have me with you forever and ever, because I will always be your Papa, and you will always be my girl. Come on. Let's see what the dinosaurs left for us to remember them by, okay?"

Grace ran ahead, and Rick took July's hand. "Still feel like a prisoner, Wabbit?"

"No. And I think you are the world's best father, Enrique Mora. One bit of understanding at a time. It will stand her in good stead."

"And you are the best sidekick ever, July Marie Kozlowski Sullivan." He helped her walk, slowly following Grace.

Chapter 26

Grace was more and more anxious to go shopping for her pony. "Can we just start looking, Papa?"

"I know it's hard to wait, baby, but patience is part of growing up."

"Maybe I don't want to grow up!" Grace pouted.

He hesitated for a minute. "Well, we can go down to the sale at that big ranch with the green gates, the one near Hooper? And, we can see who has the nicest horses. Then when you turn six, we might go to that person's ranch and see if they have a horse fit for a princess. Okay?"

"Okay. When?"

"Saturday. They will have a big barbecue lunch for everyone."

July looked up and smiled. "Papa is such a sucker." Rick responded with a rueful shrug.

On Saturday, he helped July from the truck, Gracie dancing excitedly by his side. There were bleachers set up beside the ranch rodeo arena. He settled July there, lifting her up to the third row of seats where there would be a clear view, but she was safely surrounded by people, too. He and Grace headed to a kiosk where a 4-H club was selling drinks and snacks.

Waiting in line, he greeted several old acquaintances. Wade Easterbrook spoke up.

"Got one for you, Rick. You doing any riding? There's a Senior

Circuit."

"No, we just plunk around a little on Luke Kozlowski's ranch horses. Haven't competed in almost thirty years. You?"

"Aw, hell no! Too old and slow. But I'm raising some pretty good bucking stock these days. Mainly for high school, but getting better stuff every year. I'll get some of my horses to the National Finals one of these days."

"What are you doing here?"

"Got to sell a few to buy this stallion I'm after. I'm selling three that I consider to be practice horses. Buck hard, but not stylish, you know. What are you doing here?"

"This little squirt wants her own horse. We're just starting to look around a little bit. She's not quite old enough. Still has to ride with her Uncle Rick."

"I have my own saddle for when I get my horse. And I am going to be an equestrienne!" Gracie piped up.

Wade bent down to smile at her. "Good for you, honey. Check out the ones I brought to the sale, Rick, and tell me what you think."

They watched as a few horses were auctioned off. Then Wade rode in, leading a big bay with a blaze face. The auctioneer apologized that the horse was on a lead line, explaining that the young man scheduled to ride and show off the horse's bucking skills canceled on them.

"Any volunteers in the audience?" There was general laughter.

"Oh, Papa, look how pretty that horse is! Can I have him?"

"No, Gracie. That is not a nice horse for my little girl."

A voice from behind them said, "Hey, Rick, go show her what you mean, dude."

He felt a surge of excitement at the challenge. Rick turned to July. "This is childish and stupid, but, uh."

"Yup. It is. Well, go on. We're fine here." He sprang down from the bleachers and trotted around to the arena exit gate.

"I'll ride him, Wade. You got any rigging?"

"My old rig is in the horse trailer. If you can jam your hand into it."

A few more horses went through the auction. Then the announcer said, "Some guys thrive on danger. Here is Captain Rick Mora, a high school champion thirty years ago, now of the Las Cruces Police, on that big bay bucker from the Easterbrook Ranch."

Easing down onto the horse's back, setting his hand firmly into the rigging, Rick glanced down at the cowboy running the chutes, and his eye caught an angry, hostile face in the audience. That furious look was directed at July.

"Ride 'em, Rick!" It almost caught him off guard. The chute gate clanged as it was flung open, and there was a squealing explosion. From where July sat, it looked like a thousand plus pounds of horse-flesh would go over backwards, pinning Rick against the metal stall gate. She half rose from her seat.

Rick whipped forward, his weight helping the horse to balance, and then was slammed back so far that his head almost struck the horse's hips, but he held on, swinging himself forward again when the horse reared, his arm above the horse's neck. Dust roiled as hooves pounded the arena soil. By the third jump, Rick was in perfect rhythm with the horse's motion.

The announcer called, "Time, Rick," and Wade caught up with them as Rick jumped off. He almost landed on his feet but stumbled, rolling in the dirt. Hopping up with a grin, teeth flashing white in his brown face, he dusted himself off. There were cheers and clapping from the audience as the auctioneer began his chant. Gracie was yelling with delight. "Papa! Papa!"

At the other end of the bleachers, Cindy Sanchez Mora, lonely and angry, watched her ex-husband. She thought he should have been with her, as always blaming him for her problems. But now, there was another target for her rage, the little bitch July Kozlowski. She stared at July, and her guts twisted with hate.

July found Rick's strength and skill thrilling. No wonder the Badge Bunnies picked him. How could any woman not fall for a man like that? "Your Papa is amazing, Grace."

"I know. Why don't you marry him? Then you could be my Mama."

She laughed. "Well, he hasn't asked me."

"He is kind of stubborn. Maybe you could ask him?"

July was charmed by the lack of subtlety. But before she could think of an answer, Rick climbed over the arena fence, joining them again in the stands. His hair was mussed, his shirt dusty, and he smelled of sweat. His right shoulder hurt a lot, a sharp reminder of why he was not riding broncs on the circuit, but he shrugged it off. It was fun showing off for July. There was a lot of back-slapping before he could sit down.

"Dude, you're the man!"

"Still got it, Rick! Lookin' good!"

"Way to go, Enrique!"

He sat between his girls, turning to Gracie. "And that, Princess, is why Papa is going to pick your horse out for you. Okay?"

He swung around to face July. She grinned, "My hero." Rick laughed, leaning toward her. He wanted to kiss her but caught himself, pulling back and looking away for a moment, searching the stands for his ex-wife's face. He knew she was capable of duplicity, but what else? Did he have to protect July from Cindy now?

July was looking at him with such fondness. If he was a better man, maybe she would look at him with love in those emerald eyes. He felt a confusing surge of emotions and a physical response. *Dear God, I want her in so many ways.* He wanted to hold her against his heart, whisper secrets to her, and how desperately he wanted to make love to her.

What was he thinking? She wasn't a woman to have for sport. She was a forever woman, the kind you held onto until death do us part. A strange feeling rolled up from his chest, kind of a pang rather than a pain. He cleared his throat and looked to the hills, gathering some composure. He should stop daydreaming. Getting soft would mean his death sooner rather than later, and he needed two more years if Grace's future was to be financially secure. In the meantime, he needed to make happy memories with Gracie, not dream about what would never be.

Rick made sure to spend part of every day with Grace. They

played with Topper, or he would read to her. They invited other kids to her tea parties, where Rick wowed them with tabletop volcanos of baking soda, made fancy treats, taught them songs, and took them on hikes. July was a part of every plan, every activity

"You like July a lot, don't you, Princess? It's kind of like having a big sister, isn't it?"

Gracie had the habit of tipping her chin up and pursing her lips when she was thinking. "Umm, not really, Papa. Maureen is more like a big sister. July is way too old for that. She is more like a real mama." Surprised by her answer, he tried to bury it, but it stuck in his mind. He was happy that July was healthier but dreaded the fact that soon she would not need him.

That evening, lost in thought, Rick was startled when his phone rang as he made another fruit and gelatin tonic for July.

"Detective Mora? My name is Shirley Gambino, and my brother says I need to talk to you about what happened with, you know, the bomb at the clinic?"

"Ah, Shirley! Doctor Sullivan worries about you. Where are you? We need to talk."

"Are you here in Las Cruces?"

"No. I'm on vacation up in Juniper Springs, but I can be down there in a few hours."

She hesitated. "I think it might be better if I came to you. Is that okay?"

"Sure. When? Tomorrow?"

"No. I have a day off next week. Can I call you the day before? My brother and his girlfriend and I will take a picnic and meet you somewhere."

"If you will call when you get close, I'll meet you at the Cattleman's Cafe and buy lunch for all of us. How is that? They have really good food."

"Umm." She said something unintelligible to someone else. Then, "Sure. That would be nice. We will get there around one o'clock, probably."

"Great. Doctor Sullivan will be so happy to hear that you are okay. Do you mind if she comes, too?"

"That would be good. Thanks. I'll see you next week." She abruptly disconnected. But now he had a number for her, and if she didn't show up, Rory Kincannon, with his technical know-how, might be able to find her.

Chapter 27

Upstairs, July was waking from a nap. She sat up, listening for Rick next door. When she didn't hear him, she picked up the old cowbell, made from a large tin can cut down and riveted into an appropriate shape. She rang it briefly, amused by the dull racket the bolt that served as a clapper made.

Downstairs, Rick heard a banging sound from July's room—*bonk, bink*— the cowbell. "Coming," he hollered, and raced up the stairs.

She was sitting on the edge of the bed, her hair standing on end like a red mohawk, pillow wrinkles on the side of her face, wearing his tee-shirt, as usual. Damn, but she looked cute!

He grinned at her. "How are you this morning? Hungry?"

She rubbed at her face. "I think I am finally ready to wash my hair by myself. Can you stand there near me? I am afraid that the hot water might make me dizzy."

July stepped into the shower and grabbed the safety bar. She stretched up, reaching for the bottle of shampoo, and then she slipped. Rick's instantaneous reaction kept her from falling as he grabbed her, shower curtain and all. She squeaked in alarm and fought her way free of the slippery curtain, ending up clinging to him, wet, naked, and trembling.

"It's okay. I've got you."

July began to laugh. "So, I have been worried about my lack of modesty, and now here I am in your arms, naked. Well, you might as well help me wash my hair again." And, he did, trying hard to focus on the surgical scar beside her spine, a reminder that she was still not well. She turned and gave him a crooked little grin, wrapping her arms around him.

"Careful, little girl. "

She laughed at him. "Honestly, do I look like a little girl? I thought I had a pretty good rack. What little girl is a C cup?" She looked down at her breasts.

"Geez! Don't do that. Don't talk like that."

"You don't like them?"

"Do not tease me, July! I mean it. You don't know what you're asking. Of course, I like them. But, I am just not what you think I am."

"I think you want me, and I want you. What's the matter with that?"

"Yes. I want you. And I could take you. And you couldn't stop me." He held both of her hands in one of his, pulling her hard against him. He saw the flash of fear in her eyes, but that is what he intended. She needed to be a little afraid of him so that she didn't get too attached.

"You are trying to scare me. And I don't believe you!"

"July, you know my reputation. I am not a nice guy. Don't ever pretend that I am. I am not good for any woman, and especially not Luke's special little girl. We are friends. Let's keep it there."

She sighed. "Okay. I'll try to behave. You just don't know how terribly attractive you are, Enrique Mora."

She started to push away from him, but he stopped her. "And, you don't know what you are letting yourself in for, July Sullivan. You are a terrible temptation, and you will regret the consequences of teasing me."

"Will you regret the consequences, Enrique?" She spoke softly.

"Yes. I will. Somewhere inside of me there is still a shred of morality. At least, I hope so." He could barely keep from pulling her round little bottom up against his crotch. He imagined unzipping his jeans, and …. "Okay, let's finish rinsing your hair." He ached with desire.

Rick wrapped her in a towel and guided her back to the bed, helping her with her one-armed attempt to dry her hair as she sat on the edge of the mattress. "Now, what do you want to wear today?"

"Your shirt."

"My shirt?" He smiled. "The denim one? Am I ever going to get that back?"

"Nope. It's comfy."

She didn't need his help dressing anymore, but she loved the attention. She loved any contact with Rick. July was very aware that she was falling in love with him and didn't know how to handle it except with jokes. She had never been in love before, and she found it confusing.

His shirt hung down to her knees so that it looked like she was naked underneath. She wanted him to think of her nakedness, of her availability. She gave him a speculative look.

"You are not supposed to look at Mary like that. I think you are feeling a lot better. Your patient Shirley called me a little while ago. She and her brother are coming up here for lunch in a few days. She wants to talk about the bombing at the clinic. I am meeting them at the cafe. You want to come?"

"Oh, thank God, she is okay! Yes, yes, I want to talk to her."

"Then, today, we need to work again on getting some more vitamins and minerals in you. I have some blackberry tonic downstairs. It should be cool enough for you to drink." He picked her up and strode down the stairs.

They had a wonderful morning. Down at the barn, she sat in an old sling chair watching him work with Topper. She handed him tools as he tuned up the truck. And she wielded the sander, helping to smooth the wood for new shelves in the cabin.

As late afternoon clouds built toward a thunderstorm, they sat on the house porch, Rick picking his guitar as they talked. She had been pondering what he said about not trusting him. She didn't buy it.

"Look at how that horse responds to you. That is a horse's version of love. He loves you. He trusts you. Gracie loves you and trusts you. I think I believe in animals and kids more than grown-up's opinions. You could have had me this morning, but you either don't find me attractive enough, or you were being honorable. Most men wouldn't worry about either one. They would just whip it out and have a go."

"Fortunately for you, I'm not most men."

"So, what do you do in your spare time, besides the Bunny hop, basketball, and music with your friends?"

"Music without my friends. Classical stuff, jazz, anything. I have been invited to the Santa Fe Music Festival again this year, and I am having a little trouble with the piece. But I still have a couple of months to get it right."

Rain came hard that afternoon, wind-driven, slashing at an angle, wetting the porch. They retreated to the kitchen, where Rick busied himself making biscuits and cutting up chicken to add to a stir fry. July watched him contentedly, listening to the rain pounding against the windows and running from the eaves.

"So, you never told me if you have a boyfriend." He glanced at her over his shoulder.

"No. I worked pretty much all the time. I am not one to go out to the bars and stuff. I mostly know married men, and having been the wronged wife myself, I would never do that to another woman. So, my love life has been severely limited. There is a doctor in Las Cruces that I hooked up with a few times when I was feeling desperate, but there is no real relationship there."

"Desperate?"

"Totally!"

Rick grinned. "So, is that what was going on this morning, you little flirt? Desperation?"

"No. But, you are sexy and strong and exciting and stuff. It's no wonder that you get the Bunnies that the other guys want."

Rick snorted. "I doubt that is the case. It's not like I arrange a romantic interlude in some nice hotel. You know?" He blushed. "Why are we talking about this?"

"Because you are weird. You are too shy to talk about it but not too shy to do it. It's not like you are eccentric or anything," she teased.

"Hey, most of those young squirts I work with call me the old man and think I'm crazy, so I may as well act like it."

"The Old Man? You mean you are like The Big Boss?"

"No. Eric is the big boss. He wants me to apply to be Chief when he retires, but it's not what I want to do."

"Why not?"

He paused, wiping the blade of the knife unnecessarily. "Is the fault in the stars, or in ourselves that we are underlings? I vote for the latter." He gave her a grin over his shoulder. "I have that temper problem, and that drinking problem, and that tendency to violence. I am just a problem in general."

He made it into a joke, then turned serious again. "Sometimes, I skate just within the edge of the law. I'm not good Chief material. Our police force has several captains. The others are college-educated, decent men, and would be better choices."

"Oh." She was quiet for a minute, thinking that she needed to change the subject back to something less painful. "So, you have never wanted to pick out one of the Bunnies for a long-term relationship?"

"Nope."

"Why? No flippant comments. I mean, I want to understand you."

"Well, since I don't understand myself, that might be a good trick." He chopped some vegetables. "Luke should be home soon. He likes this cabbage in his stir fry."

She sat silent, waiting.

He glanced at her. "So, you expect an answer?"

"I do."

He grunted. "I am not particularly insightful. I don't think about stuff like that. I don't have much of a vocabulary for, you know, feelings and such." He was quiet for a while, washing more vegetables.

"I told you about how my wife lied to me about being pregnant, or I would never have married her. So, I am a little distrustful. That's part of it." Chop, chop, chop.

"Most cops never get shot at and never fire their weapon while on duty." Chop, chop..

"On the other hand, I get into cases where there is a real risk of killing or being killed because I am okay with it. I guess I'm an adrenaline junkie. It has worked for both me and LCPD. But the result is that, in effect, I am a thug with a badge. That's what people I have arrested like to tell judge and jury." Chop, chop, chop.

"If I die in the line of duty, I want Gracie to get all of my insurance and my retirement. I don't want a relationship if I am not totally in love, whatever that means." He chuckled. Chop, chop, chop, chop.

"Does your recipe call for minced vegetables?"

He gave her a sheepish grin, sweeping the massacred vegetables into a bowl. "Got carried away there. I am not all that used to talking about, you know, whatever."

"Well, I know that you are very courageous, and dedicated to your job. You love Gracie and Uncle Luke, and your folks, and Maureen. You care about horses and fairness and stuff. You don't like blunt talk from a little girl, as you call me, much to my annoyance. You like sex on your own rather limited terms, but not romance. You drink way too much, you and Luke, sitting down here on the porch at night, jawing and boozing. You speak three languages, play the piano and guitar. You can sing. And you are a wonderful, thoughtful friend for wimpy me."

He smiled at her. "You aren't wimpy. You were seriously injured, had a potentially serious disease, and hardly ever complained. Definitely not a wimp. Actually, I speak four languages, including Arabic, and I am pretty good with percussion and a fiddle, too. So, now you know more about me than anyone else, even my mother. Satisfied?"

"No. Not satisfied. I don't believe some of it."

"I am not lying, July. I won't lie to you."

"Didn't say you are. Don't believe you are. I just think there is more that you choose not to look at. You hide your feelings even from yourself."

He gazed at her, thinking about what she said. If he could let himself fall in love with her. If he were ten years younger. If he had a safer job...if, if, if! "Maybe," he said.

July got up and took a few steps toward where he leaned against the sink. He held out his hands to her, pleased with her progress, but struggling to suppress his real feelings. *What will I do without my July?*

"My getting better is all your doing," July said. "You are making me better with your magic potions."

"You know that's not true. It's more that you aren't so depressed. You are having fun with Gracie, and you are eating better."

She leaned on him, looking up into those fascinating eyes. "I guess so, but that is still mainly due to your ministrations. I want to be better. I want to follow you down to the barn. I want to play in the creek with Gracie. I want to help you with the cabin, and I want to go dancing with you."

He looked away, struggling to understand himself. Was he just being an old fool? Here was this warm, soft, beautiful woman⏤funny, smart, sweet to Gracie, and she wanted him. He realized with a jolt that he was afraid.

"You scare me."

"What? Me? How can I scare you? You're kidding."

"No, I'm not. I'm afraid that if I give in to my instincts, I will be so ashamed of myself, and Luke and my folks will be so ashamed of me that I will lose what little joy I have in life. Or, I will become too attached, and you will change my life in ways that I can't foresee, and can't control."

"Do you mean, Rique, that you are afraid that you could fall in love with me?"

He stepped a few feet away and looked out the window. *Yes. That's precisely what I mean.* He turned back to her, unable to hide the desire in his eyes. "It's a battle for me, girl. You deserve so much better. You deserve a young fellow who will give you babies and be home every night, and not be that arrogant, egotistical, slimy toad that you slapped so hard. You want romance. I don't have a romantic bone in my body. I am a coyote, a predator, and I refuse to make you my prey. Got it?"

"No, Rique, I don't get it. No man has ever stuck in my mind like you have. When I was lying beside you in bed that one night, I knew that it was normal, right, where I should be. I felt attached, like we belong together. I know you drink too much. I know that you can be scary. None of it matters to me. And, you know, they did the radiation, and now the chemo." She sighed. "I can probably never have babies because of the damage done."

"Geez, July, I am so sorry. I wish it could be different. I wish *I* could be different." There was a tangle of emotions tearing at him. He could feel it in his chest, in his mind. He backed away. "I need to go down to Mom's for a bit. Will you be okay? Tom is at the barn."

She nodded, and he took off, leaping from the porch, splashing through the puddles. He ran so naturally. It was like watching some wild animal, easy in its stride despite the limp.

Chapter 27

Gisele heard thunderous piano music coming from her house and knew Enrique must be upset about something. When he was happy, he usually played Chopin, or maybe jazz. But this was a dramatic piece. She hurried up the hill from the store.

"Where is July, Enrique?"

"I left her at the ranch with Tom. I had to get away for a bit."

"What's the matter, son? You two have a fight?"

"No. Just the opposite." He played some crashing notes. "I don't know what to do. She wants me to kiss her, to make love to her, and I just can't. I can't!" His voice was an agonized whisper.

"Why is that? She is a beautiful woman, and you have kissed a lot of beautiful women. Or so your reputation would have it." She smiled at him.

"Don't tease me about that. I'm serious. I really don't know what to do. I worry about her all the time. I miss her when I am at the office. I'll be working on a problem, and I want to turn around and tell her about it, even though I know she's not there with me."

"What do you want to do?"

"Something has changed in me, and it happened so fast that I don't know how to cope. I want to be where she is. Hold her. Love her. But what I should do is get away from her. God, Mom, I am such a loser!"

Gisele gazed at her son with a concerned frown. "Enrique, you are a very accomplished musician, policeman, and quite a good carpenter and cabinet maker. Even as a boy, you were never a loser. There is a drawer full of rodeo buckles to prove it. Why are you feeling that way?"

"I don't know. It's just that somehow," he played some more notes, "that damn girl has me in a tangle. I should walk away, but I can't face it. I can't do it. In some ways, she needs me. I am something solid to cling to. I am sure that some man, or men, have hurt her very badly, and not just her ex-husband. I can feel it. She's afraid. Sometimes, I have my arm around her, and she hangs on to me like I'm a lifeboat in a hurricane. And she cries, Mom. She cries into my shirt and pretends not to."

He played a complicated passage, then turned to face Gisele. "She trusts me. I tell her not to, but she won't listen. I created a mess when all I wanted to do was help Luke. I can't bring myself to let go, but how can I be what she needs? I know she's strong and will get over needing me." He looked away. "But I'm not strong. I need her. July is the center of my life. How did that happen?"

Gisele rested a hand on his bowed shoulder for a moment. He had never been like this. Never. Always so good at problem-solving. Always so self-contained. And now, he was torturing himself with self-doubt.

"That passage in Liszt that was giving me trouble? Listen." He played the piece for her beautifully. "I've got it now. I'm ready for the music festival and totally screwed up on everything else. I should get back to work, but I can't concentrate when I'm there. What should I do, Mom?"

"Enrique, just admit that you are in love for the first time in your life, and it is not easy. True love is never easy. You are trying to hide from the truth, and that is not going to work. You have to deal with it one way or another. Seems to me like you two are a good team. Stop fighting it, son, July is good for you, and for Gracie. Let yourself be happy. It's a good thing."

He tried to ignore his mother's advice, but something happened that showed the truth of what she said. As he walked into headquarters a day later, the officer at the front desk motioned to him.

"What's up?"

"Captain, there is a woman waiting for you upstairs, and she seems very emotional. Not sure if it's anger or what."

"Which case?"

"Wouldn't say and refused to talk to Rory."

"Huh. Thanks."

He took the stairs up, doing his usual three at a time for the exercise, wondering what he would have to deal with this morning. He strolled down the hallway, hands in pockets, thinking about July, feeling like singing.

At the entrance to the Major Crimes space, Detective Eva Shannon greeted him with a raised eyebrow and a nod of her head toward his closed office door. He gave a questioning shrug, but she just shook her head.

As he opened the door, he heard a woman's quiet sob and saw a familiar bleached blonde head seated in front of his desk, short skirt revealing a well-toned leg. For an instant, he admired the smooth expanse, remembering what it could lead to, remembering his youthful lust. But then his stomach churned in disgust.

"Do you have a crime to report?"

"Oh, Ricky! I am so glad to see you. It has been a long time since we talked, and I miss you more all the time." She gave an artful dab to her eyes, careful not to disturb the mascara.

He didn't move into the room but remained in the doorway. "Do you have a crime to report, Cindy?"

"Why, no, honey, I...."

"Out."

Can't we go have a coffee and talk about the house?"

"Out!"

"Ricky! I know it has always been more your house than mine, and I thought...."

"I will build a new house for July and Grace and myself. If you don't want it anymore, sell it and give my half of the proceeds to my dad. Get out of my office now, Cindy!"

"What? A new house for that bitch and your brother's bastard? And you are still driving that old piece of junk truck? Loser! You think you are so high and mighty!"

"Q. Eva. Escort this woman from the premises."

Q said, "Ma'am, you will have to leave now."

Cindy's face contorted with fury. Rick stepped back from the doorway as she approached. Pausing in front of him, she started to speak, but instead drew back a hand to slap him. He caught her wrist first.

"Assaulting an officer is a felony."

"You would arrest me?"

"I don't need to because these detectives will. Get out of here. Stay out of my life. And especially, you stay away from July Kozlowski. Far, far away." His eyes were as icy as a blizzard.

What had he said? A house for July and Grace and himself? Was he really thinking that? There could be better men in her life, couldn't there? It seemed like something was wrenching at his chest. Tears pricked his eyes, and he turned quickly away.

"Hey, Q, can you check on Mr. Yamamoto for me tonight? Make sure that ramp is working for him? The handrail might be a little too high."

"Sure, Rick. No basketball after all?"

"Sorry, but as soon as this meeting is over, I think I need to hurry home."

Eva and Q looked at each other in surprise. Home? For twenty-plus years, Rick's home was the two-story garage behind Mr. Yamamoto's house. Now, home was what? Luke Kozlowski's old cabin? Really?

Chapter 29

Even with Rick's drinking and occasional black moods, it was the best time of July's life. There were, inevitably, days when he worked in town all day and didn't make the long drive home. July agonized over those times. They were sitting in the porch swing, July at one end and Rick at the other. Usually, she leaned on his shoulder as they swung. He hesitated a little, not sure whether to bring up the unusual distance between them.

"What's the matter, July? Are you mad at me? Did I say the wrong thing?"

"No. I am just being foolish."

"About what? What can I do to make it better?"

"Nothing. I'll get over it."

They swung in silence for a few minutes before he turned to face her. "Come here."

She shook her head, looking away, down the valley.

"Come here, babe." He reached over and grabbed her, sliding her across the swing. "Tell me what is wrong, my little wabbit."

"It's so stupid! I have no right to feel this way. I'm ashamed of myself."

"What? Feel what way?"

"I'm jealous." She hung her head, embarrassed.

"Jealous? Of what?"

"You know. The Bunnies. I have no reason to feel that way. It is not like I own your time or something. I'm sorry! So stupid and childish. I mean, we're just pals after all. I should be happy that you have Bunnies in your life." She wiped away a few tears.

"Oh." He put an arm around her. "Well, you know what? When you told me about that doctor you hook up with in Las Cruces, I felt such a surge of jealousy that if I figure out who it is, I'll probably beat the crap out of him. I should be happy that you have some jerk of a doctor in your life, but I'm not."

"Silly boy. Trying to make me feel better."

"Hypocrite. It's okay for you to call me a boy, but I can't call you a girl?" He smiled at her. "You know I never lie to you. And, I have not been dallying with Bunnies. I was just too tired to drive home. I wouldn't feel right anymore about hooking up with a Bunny. I'm not sure why. Maybe I am finally growing up, acting a little bit like the man my folks wanted me to be. Turn around here."

She turned around, curling into a ball, her head against his chest. "Thank you for not getting mad at me, Rique."

"Mad? I'm flattered!" He held her close. One foot on the porch rail, he rocked them with gentle pushes as they listened to the stream below them, bubbling and splashing over a rocky bed.

"Rique, why won't you kiss me? You kiss other women. Am I too icky?"

He chuckled. "Icky? Where did that come from?" He tweaked her nose, shifted his position a little, and stared out toward the woods. *Oh, if only you knew how much I want to kiss you, babe.* "No, you are not icky. I am not much of a kisser. Kissing is too...too intimate. I promised Luke that I would take care of you. That does not mean take you. Whatever my failings, I do keep my promises. And you are not icky, just odious."

"I thought I was obnoxious."

"That too. Maybe even... obstreperous."

"Nope, but I'm observant.

"And obdurate."

"Yeah? Well, it's obvious that you are obtuse, and, and, umm... obstructive."

"Nope, I am actually very obliging. And you are obfuscatory."

"I am not. I am just ob...ob...obsequious?"

Rick burst out laughing. "You don't even know what obsequious means, and you are definitely not that."

"I couldn't think of another ob word."

"I noticed."

She thumped his chest with her good hand. "Bully. So, you have sex with all these women but you don't kiss them? You are totally weird."

"I know. I...uh, see it's not what you are imagining. Sex is sport. Just sport. The ladies don't pick us up so they can get kissed. Besides, I don't kiss rabbits much, and wabbits? You would probably bite me, or slap me, or both. I'm afraid you would spend all your time with me curled up in a little ball like this, like someone is scaring you. I don't want that to be me or anyone else. I want you to feel safe and be safe." Suddenly, tears came. He felt so inadequate, and it hurt a lot.

"Rique? Are you crying?"

"No." He paused. "Yes. I guess." He laughed at himself. "Maudlin old fool."

"I didn't mean to upset you. I'm sorry."

"I am mostly upset with myself. I am good at all the wrong things. Not your fault, babe. Not your fault. I can't keep you safe if you aren't even safe from me, and if I betrayed that trust, you would be even more scared than you are now."

"I'm not scared."

"Yes, you are."

She didn't respond for a while, then gave a slight nod. "I guess I always felt insecure. Vulnerable to attack."

"I know something bad happened. And I don't think it was just Randy's betrayal, was it?" It took her a while to answer, and then it was indirect. "I learned to strike first, to keep them away from me. You know, arrogant, powerful men like you need to be warned away before I get hurt." She gave him a tremulous smile, deflecting his question.

"Stick with me, kid. I like protecting you. I want to keep you safe from being hurt by arrogant men like me." He held his July tight. What had wounded her so severely? He would find out and protect her from that, too, if he could. If he could.

Chapter 30

July was looking forward to getting out in public, now that her legs and arm were stronger. She was excited to see Shirley again, too. Maybe, finally, she would be able to answer a few of the questions that kept her awake at night.

They arrived at the cafe as the lunch crowd was leaving. Rick got many greetings from folks, and a few recognized July. They sat, eating salsa and tortilla chips, waiting for Shirley and her family. For a minute, July didn't recognize the girl with her shorter haircut. But, with July's distinctive hair color, Shirley spotted her right away.

"Oh, Shirley, you look absolutely darling with that haircut! Are we both trying to channel Audrey Hepburn or something?"

"I should have done this years ago. It is so much cooler! Sheena cut it for me. Good job, isn't it? You look like that little pixie from Peter Pan, Doctor Sullivan, with your red hair and freckles. It's hard to remember that you are old enough to be a doctor!" Shirley laughed.

"Well, the big guy here calls me a little brat, so I guess I should look like one, shouldn't I?" She made a face at Rick, who was rising to seat Shirley and Sheena before he greeted Abe.

"Hey, Captain. How ya doin'? This is my sister Shirley, and my girlfriend, Sheena. Sheena works for the Mesa County Sheriff's Office."

"Ladies. Abe. Nice to see you, son. What are you doing these days?"

"Thanks to you, I am the Assistant Produce Manager at the market on 16th street. We are doing good, man." They shook hands. "It is so beautiful up here. This is the kind of place where we should be raising our kids. I wish we had never moved to the city, but I guess in small towns, you have to be related to folks to find work, huh?'

"Yeah, pretty much. It's growing a little from the Hollywood set and their fancy ranchettes. Not a lot, though, because mostly they just frequent the restaurants. But up the road two miles is a big old barn-like building. That is my family's farm store. Mom is there. Go talk to her. She knows everyone and everything happening around this town. She could keep an eye out for opportunities for you."

"Hey, thanks, Captain. We will. I worry about keeping the kids away from that other side of the family, you know? So, anyhow, I have been telling my little sister that she needs to talk to you. And I need to talk to you, too."

"Yeah? What's up?"

Shirley spoke. "Well, I am confused, wondering about the fire, you know? Like, after we jumped out of the clinic that day, I looked over, and this old lady was running from the back of the building. She didn't even look around when the blast happened, so I figured that she had done it, locked us in and set the bomb off. And, I thought it was Mr. Winter's wife. At least, she wore the same kind of shoes, and had white hair. But Abe pointed out that an old lady like Mrs. Winter probably wouldn't be able to run like that, and anyone can have a wig."

Rick and July looked at each other, eyebrows raised.

"But now I am not so sure," Shirley continued. "They come to the car wash where I work, and I've watched them. She hates him. Really, really hates him. So, I thought maybe she was trying to frame him, but he is very visible and always out in front, so how would that work? Besides, after I fell, I looked around and didn't see him." Rick nodded, encouraging her.

"Then I thought maybe someone was pretending to be an old lady. But why?" She looked around the table as though for an answer. "The other day, I ran into Milly, the clinic manager. She was at the laundromat, so we had a long talk, you know, while our stuff dried. And, she was telling me about this other doctor that used to come to the clinic, giving out stuff for skin problems like you did. She showed me this, and I kept it to give to you."

She handed July a sample of a potent and dangerous acne medicine. It was labeled, "From the Office of Dr. Richard Garner."

"This doctor apparently got kicked out or something? And then, Milly started talking about how he was giving out this stuff like water and lost his license. I remembered you saying how dangerous it is for pregnant women and unborn babies, and I thought, maybe it meant something." She looked from one to the other. "I guess It just seems like this is important. I mean, it's crazy to do that, isn't it?"

Roberta. This might be the medicine Mom was talking about. Rick said, "It is very important information, Shirley. Thank you for taking the trouble to come all the way up here. Your curiosity is going to be a big help, I think. Asking questions is how we solve most crimes. But I could have gone down there to meet you." Rick smiled at her.

"Well, Captain, there is another reason for that." Abe shifted uncomfortably. "Do you remember telling me to contact you if my cousin, the guy who gutshot you, ever came back?"

Rick nodded, and his eyes grew cold and hard.

"I haven't seen him, but my bros say he is back, and I think he has been following me. Like, he doesn't trust me since you rescued me from being charged that time. So, we figured it wouldn't be safe for you if you came to meet us."

"Good move, Abe. Thanks for being so thoughtful. I will find him first, I hope."

Suddenly, Abe wasn't looking at Rick. He froze in his chair, his face pale. He opened his mouth to speak, but a voice came from just behind Rick.

"Hey, if it isn't the big hero just waiting for me. Sorry to hear that you survived. Howz about you come outside with me?" He showed

Rick a small but lethal pistol resting in his palm. "Don't want to hurt my *primo* here unless I have to. Just you, or maybe your girlfriend, if you are too slow-moving, huh?" He grinned.

Rick paused. Four innocent young people sat before him, at risk from this monster.

"Sure, sure, Aaron." He raised his hands a little in apparent surrender. "I'm coming. Let me just tell...." Rick turned as though to speak to July, then kicked out sideways with all of his strength, ramming his boot heel into the man's knee. There was an audible snap, and Aaron screamed, falling forward. Rick stabbed an elbow into his eye socket and grabbed the back of his neck, smashing Aaron's face into the edge of the wooden table. Lips drew back in a terrible grimace, and the muscles in his forearms stood out in overlapping brown bands, like layers of sculpted wood.

It all happened so fast that no one even had a chance to yell, or speak, or move. The pistol skittered under the table. Abe put his foot on it.

"I'll give you some choices here, Aaron. Shall I kill you, or lock you up with some of the guys. Like maybe Sean Riley. You remember him, don't you? I bet he would do to you what you did to his daughter." His voice was frightening in its intensity. The cafe was silent, everyone knowing that he meant it.

There was a gasping, wet sound from the ruined face. "What's that?" Rick tightened his grip on the man's neck. His teeth snapped together like the coyote threatening an enemy.

"Oh, Is it hard to talk? I'll make it even simpler. Shall I kill you now or not? Just say, live or die."

A sobbing, blubbering sound came from the crushed mouth. The hot ammonia smell of urine rose to the table occupants as a puddle spread across the floor.

"What's that? You want to live?" Rick jerked Aaron's head back, snarling. Aaron was sobbing through broken teeth in a ruined face, choking on his own blood.

Sheriff's deputies arrived, and Rick heard a voice over his shoulder, "I have him, Rick."

He let go and stood. "Better get the ambulance. His leg is broken. He has a pistol somewhere here. Too stupid to keep his finger on the trigger, or he would have had me."

"Hey, Charlie," Rick said to the bartender. "Where are your mop and bucket?"

"I'll get it, Rick."

"Nah, you get everybody's order, and I'll clean up the floor. I'll have a medium-rare rib-eye and side salad."

Charlie had known Rick for forty years. "And, a bourbon, double shot?"

"No. I think maybe a lemonade." He winked at July.

Rick tried to distract the kids from what they had just seen, asking Abe about his job, complimenting Shirley on her observations, listening to Sheena talk about how hard it was to finish her degree. And he found out a little about Eddie, Shirley's ex, who had washed out of the Navy Seals. Seals get training in the use of explosives. He would have Rory start checking this guy out. Maybe Shirley had been the target.

Rick was a good host, keeping the young folks talking about themselves. July followed his lead, and had them laughing at Rick as she told the tale of gray Captain Bob becoming an almost white bunny. Rick smiled, but he was sick that his July had seen the monster he could be. He needed a drink, and not lemonade.

Chapter 31

Rick was very quiet as they drove home, answering July's comments with a grunt. He looked so sad. She gave him that big-eyed, solemn gaze that turned his heart over in his chest and said, "I thought it might be transference, what I feel for you. Then I thought it was a daddy fixation, and although I was embarrassed by the thought, it is partly true. Luke did his best for me, but he is not the kind of man who can pick up a little girl and cuddle and comfort her. "

She paused for a moment. "I have felt at risk, unsafe, all of my life until I met you. Now, I think I am mostly safe, and I guess I feel cherished when you put your arm around me. It's like, for once, I don't have to be on guard, ready to do battle. I love how brilliant you are, and funny, and talented, and strong. I love how much you care about things. And, I don't have the equivalent of Badge Bunnies in my life. That would be what? Badge Bubbas?" That made him chuckle a little. "So, you are it, Rique. My one and only."

"Well, there is that doctor in Las Cruces."

"Oh, shut up! You saved my life, the kids' lives, and maybe more today. You are incredibly amazing, you idiot!"

He snorted but gave her a ghost of a grin. At the entrance to the ranch, he paused.

"July, is it too soon to ask what you are planning to do? Do you want to try to work things out with your old practice? Find a new practice? Do you think you will be able to do what you need to do as a dermatologist?"

"I don't know what to do, Rique. My life for so many years revolved around trying to be the best doctor, the most skilled dermatologist. Now, I don't know how much control I will ever get back in these darn fingers. I could work as a GP, I guess. I also need to figure out what to do about Uncle Luke long-term. I just don't know."

Rick nodded and took a side road, bypassing the ranch driveway. "Let me show you something."

They drove in silence, occasionally pointing to deer or elk. A bobcat ran across the road in front of them. They smiled at each other, happy to be sharing the moment. He opened a gate, and they went on, the road becoming a trail, just two tracks through the meadow. At the top of a ridge, he parked and got out. "Come with me."

He led her the few yards to a viewpoint. Far below them, they could just barely make out -the glint of sunlight from the steel roof of the ranch house. The folds of the hills hid the cabin and barn.

"Oh! It's so beautiful. I was never allowed to come up here."

"It's okay, you know the owner. We have Tom moving the cattle up here for the rest of the summer. He will develop the springs, and he hired a crew to fence the whole thing into separate pastures so you can rotate the grazing. He thinks you should get into the grass-fed beef market, with a smaller herd and use the cabin as a B&B for hunters."

"What? Cattle up here?"

"Yup. Dad and I have owned these hills and mesas all the way to Redtail Lake for years. Dad wanted me to help him buy them when they showed up in tax sales to keep them out of the hands of developers. So, we bought a few sections at a time. And there it is, home to miles of good grass and timber. Never used it for anything. Combined with Kozlowski land, it comes to one hundred forty sections. I have signed my interest in it over to you. You and Luke and Tomás and my dad should use it. If you don't want to return to practice full time, you can be a rancher and do volunteer medical stuff. Okay? So, this is an option for your future, whatever happens to me. Your domain, mademoiselle!"

His heart hurt as he held her there, knowing that by his presence, he could be compounding the risks she faced. Not just the bomber, but all the people who would like to harm him might try to get at him through her. July sensed it, the shadows coming from him, the profound depression dragging him down. She turned on him.

"What do you mean, 'whatever happens to me'? What does that mean?"

"Didn't you hear what Aaron said? He would happily kill you to get at me. Kill you! Your life is at risk not just from the bomber but from being with me. Sweet Jesus, what have I done, exposing you to this?"

"Rique! Are you afraid? Is that what this is about? I'm not afraid!"

"That's because you are naïve and foolish. If you ever grow up, you will realize that I have to get away from you and Grace. I brought this life on myself. I can't let it affect you or any of my family!"

"Am I part of your family?"

"Aren't you? I'm a very good hunter of the bad guys because it takes one to know one. I am afraid my behaviors, my history, will destroy your life and Grace's. No one should suffer for my many sins except me."

His voice was a husky growl, as though speaking was a great physical effort. The pain in his face scared her, and July did not tolerate her fears well. Her anger rose like a volcano. She attacked him with fury, kicking, stomping on his boot, hitting him as hard as she could.

"No! No! You are doing that negative, glass half empty, this is my fate thing. It does not have to end that way, you son of a bitch! Damn you, you stupid jerk!" She kicked him again, her soft-soled shoe slamming into the heavy leather of his boot. "Ow, ow, ow!"

"Don't, baby! You're hurting yourself."

She was too furious to care. "If you kill yourself, I will bite your other wrist, and drag your body through the streets, and beat the crap out of you, and, and bury you in the slime at the bottom of the pond. You stop it right now! I made the choice to love you. Do you hear? My choice. Listen up, jerk! I may not be your woman, but by God, you are my man! 'Whither thou goest', and all that."

She was so tense it made her throat sore. Her stomach hurt because she was so terribly afraid for him.

"Do you think I am just an angwy wabbit? Bubba, you will experience the total wrath of the crazy wild tiger. You hear me? You may not leave your family! Give me your gun."

"What?"

"That gun clipped to your belt. Give it to me now!"

"Do you know what...."

"Shut up!" She reached around him, snatched it out of its holster, and chambered a round.

"Are you going to shoot me? Right here, please." He pointed to his left shirt pocket. "Head shots are so damn messy."

"Don't make fun of me, sucker! I can shoot just fine. See that knothole on the tree?" She took quick aim and fired, missing by maybe an inch.

"Wow, Deadeye! Pretty good!"

"Don't you dare laugh at me! I can defend myself if I have to, and Gracie, too."

She stood there, cradling the hand with the gun, the hand that she had hit him with, trying not to cry. Her face was flushed, her hair tousled. She looked like she was ready to hit him again. He wanted to hold her, comfort her, make her happy. And he didn't know how.

"Don't beat me up, July. You're injuring yourself."

"I'll injure you, you damned idiot. Don't you dare leave me." With her chin sticking out and lips clamped tight in determination, she looked like she might very well shoot him. "I won't let you kill yourself. I won't!"

He shook his head, not knowing how to respond, then laughed a little. "Come here, baby. Give me that thing. I see that my girl also has a quote or two in her. How about this one. 'Your word is a lamp to my feet and a light to my path.' That is what you mean to me. July. You don't need this because you are a pistol." He holstered the weapon. "You are going to shoot me so that I won't shoot myself? The logic escapes me."

"I never said I was logical. It's just that...," she sniffed back tears.

"I know. I'm sorry. Come here, my fierce little wabbit."

He kissed her, ever so gently at first. She responded with fire. He grew more forceful as she gave readily to the power of his arms, the demands of his tongue. One hand cupped her bottom as she pressed hard against him. Her hand ran up under his shirt. He closed his eyes, wanting to focus on that touch, her cool hand on his burning skin. But when that hand dropped to his belt, he suddenly pulled back.

"Ah! What am I doing? No, no! Not yet." He stepped back, his heart pounding, breathing hard, holding her at arm's length. "My God, girl, your Enrique damn near lost that battle with philandering Captain Mora." He struggled with control. "I don't want to treat you that way."

Her face was flushed, her green eyes brilliant. "Oh, Rique. You are my only real love. And did you hear what you just said? You said 'not yet.' So, what does that mean?"

He ducked his head for a minute, trying to deal with a confusion of feelings surging strongly through him. It was a maelstrom, and he was dizzy, disoriented. The door he had kept closed for so long was wide open. He couldn't seem to pen up emotions for which he had no coping mechanisms. "I don't know."

"I will not allow you to mess with my feelings or Gracie's future. I will not allow you to leave your family guilt-ridden for the rest of our lives because we couldn't help you. You think killing yourself would be a selfless act, relieving us of danger. But really, it is selfish, cowardly, a way of getting free of complicated problems. Don't you dare!"

"I hear you. I don't know what is happening to me, July." Rick looked away, out across the miles of wild and empty land. It was all his, and now hers. "I thought you were safe here. I was wrong. But I guess the ranch is still pretty much the safest place around. I am going to move Tom up to the house. We will just have to stay alert and get you a gun."

"I have a gun. An S&W .44 revolver. Luke got it for me when I was seven. We used to sit on the porch and shoot at cans on that old stump in the front yard."

He laughed. "July Marie, you are amazing. Let me see that hand, babe." It was already swelling across the knuckles. She flinched as he turned it over.

"Can you squeeze my fingers?"

"Yes."

"Well, that was a pretty feeble squeeze for a crazy wild tiger. Let's get some ice on it. I don't think you broke any bones."

Chapter 32

As they drove back to the ranch, he told her something he had never told anyone. "The day after I turned nineteen, our transport ran over an IED and was disabled. Iraqis were on the rooftops, in the windows, behind cars, all shooting at us. There was blood everywhere, and bullets everywhere, and everyone was screaming. I just kept firing until there was no one left to shoot." He paused.

"That is all in the public records. But there was something else. Something happened to me. It was like when you try to break a green stick. You know, it will bend and bend and finally break partway through?" She nodded.

"It was like that. I snapped, but didn't break apart. I don't know why, and I can't explain it, but there was this instant when my sense of physical fear just turned off like a faucet. It never came back. I have never been afraid of dying or being wounded since that day. That is a lot of what made me a good law officer. I haven't had the burden of fearing the consequences of my actions. But it also made me a monster in a way. I mean, there I was, a creature in camo, invading someone else's country for who the hell knows why? I was killing, wounding, just like what happened here. The conquistadors. The Anglo invaders. I was a scrawny, ignorant, freaking crazy teenager, made strong not by superior knowledge or skill or purpose, but just by modern weaponry. And I was doing to them what my

own people suffered over the generations. Done to your Polish ancestors, too, by wave after wave of invading hordes. How sick is
that? He paused.

"To me, it felt like Sand Creek and Wounded Knee and the Long
Walk all wrapped up in twenty minutes of combat. I propped my
weapon on the back of our poor dead driver, and the broken wind-
screen, and the door of the truck. I emptied my magazine, and Ian's
magazine, and Larry's magazine, until there was no one left to kill.
It was a massacre. I wasn't sure whether I was on the right side, or
the wrong side, or even if there really were any sides. Maybe I was
just killing to be killing, like a maniac. Like a sick, crazy coyote."

He stopped the truck, leaning forward, his head resting on the
hands that clutched the steering wheel. He got out, closed the door
and said, "Here, babe. You take the truck. Drive home. Leave me
here with the other coyotes. I belong here, in these woods, with
the other wild things. I am not fit to be your man. Slide over here,
and drive away." His jaw was tight, the muscles standing out, as he
stood there with hands on hips, staring at his feet. He kicked at a
clump of grass, tearing it up with the toe of his boot.

July watched the thin roots ripping out of the soil. It felt like her
heart was ripping out of her body, and that she might wither and
die like the blades of grass.

"You asked how I became the town bad boy. It wasn't me, and
it was me. I am both Dr. Jekyll and Mister Hyde. If you and the kids
had not been there, I would have broken Aaron's neck. The only
reason I didn't is that it makes an ugly noise that you all would remember with horror. I struggle to control the mad man, and sometimes I cannot. The monster takes control. I am better than I used
to be, but it is entirely possible that at some point, I will kill or maim
when I don't need to do so, and I will end up in prison myself. Do
you understand? I cannot be the man that you love. What if I end
up bringing you harm?"

He sat down in the dirt of the little road, his head on his knees.
July waited, barely breathing, feeling the despair in him. He started
again. "I was a nice little boy until one day. One day...." His voice

trailed off. July slid down from the truck and knelt behind him, her arms reaching around him as far as they could. He covered one of her hands with his.

He started again. "I am a coyote. And the problem with coyotes is that they are excellent predators. It is their destiny and mine. One day, back when I was that nice little boy, Dad shot a rabid coyote. It didn't entirely die. Its body did, but its soul entered me and lives in me. I am he. He is me. He rages. He stalks his prey. When I say that I am a crazy coyote, it isn't a metaphor. I *am* a crazy coyote. At least part of me is. I kill, and feel no more concern than that coyote. It makes me dangerous, a monster. When Cindy lied to me, and laughed about not being pregnant after all, I could have killed her. If Eric hadn't arrived just then, I might have." He struggled to speak, his breathing heavy and his voice like gravel.

"How can I be the kind of man you want? A mental case. A drunk. It doesn't make sense. You should have shot me. The world would be a better place. So, I have that reputation for cleaning up my city, but I succeeded not because I am one of the good guys. It's because I am a badder guy than the bad guys. My life is one long lie. My ancestors called coyote the Trickster. It fits."

July leaned against him. Her cheek on his back, searching her heart and soul. There was a spark of fear, but much, much more than that was an overwhelming wave of tenderness, a desire to hold and comfort the tortured boy inside this complicated man.

"Do you know what, Rique? I know something that you don't. All through college, I worked weekends and some nights in the cardiac care unit at the hospital in Austin. I was there, holding a hand or just sitting beside people when they died. Give me your hand."

She held that warm, rough hand close to her heart. "When it is the time for someone to die, I can feel it. I feel their spirit withdrawing. But sometimes, when they have mentally given up, tired of the struggle, their spirit is still a little flame in there. You can sense it. Maybe consciously, maybe unconsciously, but you can. And you know, as a medical provider, that it is not time to give up on that person. It is not their time."

He cocked his head a little, listening.

"Rique, when it is your time to go, I will send you on your way with all my love. But, my coyote, this is not that time. There is more for you to do. Hang in there. I've got your back, and I always will have. Literally and figuratively, doofus." She pressed her head between his shoulder blades. "Got it?"

He gave a little snort. "Come here."

She moved to sit beside him. He turned to look at her. "Why do you say that I am your man? The world is full of better men than me."

"I see something else in you. I see a brainy, funny, talented man. I see someone who cares. I see that guy with the dumb jokes who pretends to shoot spider webs, or whatever it is, from his fingers and makes little kids happy with his silliness. I know a man is in here," she tapped his chest, "who is man enough to be nurturing and sweet. Besides, when he isn't in one of those grim moods, Mr. Tough Guy is very cute."

"Cute? Me? I have never met that guy, silly wabbit. I think you're imagining things."

"Nope. I'm seeing through the armor. X-ray eyes. Super girl!" She flexed her biceps.

"Huh," he said. But he almost smiled.

" You know what, Bubba? I have always liked and admired coyotes. On one level, they seem to be a problem, a threat, a bad animal to have around. But the truth is that they are incredibly smart and terribly important. I mean, they control the populations of stuff that harms us, rats and such. They provide the joy of musical nights. They are good parents and responsible mates. I think I love coyotes, one of them at least. The world would suffer greatly without them. Maybe it's because I was never real good at math, but for the life of me, I can't figure out how to shoot the coyote half of you and leave the other half unharmed. I guess I'm stuck with all of you. And all of you includes a very lovable boy."

"Silly girl. I haven't been a boy for a long, long time." It did sound silly, calling him a boy when his voice was so deep that she could feel the vibrations from it through the soles of her feet.

"And I haven't been a girl for a long, long time."

"Hah."

She gave a fake sigh of exasperation and smiled at him. "Listen up, you aren't getting away from me easily. The real problem with this coyote right here," she punched his shoulder, "is that he is so damn stubborn."

He put an arm over her shoulders, and they sat there in the dirt, watching as the sun dropped behind the trees. The creatures of the evening began to appear. Deer browsed in the meadow. Bats chased insects across the sky. And from the shelter of oak brush, a coyote family watched in interested silence.

July was quiet for a few miles as they drove toward home, then touched his hand. "I can never really understand what you have endured, Rique, but I feel it. I feel it in my heart." There was nothing she could say to heal that wounded psyche, to relieve his pain. She chose distraction. "How many were injured by the IED?"

"All of us were wounded. Some by the IED and some by gunfire. You know that this scar here in my shoulder is from that day. The round angled down, went through the bone here, and into my chest. Out of twenty, only eight of us survived."

"Do your parents know?"

"They know I came back an even worse problem than when I left." They rode home with July pressed tight against his side because that was the only comfort she could offer.

It was a lovely evening, the smell of pines filling the air. After dark a truck came up the drive, Joe Archuleta at the wheel, and a couple of fellows sitting in the bed. "Hey, Rick! Challenge you to a game of pool? Bet I can beat you!"

He hesitated, but July said, "Go. Have some fun with the guys." He jumped down the steps, vaulting up into the truck bed as Joe accelerated away.

It was still early when July and Luke heard a motor and the sound of male laughter. A pickup rolled slowly toward the house. It paused as Rick half fell out of the back, landing on his knees, and crawled the few feet to the steps before passing out.

"Well, I think our boy has had a drink or two. Let's see if we can get him out of the dirt." Luke rose with a snapping of his knees, and grabbed the back of Rick's shirt. July dumped the contents of her iced tea glass on his head. He sputtered a complaint, making it as far as the porch floor before he collapsed again. She covered him with a blanket, understanding, at least in part, why he drank as he did.

Chapter 33

It was a few nights later. July had gone up to bed. Rick sat on the porch, slowly pushing the swing, the only sound the rhythmic squeak of the chains. Luke joined him for a nightcap.

"Luke, there is something I need to understand. Do you know what happened to July in the past? Something really bad that she can't bring herself to talk about?"

"I don't think I should say, boy. There was something, and it scarred her emotionally. But until she is ready to tell you, I cannot. It was when she was in med school. That's all I can say." Rick nodded in understanding.

"July is worried about my drinking, Luke. I never used to care. I mean, what the hell, eh? Die from liver failure, being shot, or shooting myself? None of it mattered. But now, I need to live. I need to be able to take care of my girls. As much as I want her, I will not carry our relationship further until I can clean up my act and understand her fears. I am afraid of hurting her more, or again. I need to stop this nonsense." He lifted the empty glass, "And I am no longer sure that I can."

"Oh, you can, boy. You can. I think, maybe, you are just afraid to try. Drinking gets you past some big contradictions in your personality. It smooths the road a bit." The chains holding the swing groaned as he shifted his weight into a more comfortable position.

"How'd you get to be so smart, you old codger?"

Luke laughed. "Hell, boy, even little Gracie sees it. You are blind to yourself, but not to us."

Rick set his glass down without refilling it. "I have gone so long hiding my feelings, or maybe just not feeling, that I don't know what's going on with me. Maybe I'm addicted to adrenaline, and conflict, and drama, as much as to alcohol. I can't see myself as anything but a cop, but I can't imagine my life without July. One of these days, and it could be soon, I will get killed or permanently maimed. I might even end up in prison myself. I don't want her to be saddled with that. I don't know how much I can change and still be the man she wants."

"What's the matter with who you are?"

He gave a rueful chuckle. "I am almost old enough to be her father. I'm a target for every gangster in the region. I'm a frigging drunk when I'm not at work, and sometimes when I am at work. Being a total louse, I spend my spare time screwing whatever is available and compliant. Then, of course, there is that little matter of my being paid to kill people." He sighed.

"I was holding her in my arms, and part of me…I don't know. It was like nothing mattered but July. Her goals, her career, matter much more than mine. Sounds like the theme for some schmaltzy TV movie, doesn't it?" He picked up his glass, but put it back down, still empty. "I am good at hunting the bad guys down. I am an efficient manager and an accomplished killer. I was sort of okay with my failings for all these years. Then came July."

Luke sat silent, letting Rick pour out his feelings. "What I am not good at, Luke, is being a decent human being, and that is what July needs, deserves, in her life."

"You think you can tell that girl what is best for her, Rick? You've got another think coming."

The old man rocked for a few minutes. "When I was a boy, your grandfather was an old man but still straight and strong. He was a real hero, a true warrior. An Army scout behind enemy lines. He earned a chest full of medals. Some were never awarded because, you know, he wasn't white. I worked for him when he was foreman on the Campbell Ranch."

Luke rocked and sipped for a few minutes. "Maybe you are a warrior, too, son. A modern kind of warrior, keeping the weaker, slower, less aware folks safe. Have you thought of that? I am pretty sure that is a good thing."

They listened to the breeze in the pines, the creek's murmur, and the horses' shifting in the corral below. Rick struggled in silence. He had tried for most of his life not to look too carefully at any kind of feelings. In recent years, his emotions were reserved mainly for Gracie. He just did his job and went on, day after day after day. But now?

"Damn it. Somehow, I have gotten so tangled up." He paused. "She is better, stronger. I suppose she will leave pretty soon. What will I do without my July?" He wiped his eyes with a finger.

"You know, Luke. I usually think of myself as a savage, a wild animal, not someone with much emotional depth. I am often disgusted with myself for some of the reckless things I do, but...." He paused for several minutes, not knowing how to say what he meant.

"I think I understand, Rick. You like your power. You like winning." He watched the younger man's face, seeing bitter recognition of the dilemma.

"Think of Greek mythology, boy. We still refer to those characters, don't we? Most were half-man, half-god beings in the stories. Not really gods, of course, just men, but different men. It's humanity's recognition of the power some men have to both build and destroy. Some unusual men like you. All the good people who need protection from murderers and rapists and such need you. You know that thing about how some have greatness thrust upon them? From Shakespeare?

Rick smiled a little. "Sure. Twelfth Night."

"Old Will wrote for the common man. Men like me. So often, what he said was true. You have taken lives, but I wonder how many lives you have saved by your actions? You haven't been in this nursemaid role for very long. Give yourself more time."

Rick sat silent then, listening to the night. "Luke, I have to find out what I am, what's inside me, starting tonight. And give July time to think about what she wants, too. I'll be back in a week. Can you or Tom be here every day until I get back? I have a gig with Q and Sharon in two weeks, doing a fundraising thing at the Policeman's Picnic. I want all of you to come to the picnic if you can. We can stay in the hotel for a few nights, have fancy dinners, and go out dancing or something. Kate will like it. I'll have Sharon call you about arrangements. Okay? Tell July that it's okay. It's not my time. I'll be back."

Chapter 34

Rick packed supplies into the outer pocket of his camel backpack and filled the water pocket with ice, so he would have cool water to drink as it melted. The backpack went into a plastic garbage bag tied tightly shut to keep things dry while crossing the river.

The sky was already beginning to lighten. Anxious to reach some higher country to get out of the heat as soon as possible, he swam the river instead of going all the way down to the bridge. The current was strong from the summer rains, carrying him downstream a little way before hitting a backwater where he could make some progress. He climbed out onto rocks at the base of a cliff, short of breath, and rested for a few minutes, examining the barrier in the growing daylight.

There were enough possible hand and footholds. With a running start, Rick leaped up, just catching a protrusion with the fingers of his left hand. The wrenching pain, as fingers and arm took his body weight, jerked a gasp from him. He hung there for a moment, then swung so that his right hand could find purchase a little higher up. From there, he climbed to the top with only a single scary gap where the stretch to the next handhold was almost too far.

He rested a moment after reaching the mesa top, then began jogging. Wet jeans restricted movement a little bit. As the route leveled out and his clothes dried, he picked up speed and was soon running, dodging around saltbush and chamisa, leaping over rocks and logs. He headed for a grove of piñon, its shade inviting in the heat.

There was already an occupant. A fat rattler lounged on the rock Rick had chosen as his seat. He broke a dead branch from one of the trees and gently poked at the snake. It slowly uncoiled, then in the blink of an eye, was off the rock, striking at Rick.

He leaped sideways, laughing, using the branch to confound the snake's strikes. It was a dangerous test of lightning-fast reflexes against lightning-fast strikes. After a few minutes, the snake conceded the field and moved away, disappearing down a small arroyo.

Rick rested on the rocks, sipping a little water, trying to empty his mind of anything other than his surroundings. But he couldn't help wondering why he needed to take those risks. Climbing the cliff? Competing with the snake? Both actions were really just stupid. What was he trying to prove? He shook his head, rose, and ran on.

The sun dazzled his eyes, even through the dark aviators. Sweat soaked his shirt. Rick sought a little shade beside a sagebrush, there being no trees for several miles as he crossed an area of grassy plain. He scraped a small patch clear of pebbles and lay down, his head in the shade.

The tickling of ant feet on his arm woke Rick. He was nauseated and shaky. He rose and walked for a while, trying not to vomit. It was still quite hot. A breeze dried his sweat, offering a bit of coolness. Running again, he set his sights on a dark spot far ahead, assuming that it was a patch of trees, but long before he reached his goal, he was on his knees, vomiting. The full moon was at the meridian before he dragged himself into the grove of pines.

He slept until the scrabbling of small animals in the pine needles woke him at dawn. He staggered out to greet the rising sun, pulling off his shirt, feeling a need to have the first rays strike his bare chest. There was a whisper of something on the breeze, very faint. Tap, tap, tap like a drum. Rick cocked his head, straining to hear. The rhythm of his stride was like that distant drumbeat. Tap,

tap, tap, tap. His heartbeat seemed to match it. His thoughts began to take a rhythm, too, like a chant.

Climbing down into the bed of Willow Creek changed the hypnotic effect of his trotting. There were a few large trees and many small pools of clear water. He filled his water bag, added the necessary sterilizing tablets, and sat. Cool water on his bare feet and a slice of jerky held between teeth and cheek restored some energy. A few minutes rest, some dry socks, and he was up and running again. Tap, tap, tap, tap, the steady rhythm of his feet.

The mid-day heat made him dizzy. The lack of his daily ration of alcohol made him try to vomit again. But it was all dry retching, almost painful in its intensity. He stuck the flexible straw of the camel pack in his mouth and sipped. Tap, tap, tap, sip. Tap, tap, tap, sip. He ran on and on, eyes dazzled by the sun, mind numbed by the rhythm, following a deer path. Suddenly, there was a flash of light, and then nothing.

Pain in his arm and side woke him. Was someone kicking him in the side? And none too gently, either. But there was no one there. He had a throbbing pain in his ribs and an actively bleeding cut on his shoulder. Broken branches of a dense shrub hung over his head. His shirt was torn and bloody in places. Touching a crust of dried blood on the side of his face, he looked around, gradually realizing that he had somehow managed to run off a small cliff, his fall broken by the shrub above him. He could hear the murmur of running water somewhere nearby.

Slowly, painfully, Rick got to his feet and re-filled the camel. He gathered some pine needles with a few twigs and small branches. Using a lens of his bifocals, safe in the hard-sided case in his pocket, he focused the rays of the sun on his little cache. Focus your energy like the rays of the sun, he told July that day in the hospital. As he thought about her, something bubbled up. Some pain, or fear, or something he did not understand, and he sobbed, startling himself. He didn't know if he should laugh or cry.

It took only a minute or two to get a small flame going. Rick smiled a little, remembering all the times his mother had gotten after him for doing this. He dipped his shirt in the creek, using it to wipe his face and chest, the cold water stinging multiple cuts and scratches. Rick rested on a rock, his feet in the water. Crawdads began to move in the pool beside him. Using his shirt, he made a little dam to keep them from escaping, and with fast hands, scooped a dozen of the larger ones up onto the sand. He quickly pitched them into his little fire, and almost as fast, fished them out to cool. It was a good dinner. Crawdads, dried apricots, and water. He fell into a restless sleep, his wounds throbbing, stomach cramping, muscles spasming.

When he woke, the sun was already peeping into the canyon. He thought there was a voice. "Get up, grandson. Get up and run, like a warrior." But, of course, there was no one there, just the faint beating of a drum. He could feel it, couldn't he? Feel it through his body, hear it on the breeze? He cocked his head again, listening. Or was it the throb of injured ribs that he was feeling, imagining the sound?

He moved carefully, stiff and very sore, but he moved. Snail slow at first, he was trotting again by noon, following a rocky wash through the widening canyon, a stabbing pain in his side at every step. His goal was an ancient ruin built into shallow caves in the canyon walls.

The cliff dwelling was in fair shape. The kiva ladder looked like it was replaced within the last year, probably by archeology students from the U. He climbed down into the half-light and squatted on his heels. In spots, the circular walls showed faint traces of murals that had decorated the interior for hundreds of years. These were not his people, yet he felt an affinity somehow.

Rick rested there, eventually lying down in the dirt, looking up through the overhead entrance, letting his mind roam. Half asleep, the drum beat through his body, and he thought he heard chanting. He imagined the residents preparing themselves to repel raids by his ancestors. Did they purify themselves with emetics or the smoke from sweetgrass bundles? Did they share tales of previous battles, recounting successes? Did they talk to their gods?

Startlingly white puffs of clouds drifted slowly across the deep blue sky overhead as the light began to fade to the orange-red of sunset. He climbed up into the cooling air, trotting again, and found himself chanting in rhythm with his stride.

Rick sensed Iron Horse running beside him, matching him step for step. The life around him touched his soul. He knew he was hallucinating, but he didn't care. Lizards nodded to him. Ravens spoke to him from above. Flowers bloomed just for him. Bees buzzed secrets in his ear. A doe, startled, sprang up from drinking in the river, then stood and watched him pass by.

He ran on as darkness reached him, his only light from the emerging stars to the east and the fading glow in the west. He was one with it all, feeling a part of the creatures, large and small. The healing white light of the rising moon brought him some peace.

Chapter 35

"Oh, Luke!" July slumped into a kitchen chair. "I am so afraid for him! He gets in those black moods."

"I know, honey. He'll be back. I have been saying silent prayers over that boy seems like forever." He sighed. "Rick is deeply wounded, July. I have seen that despair in him so many times, and feared what a man like him might do when alone with a gun. But, I don't think he will leave Grace without her Papa, and he doesn't want to leave you."

"Where is he, Luke? Where did he go? Will he call me?"

"Probably not. You know, he's a pretty confused fella. He needs to get his head on straight. You are all mixed up, too. I can see that you're in love with him, but what does that mean? Do you want to try to keep that fellowship in London? Do you want him to give up a twenty-three-year successful career and follow you? What would happen with Gracie then? Do you want to give up your career for him? Can you tell me, right now, how you see your future with Rick?"

"I know that I want to be with him, but I don't know how to make it work for all of us."

"Exactly. You know, July, I never figured out what to do for you. I think I was a failure as a father substitute." He made a hushing gesture when she tried to object. "It is probably a good thing that I never married. I just wasn't ready. And, in some ways, I think you are still not ready."

July flushed pink and then turned pale. The truth hurt.

"Intellectually, you are amazing. And you are tough, strong in a lot of ways. But, honey, in other ways, you are still very young, much younger than thirty-two. If you love Rick because he is the papa you never had, you need to deal with that damn quick. It's not enough, July. It's not enough for you or for him either. Do you understand what I mean? He loves you partly because you are young and beautiful, and he feels good about taking care of you. Is that enough? He would not be the first man to sacrifice his life for the sake of a pretty girl, but that might be what is happening. Can you see him being happy as a carpenter or a cowboy? He is a tornado, baby, not a summer breeze. And what about your life? If he gets wounded and is not so strong anymore, can you pick up the pieces and carry on for both of you? You need to be absolutely positive that you love the man within the man. Consciously or not, you have roped him, but you mustn't even try to tie this wild one. He needs a loose rein or no rein at all. You both have enough wounds already."

Luke paused, leaning against the sink shelf, smiling at his grown up little girl. "You know that Rick is a different kind of man. He reminds me of old Iron Horse. Do you remember, when you were little, how I told you stories about Iron Horse?"

"Kind of. He was like a big hero to you and your friends when you were kids, wasn't he? I never understood why."

"Iron Horse was our hero, for sure. Rick is a lot like him. He is Iron Horse's grandson, you know."

July looked up, startled. "He is? Rick is? He never mentioned that." She paused. "He did say his granddad was a well-known horseman, and he hoped he had some of that man's instincts."

"He has lots of his granddad's instincts. Rick was observant, analytical, and very intelligent even when he was a little boy. He sees with other eyes, and hears with other ears, like a wild animal. He is just not like other men in many, many ways."

Like a coyote. Tears welled in July's eyes. She missed Rick terribly. The day stretched before her, empty, dreary, despite the brilliant summer sunshine. There seemed to be a hollow place where her heart used to be. It took Gracie's late afternoon arrival to snap her out of it.

"Hi, July!" Grace raced up onto the porch and flung herself onto the swing next to her friend. "Well, Papa did it again! Took off." She looked at July's red eyes. "What's wrong?"

"I guess I'm just missing Rick," she smiled, but it was a little shaky.

Gracie patted her hand. "Papa just disappears sometimes. Gotta get used to it." She grinned at July. "When he comes back, he will bring us cool presents. Or take us someplace cool."

"He will?" Gracie's enthusiasm was charming, and July found herself grinning back.

"Really, really coo-oo-ool. One for you, and one for me, and one for Grandma Gisele, because we are his girls, and he loves us,"

"Am I his girl? Does he love me, too?"

"Oh, July! You are so silly sometimes." She sighed dramatically, flinging her arms out in exasperation. "Papa called me before he turned off his phone. He said I was to take good care of you and help you get your legs real, real strong."

She sprang off the swing, bouncing down the stairs to the truck. "Look, July!" She shouted over her shoulder. "We brought supper and a movie."

"Don't worry, July," Gisele said. "My Enrique is a strange man. He has to do things his way. He was always a wild boy, spending as much time alone in the forest as at home. He will be fine. I think he loves you very much."

"Do you really think so? He says he is incapable of romantic feelings."

"Pooh, girl! Surely you feel it? Maybe he is not romantic in any normal way, but he is obviously all tied up with you. Do you remember how Hamlet said he must be cruel to be kind? That is Enrique. He is very hard to understand. He is a paradox, that man."

"He tells me that I'm too young for him. He says he is a bad guy, and I should stay away from him, Gisele. He rarely even holds my hand in public, and he won't kiss me."

"Not at all?"

"Well, once. Just once."

"And?"

"And, it was amazing, wonderful, and very, umm," she looked at Gracie, opening the pizza box, and instead of speaking, made a gesture like fanning her face.

Gisele smiled, understanding the meaning.

"Well, it is true in some ways. He can be a bad guy. Enrique has always had that dangerous temper. You know about Romulus and Remus, or Kim, being raised by wolves? He was like that in my mind. No matter how hard we tried, he was always wild."

She sighed a little. "He is so smart. Sometimes, he would come home from school angry because he knew more about geography or biology or history or whatever than the teacher, because he reads so much and remembers pretty much everything he reads. Some teachers encouraged him. But others were embarrassed when he would say that on page something in some book or other, it said a different thing than what the teacher was telling them." She laughed a little. "It was hard to take. He would almost fail a subject because he would run off to the woods instead of going to class. But then, he would take the final exam and do so well that they had to pass him."

She smiled at July. "There is a devil in him and an angel. I think it is why he drinks so much. But, right now, let's watch a movie."

They brought an old Fred Astaire musical. July vaguely remembered watching one of those classics before. But she spent so much of her life studying and working that she never took time to appreciate glamour or romance. It was a cute story, and she really enjoyed it.

"Maybe if I were more romantic myself," she said to Gisele and Gracie. "He says I am crass and crude, and he should wash my mouth out with soap. He blames the generation gap, but I think it is just me."

"You can't change a man, but you can change yourself." Gisele smiled at her. "I think you and my son have more in common than you realize. I remember how solitary you were. The little orphan with no parents and few friends. Enrique was also alone most of the time, isolated by the insults of other kids. They called him Chief or Crazy Horse or Half-breed. When he was little, they would gang up on him, and he would come home with his clothes torn and a bloody nose or something." She sighed.

"Growing up here was hard on you. Luke tried, but what did an old bachelor know about raising a girl? You became strong and independent. That is good. But you were also not able to associate much with other kids. Luke was too busy, seven days a week running the ranch, and that was not good. All those silly things like slumber parties and basketball games and proms help us decide what we want in life. Now, you seem to want Enrique, and I wonder if you know why?"

"I wonder the same thing. Most of my experience with men has been bad, sometimes really bad. Why this scary guy? Rique is so damn smart about things that I should know but don't. At first, I was intimidated by him, which made me mad. Then, one night at the hospital, I woke up to find him sitting by my bed, humming. He was so drunk that he didn't even know how he got there. I should have been frightened, but I wasn't. He told Dr. Moussa that he just came to sit with me because I was alone." She teared up a little.

"It was such a kind thing to do, Gisele. He was injured, bleeding all over the place, but he chose to sit with me. I have been so mean, mocking, even hitting him. He has been steadfast, patient, protective, tolerant. He is so much more everything than I am. Uncle Luke told me that, in some ways, I am too young for Rick. I mean, you know, too immature. He's right. Rick has told me many times that I am too young for him. But I can change that, put my fears behind me, and not be so dependent. He needs a woman, not another child. I can change, and I will."

When they were not watching a movie, Gisele and Gracie taught July line dancing. She soon was boot-scooting with the best of them. Tuesday night, they were whooping it up with other ladies and a few men at the Cattleman's Cafe, stomping and clapping as they followed the steps. Rafael and Gracie sat on the sidelines, happily munching chips and salsas.

Rick's ex-wife, Cindy, watched July with glittering, angry eyes. She joined the line in a spot next to July and hissed, "Rick's little whore, July? What does your uncle say to that? I thought you were some high mucky-muck doctor, but you are just another cheap piece of ass, aren't you!"

She turned to look at Gracie. "Taking care of that little bastard, too? And, keeping Rick from getting his fancy house back." She sneered, "My, how far the mighty have fallen!"

July flushed with a massive surge of fury. She almost slapped the perfectly made-up, hostile face, but with Grace there, she smiled instead. "Not a bit cheap, Cindy. With my doctor's income, I come pretty high priced. Gracie, Rick, Uncle Luke, and I are quite happy as a family." She put heavy emphasis on the word family. Tears glittered in Cindy's eyes. July felt a stab of sympathy. "Sorry, Cindy. You reap what you sow. I hope life gets better for you."

She stepped in time with the other dancers and turned away. When she turned back, Cindy was gone, but Rafael was smiling at her. "I heard. That was a good way to handle it, July. Cindy wants Rick back, but he will have nothing to do with her. It's good for her to know that he is part of your family now. Maybe she will stop pestering us about him."

Gracie piped up, "Did she mean me, Grandpa Rafael? Did that mean Cindy say I was a bad surd? What does that mean? Is it bad to be a surd?"

"No, sweetie. She was trying to say that you are a little girl with no father, but that isn't right, is it? You have your Papa."

"Oh. She must be a silly lady!"

"Yes. Yes, she is."

July wanted to hug them both.

Chapter 36

The nights were cold up in the high mountains. Rick walked and ran each day until he was ready to collapse from fatigue. It was time to work his way down to the low country and get on home. The tremors and cramps were gone. There was no actual physical craving for his bourbon, But he knew it would be weeks before he was free of the habit. He could do it.

So, he had gained control over that part of his life, but what about the rest of him? He wasn't the old familiar Captain Mora anymore. Who was he? What was he? The mental picture of himself as strong, logical, and competent, the image that had stood him in good stead for so many years, was blurry, shifting, like something seen through a stream of running water.

Rick sat on a rock, gazing out over miles and miles of forested wilderness, down to the sagebrush flats below. Tomorrow, he would run down to the town and confront whatever the future held. He spread his little fire out across a few feet of bare ground. When it burned out, the hot ground underneath would keep him warm much of the night.

A movement in the trees caught his attention. He sat still, like an extension of the rock, watching. Minutes passed. Then a big old bull elk stepped into the meadow. It snorted, stepping closer, shaking velvet-covered antlers. Rick couldn't hide or out run or out fight a bull elk. Instinct took over. He stood and spoke.

"Hello, friend." He wished that he knew some words in Nde, his grandfather's native language, but he only knew the standard greeting in Navajo. "Yá'át'ééh shi'kis," he said, spreading his hands open in the universal sign of peace. The elk gazed at him for a few minutes more, then went to browsing willows along the little brook. Watching this new companion, Rick went about his preparations for the night, acutely aware that a bull elk can be terribly dangerous. But, as the animal munched its way along, occasionally pausing to regard him with a dark eye, something happened. A quiet calm wormed its way into his soul. He felt a kinship with this neighbor, and thought about spirit animals, guides, protectors. Was this elk a spirit guide? Had it just shown him a new way? He talked out loud, singing to the big animal as it ate, drank, and finally lay down just a few feet away.

Despite the cold, Rick slept well, comforted by occasional sounds from his four-legged companion. Pre-dawn twittering of a tree full of little Pine Siskins woke him. He stretched and rose, going first to the creek for water. The elk was still there, lying down, its antlers looking like a shrub in the half-light. Rick almost ran into him. Startled, he stopped, holding out a hand toward the animal, warding him off, or greeting him? He was not sure himself.

The elk made a snuffling sound. A return greeting? Rick moved slowly past his new friend, kneeling by the brook to wash his face and take a drink of the icy water. There was a loud rustling behind him. Rick whirled around to see the bull trotting off. It paused at the tree line, giving a soft whistling grunt before disappearing. It seemed like a friendly comment, a farewell.

Rick smiled. A new dawn. A new day. A new man. He grabbed his nearly empty pack and began to trot down the mountain on his way home to July. As the sun rose, he raised his arms in some ancient ritual. Gathering the sun's rays symbolically with his hands, Rick poured them over himself, hoping to wash away depression and despair. The drum beat in his brain and his heart. His feet moved in time, down the faint trail left by some forest dwellers.

Dusk found Rick trotting beside the road almost at the edge of town. A police cruiser passed him, then stopped and swung around.

"Hey, Rick! Is that you, man? What are you doing up here? Been hiking?"

"Hi, George. Yup, hiking trip. How you been?"

"Good, man. Hop in. The girls are at a school event, and I am just on my way to have dinner. Join me?"

"Geez, yes! I'm starving!"

"You look good, dude. Wish I had a flat belly like that. My six-pack comes with cans." He patted his bit of a paunch. The interior light showed the multiple scratches outlined in red on Rick's arms and face. "Shit, man, what did you do? That is ugly!"

Rick laughed. "Yeah, well, fell off a cliff into some brush."

"What you doing? Back to the old Apache ways? Did I ever tell you that my granddad knew old Iron Horse? They were like clan brothers or something. He told us lots of stories about your grandfather."

"Really? I never knew much of anything about him until a couple of weeks ago. Remember Luke Kozlowski? I spent most of my vacation on his ranch, remodeling an old cabin for him. He told me more about my ancestors than my folks did."

"You didn't quit, did you? I mean, you are a great cop, a natural, and you are younger than me by a lot."

"Not quitting yet. Thinking about it. I have twenty-three years with the city, you know. Realistically, I should stay on another two years at least, but I don't know."

"You getting burned out?"

"Yeah, but not just that. I met this terrific woman, and I want her to have a better life than as the wife of the cop everyone hates. You know? I mean, if she will even have me. Being with nasty Captain Mora puts her in danger from all those yahoos that are after me. Scares me, but not her. She is tough! Hey, you sure you want to be seen with me?" He pulled his clean but very wrinkled tee-shirt from the backpack, and ducked out of the dirty, torn rag he was wearing.

"The tourists will think you're some eccentric artist. Probably ask for your autograph. Come on. Tell me about this woman in your life."

Knowing that his stomach capacity shrank during the last few days, Rick ordered from the appetizer menu. Shrimp ceviche, tortilla soup, a small salad, and tea. Gracie would be so proud of her Papa drinking tea.

As they ate, Rick found himself sharing much more about his life than he was usually comfortable mentioning even to George Dobbs, who had been his training officer when he joined LCPD. George listened in interested silence as Rick went on and on about July and Gracie and the ranch and the cabin.

"So, describe this July to me."

"Well, she is complicated. Sometimes, even though she is very smart and educated, she seems kind of naïve and helpless. Sometimes, she's like a shy little critter. A kitten or a puppy, hiding in my arms. And then she comes out with some brilliant observation, or she turns into this tough, in command, wild woman. The other day, she beat the crap out of me, and even pulled my own pistol on me."

"Cripes, man!"

Rick laughed. "Yeah. Just grabbed it off my belt. I thought she was going to shoot me. Shot at a knothole in a tree about fifty feet away instead. Hardly even aimed and only missed by about a finger width. She said that old Luke bought her a .44 revolver when she was seven. Can you imagine? July is something else, George. And absolutely gorgeous, too. Hey, I'm sorry about babbling on like this."

"Don't be sorry. I am enjoying you being something other than Old Stone Face. Have you called this girl yet? Told her you are on your way back?"

Rick shook his head. "My cell phone battery is dead. I'll charge it tonight."

"You chicken shit! Here. Call her." George tossed his phone across the table.

Rick hesitated, drew a deep breath, and dialed. Three rings, four. Then a hesitant "Hello?"

"July."

"Oh, Rique! Are you okay? I have missed you so terribly! Where are you?" There was a pause. "Are you coming back?" Her voice trembled.

Rick was so relieved. Neck muscles that were unconsciously tight suddenly relaxed. He took another deep breath. "I'm fine, Wabbit, on my way home to you. Are you okay?"

"I will be fine. As soon as I feel your arms around me, everything will be fine. Hurry home!"

"I'm coming. I'm coming. I'll be home tomorrow. We have a lot to talk about."

"Yes, we do. Sharon Reynolds called to tell us about that gig at the picnic. Listen, your mom and Gracie and I plan to be in Las Cruces tomorrow. We are going to shop for some new clothes, and take Grace to the American Girl shop. So, where will you be?"

"Great! Then I will be at the office by two. I want to go shopping with you three. I love going to American Girl with our Gracie. I can't miss that. And can you spend the week with me?" He held the phone after they finished the call, just staring at it.

"That's how you talk to your woman? For Pete's sake, I am more lovey-dovey with my dog. What's American Girl? Isn't that a doll or something?"

"I know. I just can't seem to find the right words for her. I am such a loser sometimes. But I am an expert on American Girl dolls and their wardrobes." He gave George a grin.

"Mind if I make another call, George?" He dialed his folk's number.

"Mom? You two okay? I'm good. Dirty and tired, but good. A few scratches. Yes, I called her. Listen, Mom, can I have that ring that grandmother always wore? The one with the emerald. I want to give July something special. Do you think she will like it?"

"I am sure she will, Enrique. Is it intended as an engagement ring? It was your grandmother's engagement ring."

"I'm not sure, Mom. I am trying not to act like the boss. I want her to choose whether she wants me around permanently or not, and whether…ah." He paused.

"Enrique, *mijo,* sometimes you think too much. I am sure you misunderstand our July. I think you should just sweep her off her feet, marry her, and be done."

"Yeah. Well, the secret is out. I am a coward at heart. I mean, what if she says no?" He listened for a minute as his mother scolded him.

"Then you will wait, and ask her again."

"Okay, Mom. George said pretty much the same thing." He laughed a little. "I am such a wreck. Geez, I have a yellow belly a mile wide. See you tomorrow. I am not going to miss shopping with my Gracie."

George smiled at the younger man. "Come on, Rick. You can sleep in Junior's room. Save your money for buying your girls clothes. You are going to need it."

They sat out on the patio, waiting for George's two to come home. The older man noticed Rick's silence and thoughtful expression.

"Penny for your thoughts."

"I had this experience when I was on the mountain, George. It was this old bull elk. I feel like he spoke to me, and something in my heart, soul, or whatever, changed. It felt almost like a physical change. I don't know. Was I just hallucinating? Was it delirium from my body not having the alcohol? But that elk brought me a kind of peace. He slept within a few feet of me." He shifted in his chair and leaned forward, elbows on knees, seeking an answer to his confusion.

"Remember, Rick, when you used to tell me that you did something because it was just a gut feeling? It seemed like you were more tuned in to our surroundings, the mood or the atmosphere, or something than the rest of us. You picked up on stuff I was unaware of until you pointed it out. And you were almost always right. Being aware of your surroundings like that, I mean, that is how our ancestors survived. I can't observe and understand what I see like you do. Most of us don't. It made you an outstanding cop. And now, you have an element of peace in your soul. If it came from an elk, maybe that's a good thing. A spirit guide. So, what has you hesitating now? I think you are scared of this girl, and I've never seen you scared of anything."

"Well, she's used to being in charge, and I am used to being in charge, and...." He went silent in mid-sentence. "I am scared. She should reject me, but I don't know how I will manage if she does."

"Sometimes, Rick, you think too damn much. Follow your instincts, man."

Chapter 37

"Luke! Luke! Oh, thank God, he's coming!" July flung herself down on the old porch swing next to her great uncle. "Gisele and Gracie and I are going to meet Rick at his office before we go shopping."

"Great, honey, but shouldn't one of us go along? You know, Rick worries about you not having a man around until they catch that bomber."

"Uncle Luke! That is an absolute insult to Gisele and me. We are a couple of tough birds, you know."

"I know, honey, but...."

"You and Tomás can go down to the café for dinner. You guys need a nice steak anyway, hey, Tom?"

"Sounds good to me. So, Rick is on his way home, July? Where has he been anyway?"

"Don't know. He called on someone else's phone. George Dobbs, the ID said."

Luke whistled. "Wow! He ran a long, long way. George lives way the hell up north." He patted July's hand.

Tomás was a little worried. "I'm glad he is coming back. I don't like how that car has been hanging around all day. I'll be glad to have the Captain here. I don't want to leave even for a few minutes until they are gone. Suspicious, I think."

"What car?" July asked.

"Oh, a fancy silver thing. I think it's a Cadillac. I tried to talk to them a few times, but they hurried away every time I walked toward them, so I couldn't get a good look at them. Sheriff says he can't stop anyone from parking in a pullout on a public road. Says they are just doing some bird watching, but I don't know. I don't like it."

Tomás was genuinely uncomfortable. Something did not feel right to him. Who was it? Why were they really there? There were lots of places along the creek better for birdwatching. It looked a lot like Cindy's car. Everyone in town had seen her new silver Cadillac, but she was no bird watcher. He continued sitting on the porch after the others went up to bed, and after a while, walked down to the tack room. He could see that the silver car was gone now, but things were not quite right. Gathering up some old saddle blankets, he spread them on the front porch and settled for the night, on guard against he knew not what.

With the morning, the car was back, a young woman sitting on a log beside the creek, apparently watching the birds. Tomás determined that he would work around the barn as long as that car was in sight.

Bebe clutched Roberta's wrist, fingernails digging painful grooves in her soft skin. "Are you sure this is the right place?"

"I told you. This is where my auntie says July is staying. And, that is the same thing that Mr. Cannon, your private detective, told you. That is all I know. It is her great uncle's house, where she grew up."

Roberta was trying not to sound impatient or angry. She told Bebe this same information several times yesterday. But Bebe had grown increasingly strange in recent days, threatening to keep Roberta from seeing her son if she didn't help with the smoke bombs. Roberta was becoming frightened about her relationship with this woman. And it seemed odd that she used her maiden name at work. Something was very wrong.

A brown truck came up behind them. Roberta thought she recognized it as the Mora's, from the feed store. She raised binoculars to her face, watching the heron hunting in the creek. But out of the corner of her eye, she saw the truck turn in Kozlowski's driveway. She retreated to the car.

Bebe, watching the truck pull up to the house, reached into her pocket and brought out a pistol. The slight sound as she released the safety seemed to echo through Roberta's brain. She felt a stab of panic. "What are you doing? Why do you need a pistol? Why are we hiding here?"

"Stupid girl! People like you and July cost my husband his license. If little bitches like you had done as you were told, you would not have had a deformed baby, and my husband would still be practicing medicine. The bomb did not work well enough. July survived, so I have another solution!" Her smile, so cheerful and gay, sent chills down Roberta's spine.

Survived? We are supposed to hurt people? Kill people? It wasn't an accident! Oh my God! "So, our goal is to...."

"Yes, I will have my revenge! My husband gave you the acne medicine, and look how beautiful your skin is now. If you just had not gotten pregnant. He warned you. He warned all of you. But people like July blame it on him when you are the ones to blame! You!"

Her eyes glittered as she raised the pistol toward Roberta.

Just then, they heard the rumble of a truck engine, and the brown Ford pulled out of the drive, heading east toward the highway. The bright red hair of the driver was plainly visible.

"Look, there she is." Roberta pointed.

Bebe paused, staring at Roberta but not seeming to see her. After a moment, she turned the car around and followed the truck, still gripping the pistol in one hand.

Chapter 36

Rick unplugged his phone from the charger, and started to stick it in his hip pocket, thinking about what he would say to July. The little message icon caught his eye.

"Captain, call ASAP!" He dialed Rory Kincannon's number as he climbed into George's truck.

"Sorry, Rory, my phone was dead. What's up, Lieutenant?"

"There was a silver car, maybe a Cadillac, seen parked around the corner from the clinic before the bomb went off. People noticed it, and we investigated, but nothing tied it to any of the demonstrators or previous patients or anything. No one noticed the license number, of course."

"But, in the bombing of another clinic, in Phoenix, there was a silver car, maybe a Cadillac, parked around the corner. In both cases, the car pulled away almost immediately after the bomb went off. Here is the kicker. The person killed in the Arizona bombing was a dermatologist, Dr. Grammage. I know it is an unlikely connection, but since Dr. Sullivan is up there with you? Well, alarm bells, you know."

"Yeah." Rick hesitated, mind racing. "At the moment, she is not with me. She and my mother, and Gracie are on their way to Las Cruces from Juniper Springs. I am up north with George Dobbs. Contact State and alert whoever is on patrol along their route. They will be in a brown Ford F350 crew cab. I'll have my mother watching for anyone following them. It is unlikely that they will know where to look for July, if she is a target, but can you work your magic and track my family? You have my mother's number, right? Thanks, Rory."

He turned to George. "You got any noise in this wreck? Suddenly, we are in a hurry."

Before Rick had even closed the door all the way, George was rolling. As soon as they hit traffic, he had the lights behind the grill flashing, the siren wailing. They were quickly away from town, roaring south.

Rick dialed his mother's cell phone but got no answer. He waited impatiently, his mind full of what-ifs. His stomach muscles clenched as his mouth filled with saliva. He swallowed convulsively. He had better luck contacting the sheriff in Juniper Springs. "Listen, Billy, I am probably a complete fool, but that fancy new Caddie of Cindy's? Do you know where it is right now?"

"Yup. How is that your business, Rick? I mean, come on, man. She is out of your life, isn't she?"

"I get it, Bill, but when she was in my office a few days ago, she showed some real hate for July Kozlowski. You know that July's injuries resulted from a firebomb, right? And the bomb may have been planted by someone driving a new silver Cadillac."

"Well, Cindy is a vicious little bitch, but that seems like a pretty extreme action, even for her. Anyhow, right now, Cindy is over at the coffee shop."

"Thanks, Billy. I guess I am just paranoid." He dialed again and again, staring at the screen, gripping the phone so hard that he accidentally turned it off a few times. Finally, Gisele answered.

"Mom, I don't want July or Grace to know this is me calling."

"Yes, I understand," she answered.

"Are you driving?"

"No, not right now."

"Good. Listen, there is probably nothing to worry about, but just maybe someone is after July and driving a silver car. I want you to watch for anything of any color that seems to be following you or pacing you somehow. When you stop, if you do, be sure that it is only where there are a lot of people around."

"I see. Yes, I can do that."

"Don't hang up. Just put your phone carefully on the seat by you. Kincannon will tap into it and track your location, just for safety. George and I are on our way."

"Okay. Nice talking to you, too."

Rick looked at George. "Mom catches on to everything so fast. I wish I had her brains. She is the salt of the earth."

It was an hour before Rory called. "I have locked on to your mother's phone. An Officer Casaus from State picked them up and followed them for about forty miles. He did see a silver Cadillac. He slipped in between them and slowed down until the truck was out of sight. The Cadillac did not try to catch up to the truck, so that was probably a false alarm. When they get real close, I will send Eva Shannon out to trail them. I don't know. Everything seems fine, but I have this feeling."

Chapter 39

Bebe accelerated as soon as the police car turned off, and in a few minutes, the brown Ford truck was again in sight. She shortened the distance as they came into the city's outskirts, staying within a half-block of her prey. They turned in at the Super Mall. The little red-headed mouse was almost in her hands. She did not notice that the plain sedan driven by Detective Shannon followed her. Nor did she see the white Grand Caravan that followed farther behind.

But Jack Cannon noticed Bebe and Roberta. He had tailed them from Juniper Springs. It looked like what Mrs. Gauthier hired him to do, to photograph her husband and July Kozlowski, his supposed mistress, was not really what she wanted. Had she hired him just to find the Kozlowski girl? It was starting to look that way. He pulled into the parking lot and strolled into the building behind July. The security guard near the door was another police retiree.

"Hey, Joyce," Jack said. "Hooked yourself a man yet? Or are you still drooling over that TV actor?" He grinned at her.

"Hi, Jack. Found a good woman yet? How's retirement?"

"Oh, I get a little bored sometimes. Gotta stop and see my old buddies. So, what's new?"

They chatted for a few minutes as he kept an eye on the shoppers, turning his back when the Gauthier woman came in with the younger girl.

Eva Shannon was also watching. She was not a new officer, and was not easily fooled. The ladies in the Cadillac sat in the car, the older woman talking, the younger almost cowering in her seat. As the two walked toward the mall entrance, the young woman looked nervous, the way she held her shoulders and looked down as she walked. Eva watched for a minute from where she sat, her car partly hidden two rows over.

"Rory, they are at the Super Mall. It doesn't seem like they could be following Rick's mother. They sure aren't keeping close. But something looks wrong. I am going to trail them."

She tied her hair back in a ponytail and took off her blazer, revealing a sleeveless top. She looked like any soccer mom going shopping. Slinging a fat purse over her shoulder, Eva followed the two women into the building.

Bebe slowed at every little shop, checking the interior through the windows. She called her husband. "The little red worm is here, no more than a mile from the house. Get over here now. This may be our best chance." They argued. "No! Right now!" Bebe's eyes squinted nearly shut, and her lips pressed tight together. She was furious.

She gestured to Roberta to come closer. Roberta hung back, confused and frightened. She could hardly believe that Bebe was really going to shoot anyone. Still, there was that crazy laugh, her apparent familiarity with the revolver in her purse, and her palpable anger.

"You will stay here in the middle of the mall and watch for the bitch. Call me on my cell as soon as you spot her. My husband will be here in a few minutes. Do you understand? If you try to run...," she laughed. "If you try to run, you know what will happen to your baby!" The last word came out in a hiss. Bebe grabbed Roberta's arm, digging her fingernails into the tender flesh just above the elbow.

Roberta nodded, speechless. She jerked her arm away. Bebe walked off, checking each shop for her prey. Roberta wiped her eyes with trembling fingers, not wanting to attract attention by crying.

But Eva noticed. She feigned fatigue and sat to rest on a bench just behind Roberta. Jack and Joyce strolled slowly past, still chatting, keeping an eye on Roberta and Bebe. When Bebe turned down one of the side hallways, they exchanged glances, and Jack whispered that he did not want to be recognized, so Joyce continued walking along, trailing Bebe. Jack sat on a bench near Eva, apparently absorbed in his cell phone.

A tall, gray-haired man stopped by Roberta. "Where is my wife?" He seemed nervous, sweating. She pointed down the side hall, and he hurried in that direction. Obvious fear in the girl's face alerted Eva. She rose, ensuring with a quick nod in Roberta's direction, that Jack would keep an eye on this end of things, then strode quickly after the agitated man.

Jack moved to Roberta's side. "Do you remember me? I am the private investigator hired by Mrs. Garner." Roberta nodded as he showed her his ID. "She said she thought her husband was having an affair with that little redhead, but that isn't what is going on, is it?"

Roberta could not hold back her fear or her tears. "She is threatening to shoot Dr. Sullivan! She's crazy!" She whispered, her voice squeaking with fear.

"How is Captain Mora involved?"

"I don't know, but my aunt says Dr. Sullivan is his girlfriend."

Jack whipped up his cell phone, scrolling contacts down to Mora.

"Rick? Jack Cannon. At the Super Mall. A nutcase is stalking your redhead. Eva Shannon and Joyce Costanza are following them. They are in the east wing. I am on my way to back them up." He started down the hall at a rapid walk.

Q and Rory stood in the office window, watching kids playing in the park across the street. The detectives chatted idly, Q eating a late lunch. His phone vibrated. "It's Cap." He put it on speaker.

"Something's going down at the SuperMall. Eva is there, with Jack Cannon. And my family is there. Move it!" In less than five minutes, three police cars pulled into the parking lot, right behind

George and Rick. Rick gestured as he dispersed his crew, sending a car to each mall entrance. Jack called again.

"I am following Eva down the east wing. The Garner woman and a man are turning into that western wear store. Your mom and your niece are headed toward the pet store, but the redhead is not with them. She must be in the western wear store."

"I called Eva. She is not to act unless forced to. I am almost there." Rick's voice was harsh, his words clipped.

Inside the store, July picked out a new scoop-necked blouse and a pair of jeans. She thought they would look good on her, keeping Rick's eyes off what she imagined would be the younger, prettier ladies who were sure to be at the police picnic. A pair of low-top boots with stitching in a cactus pattern slipped easily onto her small feet.

She picked up a heavy silver belt buckle with a deeply carved, stylized figure of a quail. It was very pretty, but the scalloped edges were too sharp. July turned it over in her hand, thinking that Rick would know how to file down the sharp spots without affecting the piece's overall look. *Or, I could just chop wood with it.* She smiled at the thought.

There was a sound of whispered arguing behind her. And, there was Bebe, glaring at a graying man who snatched something from her hand. July quickly turned back to the display of buckles, not wanting to speak to Bebe, hoping not to be noticed. Too late.

"July, darling! How nice to see you." Bebe grabbed her arm. "Come have lunch with me. There is so much to discuss."

"No, thank you, Bebe. I am here with friends. They are down at the pet store looking at the tropical fish, and I need to join them as soon as I have paid for these items." She smiled, holding up the buckle.

"You will come with me! Now!" Bebe's voice was a growl. Her eyes squinted with rage.

"No!" Alarmed, July backed quickly away. Just then, there was the sound of running footsteps in the hall. It was just a couple of kids, but Bebe turned pale and started toward the store exit. A soccer mom in a sleeveless top, blocking her way, asked her about something that Bebe, in her panic, could not understand.

"Get out of my way!" She tried to push past the younger lady, but found herself tangled in the long shoulder straps of Eva's bag, the contents spilling on the floor at her feet.

"Look what you have done!" Eva grabbed Bebe's arm, shaking it in mock anger. Bebe screamed with rage, struggling against the superior strength.

An arm went around July's neck, and she was pulled roughly back against Bebe's husband. He smelled of sweat. Pressing a pistol to July's cheek, he shouted at the woman restraining his wife.

"Let her go. Let her go, or I'll shoot!"

Eva let her go, reaching for her own weapon. Customers and clerks ran out the door, some yelling about a man with a gun. Rick appeared beside Jack Cannon.

"Thanks, Jack," he said calmly. "Please clear the area, Joyce. George, take my gun. See if you can get a different angle on that guy than Eva has."

"Wait for SWAT, Rick!"

"Can't. He's choking her." He strolled into the store as casually as if he were on a shopping trip, but his heart was pounding in his ears, and there was icy sweat between his shoulder blades. *Hang on, baby.*

"That's my girl you're threatening."

"I'll shoot!" The man's voice was shaky, but his hand was steady as he kept the gun pointed at July's face.

"It won't do you any good, you know," Rick said as he moved slowly through the displays of saddles and clothes, boots, and jewelry. "It's me you need to fear, not a little girl."

The pistol turned toward him. Rick stepped forward, empty hands at his sides, trying to draw fire away from July. Eva aimed at the man from the doorway, but she couldn't risk a shot given the angle. Rick was so close to the man that he blocked George's line of sight.

July saw the gun extend toward Rick. *No, No. Not my toad.* She stiffened her neck muscles even more, fighting to stay alive.

"Take care of our Gracie for me, Wabbit. Close your eyes. Don't watch. Don't remember me this way." *Goodbye, my love. Goodbye.*

July's vision was growing fuzzy around the edges, narrowing to a black-and-white tunnel. The arm tightened even more across her throat, cutting off her breathing. She was close to losing consciousness. She clenched her hand, feeling the sharp edge of the buckle crease her palm, and realized that she had the power to stop this. She had no air left, but there was still some strength in her arm. She brought her fist forward and suddenly slammed back with all her remaining strength, digging the sharp edge of the buckle into the man's crotch. She barely heard his shriek in her ear. Reflexes caused the gun to fire, the round thudding into a wooden display case.

As Dr. Garner doubled over screaming in agony, July fell, unconscious before she hit the floor, landing on her right elbow. Rick slapped away the gun and knocked the man unconscious with one fierce blow to the temple.

He dropped to his knees. "July?" She was pale and unresponsive. "July!" He shook her, but she was limp. "Call an ambulance! She's not breathing! Oh, Jesus, July! Breathe, baby!"

His long experience took over. He checked ABCs and began chest compressions. But inside, he was screaming. *Don't leave me! Don't leave me!*

Rick was only dimly conscious of the *whoop, whoop, whoop* that characterized ambulance sirens until Eva said, "Here they are." He didn't pause, but continued the compressions.

The older paramedic knew Rick well. "Who is this, Captain?" he asked as he and his aide took over, preparing to hook up the defibrillator.

Gisele and Gracie stood just inside the door to the pet store, watching wide-eyed as Lieutenant Q guarded the hallway outside. "Q? What has happened?" Gisele surged through the crowd as she saw the paramedic and her son run past with July on the stretcher.

"Not sure, Mrs. Mora. Stay with me, and we will get it all sorted out."

"There was a lady in a silver Cadillac with a younger girl, Lieutenant," Eva said. "She is involved in this, too."

"Yes," Jack added. "The girl is in the center court. Her name is Roberta. She is the one who alerted me. And that lady's name is Mrs. Garner. She might still be here in the mall. She parked in Section C."

"You know her, Jack? You and Eva stake out that car. I'll find the girl," Q said.

But, despite Roberta's cooperation, and experienced officers looking for her, there was no Bebe to be found. When the mall closed for the night, the car remained untouched. Lieutenant Quintana ordered it impounded, and an APB was issued for Bebe.

Chapter 40

In the ambulance, July suddenly coughed. Her eyes flew open. "Rique, are you hurt? What happened?" Her voice was a raw whisper.

"Thank God! You scared me silly, Wabbit. I'm not hurt. He shot a display case. I'm okay. You will be okay." His face was almost gray with anxiety.

July's eyes were huge in her pale face. "I don't feel good, Rique. My chest kind of hurts, and my arm...." She started to lift her right arm and let out a sharp squeal. Her eyes rolled back in her head, and she fainted just as they pulled up to the Emergency entrance. He leaped out of the back, grabbing the end of the stretcher.

There was a question in Arabic, "What happened?"

He replied in kind. "It's my July, Mo. He choked her! And, it's that right arm again." His throat was so constricted with fear for July that he could barely speak.

"Let me have her, Rick. Let me have her." Mo's voice was calming.

Rick reluctantly relinquished his grip on the stretcher, holding July's left hand instead, controlling himself with difficulty. The paramedic recited July's vitals to Dr. Moussa as they wheeled her through the sliding doors.

"She woke for a minute, Mo. Recognized me, spoke to me. But, when she started to move that right arm, she cried out and fainted."

Mo checked the IV, adding something through a port in the

tubing. Then they were rolling down the hall to that familiar X-Ray room.

"Captain Mora." The rad tech greeted Rick.

"Lorena."

"Captain, you need to stand back behind that wall."

"No."

"Rick!" Mo stood in the way, arms folded across his chest. "Go!"

"She might wake up."

"She will not wake up until I let her wake up. Scoot so we can see what is going on with that arm. Go. Now!" He gave Rick a gentle push, rolling his eyes at Lorena.

The two of them carefully placed her elbow in various positions, ninety degrees, fully extended.

"Well? Let me see!"

Mo nodded at Lorena, who turned her screen so that Rick could see the mess of splintered bone that was July's former elbow. The pins placed after the earlier fracture no longer held much together.

Rick needed no explanation. He could see for himself. His belly muscles started to tremble, and he could not breathe for a minute.

"I should have killed him!" He drew back a fist.

Mo grabbed his arm. "Don't hit the wall, you dumb shit! You need both hands to take care of her. Take her back to the ED. I need to call for a consultation. Lorena, follow him."

"I can do it!"

"Oh, I know you can, but I do not know that you will control your temper along the way. So, Lorena will follow you in case we have to call Security on Captain Asshole." He stood on his toes, glaring at his angry, dangerous friend.

Rick rocked from foot to foot for a moment, trying to control himself, then suddenly went almost limp. Tears streamed down his cheeks.

"She won't be able to do her surgery, Mo. All those things she is so proud of having accomplished. My poor baby! My poor little wabbit!"

Lorena stood there dumbfounded for a moment, unable to

believe that this was the hard man she had seen so many times, stoic in the face of his injuries. She grabbed a towel and held it under the cold-water tap.

"Here, Captain. She will need you to be her anchor when she wakes up." She wiped his face with the cold, wet cloth, just as she did those of her two boys when they were hurt.

Rick took a few deep breaths. "Right. You are right. I'm sorry. My God, I'm such a mess!"

"Yes. You must love her very much."

He nodded, biting his lip. "This is it. No more. My girls need me."

Chapter 41

Dr. Moussa sighed. "Poor Rick! He doesn't know how to handle this kind of emotion. I'm afraid there will be a dreadful drunken brawl or some other violent outlet for those feelings. Someday, LCPD will probably have to fire their wild man. It's all about political correctness now, and you know the Captain. He is far from compliant."

"I know," Lorena said. "He's a very kind man, a good man, even if he is kind of, you know...a drunk. I like him."

"Yeah. Me, too."

The overhead pager sounded. "Dr. Moussa, to your office. Dr. Moussa." Finally, the orthopedic doctors were there. He glanced at his watch. Only four hours. Not that bad. As it turned out, one of the orthopedists had gone to medical school with July.

"This is going to be tough," Dr. Patel said. "You know, she was the most sought-after doctor for a dermatology residency. Everyone wanted her. And, I saw in the alumni magazine that she won a London fellowship for next year. She is real good. Was real good." He shook his head. "Well, we may as well bite the bullet. It won't get any easier."

As they walked toward the room where July was resting, they could hear singing. "You have a sound system?" one asked.

"No. That's our bad boy. Listen. Don't say anything to antagonize him. He is used to doing things his own way, and is really on edge about this. He's very much in love with Dr. Sullivan, and he is somewhat unpredictable."

"Oh." They paused. "Do we need to call the cops, then? Have them on standby?"

"Thing is, he is the cops. Look, he is an incredibly brilliant, brave, and accomplished man. But sometimes, he sort of teeters on the edge of sanity. Just don't antagonize him. Okay? He is emotionally fragile right now."

"You are talking about that Mora guy, aren't you?"

"Yes."

"My dad thinks Captain Mora is God's gift to the world. You might know my dad, Ernie Patel? District Fire Captain?"

Mo nodded.

"Man, I will be glad to meet the famous, infamous Enrique Mora!"

"Just a word. He is not into adulation. Okay?"

July was not in the bed. A pair of running shoes attached to some denim-clad legs was propped on the edge of the bed, and a small red-headed person, curled in Enrique's lap. Her head lay on his shoulder. He was lounging back in the chair, one arm curved protectively around her back, the other poised to support her arm. He was singing an old country song to her.

"Did she wake up?"

Rick nodded.

"You singing her back to sleep?"

He nodded, looking down at her with such tenderness that it was almost embarrassing to see. "July, the ortho guys are here."

"Mm." She stirred and opened one eye. "Oh, Marcus! Why are you here?" She was terribly nauseated, dizzy, dopey, but she was not going to be a weakling. She sat up a little.

"Ayisha wanted to be somewhere warmer than Chicago, so we moved here last month. And we have a girl now, too. How about you?"

"July has a lovely, brilliant, almost daughter. Don't you, babe."

She tried to smile, but it was a little trembly. "Well, yes, almost.

Gracie is Enrique's niece, but I love her like a daughter."

She turned to the other man. "I recognize you. You are Dr. Martin, aren't you? Big guns for little old me."

He stepped forward and extended a hand to Rick, who rose, maneuvering around the IV pole, placing July carefully on the bed before shaking hands.

"So, gentlemen, what can you tell us?" Rick asked, keeping one hand on July's back, steadying her.

Marcus cleared his throat, looking at his mentor, Dr. Martin, who just nodded to him.

"Well, July. There is not much to work with in terms of replacing the joint. Do you want to see the x-rays?"

She hesitated, and the fear showed in her face. "Did you see, Rique?'

"I did. Let's leave it for now, okay? It's not going to make anything better, so let's just leave it." Rick could see that she was struggling to pull herself together, preparing herself for some very bad news. He kept an arm around her.

"Okay, what's the story." Her voice was a little shaky.

"Amputate or let it fuse," Marcus said. "I am so sorry, July! There is just not much we can do." His face showed how terrible he felt for his friend. Dr. Martin nodded in agreement.

The room was very quiet. They could hear the hum of the air conditioning, the sound of footsteps in the hall, a faint murmur of traffic in the street below. She leaned her head on Enrique's chest, listening to his slow, steady, comforting heartbeat, then looked at the expressions of three men in front of her. Mo with a sympathetic look. Marcus, his hands spread in helplessness. Dr. Martin's head tilted in a gesture of 'it is what it is'.

July glanced up at Rick, his face full of anguish, and realized that it was time for her to step up and be the comforting one. *I am not a child. Where is my courage?* She composed her thoughts as best she could, fighting down the dizziness, the nausea, and the dread.

"Don't worry, Rique. It's just my arm, after all. If we let it fuse, I can still do most things, just not surgeries. I will manage okay. Really,

I will. And, I will not be the dependent little worm I have been."

"July."

"Because I can probably get a teaching job, or maybe just work as a GP."

"Stop, July."

"I bet the clinic in Juniper Springs can use someone, and I promise I won't ruin any more of your life, and you will not need to take care of me all the time."

"Goddammit, July! Stop! You have never been a dependent little worm. You have not ruined my life. I like taking care of you. I want to take care of you. Who was it that took care of me?"

She looked down at their linked hands, not knowing how to respond for a moment. "That was just kind of an accident. I didn't plan it. It just happened."

The three doctors stepped quietly out of the room, not wanting to intrude on an intensely emotional moment. Rick shifted from foot to foot. "July." He cleared his throat. "July." He chewed his lip. "I, uh, I don't know what...how to tell...." He swallowed. "You mean more to me than I know how to explain. I want to always be with you. But I cannot promise that I will change. The coyote is growing smaller, but he is still there."

July looked at him in silence, then squeezed his hand with her own uninjured one. "Rique, there is so much more to you than that coyote. I have been a whiny child leaning on you these last weeks. I was full of pain and fear and despair, losing all that I had worked for during the last twenty years. Then you came into my life, and dragged me into a new reality, a different future, a new set of goals. We all have a dark side. Most of us are too dishonest or too afraid to confront it. This sounds theological or something, but there is bad action, and there is evil action. You don't have the makings of evil, and at least some of your 'bad' actions have a positive result."

His heart thudded in his chest, and it was hard to breathe. Where were the smooth words? Where was the clever coyote? What could he say? Or do? It came out in a hoarse whisper.

"July, please don't leave us. I have never been happier than these last weeks with you. My little wounded warrior wabbit, you are brave and smart, and sometimes a totally obnoxious little pest, but always, always, amazing. I want to cook for you and laugh with you, or maybe sit on the floor and play jacks with you. Something. Anything. You are my family. My folks and Luke and Grace, and you and me. Family. I don't know how to make it work, but you said you've got my back and you proved it. Well, I have yours, too."

She placed her hand on his chest and gave him a shaky little smile in return. "Yes. Family." She was starting to wobble a little bit from fatigue and medication. "I don't feel so good, Rique."

"What would Dr. Sullivan say? I bet she would say let these guys operate on that arm. When you wake up, I will be back. Okay? We have so much to talk about. And as soon as Mo lets you out of here we need to go shopping." He gently ruffled her hair. "You know what, babe? You are going to have to shoot me with your old .44 caliber if you want me to go away, and you know how hard it is to kill me." He grinned that lop-sided grin, dazzling white in his brown face.

Mo, was waiting in the hall as Rick left the room. "How is it going to work, Mo? Do you think it will need to be amputated?" There were still tears in his eyes, ones that he had suppressed in front of July. "I need to take care of her, and I'm not sure what to do."

"We have to wait, Rick. It's all a gamble from this point. She is young and very strong. She will recover in one way or another. Go on, now. There is nothing more that you can do until tomorrow. She will be sleeping for quite awhile. Go on. Get some rest." As Rick dragged himself down the hall, Mo stepped up to July's bed, checking the IV drip, increasing it a bit.

"Time to doze," he said, clicking the side bed rails into place. "I sent Rick home to rest. Are you warm enough in that gown?"

July looked at the hospital gown that wrapped nearly twice around her. "Heck, it practically smothers me! But I will be fine. Really, really fine."

He gave her shoulder a pat. "They will come for you soon."

Chapter 42

Rick was on the phone as soon as he left the room, calling in some favors from the manager of the hotel where the Governor's Ball was always held the night after the Policeman's Picnic, booking a room with a balcony for himself and July and a large suite for the rest of the family.

"But that is the room where the Governor always stays," the manager protested.

"Put the Governor on the other side, Stacy, overlooking the city. His constituents are down there, after all, and I tip better than the Governor anyway." She laughed in agreement.

"And where do we go to buy my girl a gorgeous gown for the Ball, Stacey? Something exceptional? Oh, I don't care how expensive. I have to make an appointment? Are you kidding? Okay, I will call them. Appointment. Huh!"

Rick sat in his truck for a few minutes, parked by the bridge, watching the smooth run of the river, listening to the crickets and soft murmur of water through the reeds. What an enormous change he was about to make! It was more than a little disconcerting. Twenty-three years with LCPD, and now an uncertain future. He searched his soul for doubts, but there were none. His guts said this was the right thing to do.

He picked up his phone. "Mom?"

"She will sleep through the night, son. Dr. Moussa sent us on our way. This is a very nice suite, dear. Can you afford this?"

"Yes, I can afford it. You just enjoy the vacation. July and I will be right across the hall. I wish Dad had come, too. Can you talk him into it? You know Tomás and Maureen's brothers can run things for a few days. I want Dad here in case July agrees to marry me. I am hoping that we can do it right away, when all of us are together?"

"You haven't asked her?"

"I almost did, but she has a lot to deal with right now. I don't want to add any pressure."

He could imagine her shaking her head. "You think too much, Enrique. But we all love you, and especially July. She is almost as odd as you are. So, who knows, maybe your lack of a plan is just right."

"I am scared to death that she won't want me in that way, you know? I started out being the big brother, and when she wanted more, I put my foot down very firmly. Now, I am the one who wants more. I don't know how to handle it. And, for the Ball, could she wear Grandmother's ring?"

"Sure! I brought it. I would like for her to have it anyway. Grace wants to tell you something."

"Papa, if you don't know what words to say to July, why don't you sing them to her? You know, like Fred Astaire."

"Yeah. Okay." He laughed. "You are amazingly smart, Graciela Mariposa Mora."

The old truck started up right away, and he drove slowly across town. It was his town, his domain. But now, he just saw a city like any other city. He smiled, pleased by the change.

Chapter 43

Eric's car was in the Chief of Police's reserved parking place. Rick didn't want to have this confrontation right now, but maybe it was best to have done with it. He took the stairs one at a time.

"And, speak of the Devil, here he is." The Chief was leaning against a desk, arms crossed over his chest, ankles crossed, too. Q was tipped back in a chair against the wall. Rick felt immediate relief that they weren't waiting to beat up on him verbally.

"What am I going to do with you, Mora? You keep stealing everyone's thunder. The reporters have been after me all day about the infamous Captain Mora." But he was smiling.

Q tossed a peppermint candy at Rick. "Here. Suck on something sweet, you nasty bastard. I was too busy to notice. Were you really unarmed?"

"Yeah. But what choice did I have?"

"Oh, I don't know. SWAT maybe? Cripes, man, you are a frigging idiot! What makes you think that walking straight at a guy who has a gun in your face is a good idea?"

"Trafalgar."

"Who?"

"Lord Horatio Nelson and the Battle of Trafalgar, 1805."

He got two blank stares for a minute. "Something about Napoleon?"

"Yeah. Napoleonic Wars. Combined fleets of Spain and France against England. Thirty-three ships. Nelson had twenty-seven ships, most of them smaller, with fewer guns. He said, 'England expects every man to do his duty' and sailed his ship, the Victory, straight into the front half of the enemy fleet."

"What happened?" the two said in unison.

Rick smacked his forehead. "England won, you dimwits! Sheesh!"

"But didn't Nelson die in that battle?" Q asked.

"Well, yeah, there's that," Rick answered with a grin.

"I can see you now, sails snapping overhead, cannon fire, black smoke billowing, sword drawn, you point at Doctor Garner and say...."

"Fuck off, Chief!"

"No, that's not what you said."

"Okay, okay, you two. Enough."

They laughed.

"Look, I have something serious to say."

"Like, how Las Cruces expects every man to do his duty?"

"Oh, shut up. Geez, you guys are a pain in the ass. No, really. I'm serious. This is it. I am resigning, effective ASAP. And, I have an idea of how to make this outfit better with me gone."

They just looked at him in astonishment.

"You both know that I am aging fast. I am a worn-out war-horse. And, you know better than I do that things are changing in law enforcement. So, I propose that Major Crimes continue under the direction of former Lieutenant, to be newly promoted, Captain Quintana." He slapped Q on the back.

"And that we split off, I mean you split off, a new division, Cyber Crime, under a newly promoted Rory Kincannon. Add a couple of the tech guys we use as consultants now to help Rory. You would have to pay them less, but they would have city benefits to make up for it. No need for any new facilities, just upgraded equipment, and it will be much more effective."

"So, are you considering the Chief job after all, then Rick?"

"No, Eric. I don't know where I will end up or what I will be doing, but I must get away from this job. It's not who I am. I don't know who I am anymore, but I'm not old Captain Mora."

"What happened? What's going on?"

Q spoke up. "Methinks there is a little redhead behind this."

"Yeah." Rick smiled and sat on the desk, looking from one to the other. "That's not the whole story, though. I went to the mountains and ran. I ran almost all day for seven days, all the way to George Dobbs' domain. I heard something strange. It was like drums beating in the canyon ruins, in my head, maybe in my soul, or whatever. I imagined my grandfather running beside me. I spoke to the ravens, the lizards, the deer, and they spoke back. A bull elk slept beside me. A real one. Not an hallucination."

He paused, looking out the window to the lights below. "I am just not who I was, Eric. I'm completely sober. Imagine that. I want to stay that way. I want to marry July and adopt Graciela. It is not the time for me to be a cop."

"What will you do, my friend?"

"Rick is a great cabinet maker, a wonderful chef, a halfway fair musician, and *un gran jinete.* He will survive." Q interjected.

"Jinete?" Eric asked. "I don't know that word."

"A horseman."

"I thought that was a caballero."

"Nope. A caballero is a gentleman, and Rick is not one of those, for sure."

Q laughed as Rick gave him a middle finger. "But he had better not be pulling out of the band yet."

"Not as long as I am within driving distance of you and Sharon."

"But," Q went on, "what are you planning to do, Rick? Really."

"I truly don't know. I'm probably moving back to Juniper Springs for now because that is where July and Gracie are. You want my apartment, Q? No rent if you do the maintenance for Mr. Yamamoto. Sharon's boys already know the place so well that they can help you. I need to find someone reliable to replace me before I can move."

"Hell, yes! After all the work you did on that old garage? It's a great place. With all that room upstairs for the boys, maybe I can finally get Sharon to marry me. When are you picking up July?"

"Mo will let me know when she's ready to go. I will have to keep her doped up for a week or so. Her arm is terribly damaged. She won't be able to do the surgeries and such. So, we are both setting out on a new course, with no compass yet."

The shift changed as they talked, the morning crew arriving. Rick sought out Kincannon for some help. "Rory, I need your expertise for a few minutes. Something terrible happened to my July in the past, and I need to understand how to help her deal with it. You are faster at searching the internet than I am."

"Sure, Cap. Where do we start?"

"Austin, Texas. Eleven years ago."

Rory's knowledge of search engines and keywords quickly found a back-page paragraph in the city newspaper about Douglas Gilman, Junior, accused by J.M. Kozlowski of a violent rape.

"This is the only notice, Cap. And that is very odd. Either the charge was dropped or moved venues, or some powerful party managed to suppress anything more."

"Can you check court records?"

"Not quickly, but I can check arrest records in the city and county pretty fast."

It only took a minute or two, and there it was, complete with the names of arresting officers. It was a very detailed report.

"Oh, my God, Cap! That poor girl!"

No wonder July clung to Rick so tightly sometimes. No wonder she was afraid. He picked up the phone and dialed. On the Austin end, Captain Mohedin remembered the case well. It had been very frustrating for his team when it ended in a hung jury.

"Everyone knew he was guilty, Captain Mora. We all believed that Dougie's father paid off the jury foreman. It was not the first time daddy bought the little shit out of trouble. That girl weighed less than a hundred pounds, and Doug was at least two-fifty. Tough little thing."

"Yeah. She still is."

Rory kept searching while his boss made the call. He turned the screen so that Rick could see the face. Cold, hard rage nearly consumed him. *Douglas Gilman, Junior. I'll find you one of these days. I'll find you and you will suffer terribly, if I let you live.*

Chapter 44

Waiting to hear from Mo, Rick returned to his apartment. He thought he would just lie down for a few minutes, but emotional stress was more exhausting than he thought. He slept for almost twelve hours, then waited through the next day and night, sitting beside July as she slept, woke briefly, and slept again. Rick realized that for the first time in twenty five years, he was a nervous wreck about pretty much everything. He laughed at himself. *Chicken!*

The fourth morning, he sat on the other bed, watching his mother's flying fingers as she knitted. He sank back, curling onto his side, facing July from a few feet away, and was almost instantly asleep again. Gisele smiled to herself, watching her two sleeping charges. Rough Rick always looked so much younger in his sleep. And July, their lIttle July, squeaked a tiny snore.

Dr. Moussa strode in, clipboard in hand, grinning at the tableau. "Hey, you!" He smacked Rick's boot sole with his clipboard. "Get your boots off the bed."

Rick jerked awake, smiling at July as she opened sleepy eyes and stretched out her good arm to him.

"Hi, little wabbit. How are you feeling?"

"Shezwam."

"Shazaam?"

She laughed, shaking her head.

"Sheezwaaam," she said, trying to enunciate, pushing herself to a wobbly sitting position, and giggling again. "No, mensheezwam!" And, she doubled over in a fit of giggles.

Rick crouched by her bed. "I think you are higher than a kite."

Another burst of laughter from her. "Ah, hah, hah, Can't feel my lips.Thz shoes wand!"

"She means the sheet is too warm." Mo unwrapped her from the tangle of sheets. "There. Better?"

July nodded, still giggling, and leaned against Rick. She pointed to her cast arm, and gave Mo a questioning look.

"It will be a slow recovery. Maybe three months, even more. You can't voluntarily move the joint. I hope you will have some grip strength, but there is nerve damage, so as you know, we just have to wait and see. PT might help, but not until we get some healing going. Okay?"

She turned her head for a moment, burying her face in Rick's chest, but then rallied. "K. Will make it work." She smiled a little unsteadily at her man, and said, "Lez go."

"Isn't it too soon, babe?"

She shook her head and enunciated carefully. "Hospitals are for bad memories."

He saw it in her face, the pain of that time in Austin. "Okay, babe. Is she okay to do stuff, Mo? Can she eat and drink whatever now? And clothes? Where are your clothes?"

Gisele lifted a shopping bag. "I threw them away. When Grace and I went back to the western store to get July's purse and the truck keys, the clerk said that the pretty lady was about to buy these things. So, Grace and I washed them yesterday." She held them up for July to see. "And, new boots." Gisele smiled at July's enthusiastic nod. "Okay. You men clear out now."

"But, what if...."

"Out, son. We can manage. I won't let her fall. You get whatever prescription July will need from Dr. Moussa while I help her dress."

"I'll check that arm tomorrow, Rick. Then next week follow up with Doctor Patel."

Rick stiffened.

"You jealous idiot! Behave yourself. Relax and enjoy. She obviously is in love with you, although I cannot imagine why. She will forgive you your trespasses, or whatever it is that you Christians say."

"Okay, okay I get it. Kind of. Mo, after twenty-three years, as of Sunday midnight, I am no longer Captain Mora, and I hope she will marry me."

"You resigned before you even know if she will marry you? That sounds like the definition of stupid. But, maybe you will live long enough to see little Gracie grow up after all." He patted Rick on the shoulder.

The room door squeaked open, and July stood there in her new outfit, knowing that despite the cast, she looked okay. Gisele understood men very well and had helped July achieve that special something. The turquoise-on-cream striped shirt tied just above her waist, the scoop neck just low enough to show a few inches of cleavage. A small swathe of pale skin showing between shirt and pants was tempting, without being blatantly sexy. Jeans fit tight to her curves. Boots gave her an additional two inches of height, making her shapely legs look longer. Her eyes were brilliant, sparkling green in her freckled face, and they appeared even larger than usual somehow. Gisele slung her own navy sweater over July's shoulder, draping it to hide the cast.

Mo complimented her, but although Rick was momentarily tongue-tied, his flushed cheeks under the tan were very revealing of his feelings.

"You go to that fancy hotel and order this girl a big breakfast, Enrique. She is hungry. "

"Okay, Mom. Where is my little princess?"

"She and Maureen are up at her other grandparents for a few days. Go on now. Shoo!"

July took him by the arm and just began slowly walking down the hall, rejecting the offered wheelchair. Rick almost stumbled at first, but quickly caught himself, matching his steps to hers. She was still a little woozy, needing his supporting strength. He wanted to hover, to coddle, to baby her. But something told him this was not the time. She was proudly in charge, her natural shyness overcome by the effects of pain killers and the open admiration of the men. He covered her hand with his.

Gisele and Dr. Moussa looked at each other with mutual understanding. "It is not going to be an easy transition for either of them. But, they have each other," he said. "They will make it okay."

"I have always wondered, Mo, whether my boy is crazy? One minute so violent and the next so kind, even sweet. I mean, medically. Is he?"

"I would say something like high functioning PTSD, Gisele. Borderline sometimes on the sanity scale, but very high functioning. He will be okay. I think July helps stabilize him, don't you?" He smiled at her, understanding her concern because he, too, worried about his friend's mental health.

Chapter 45

Far to the north, Governor Leo Durbin stood in his office in Santa Fe's Roundhouse, the state government headquarters, looking out over the capitol city. The sunlight was brilliant, making adobe buildings glow warm brown. Aspen leaves shimmered in a faint breeze. But, the atmosphere in the room was gloomy.

"It has to be someone that the voters will trust. Someone empathetic. Someone unlike me, and who is not after my job. I don't want to be fighting internally while I am campaigning externally."

"It is a little more than three years until the elections. You have plenty of time to repair the voter's image of your administration. But you can't do it with another career politician on your staff. This scandal with the Lieutenant Governor will be bad for you unless you pick a replacement soon. Someone who is absolutely incorruptible. I'm telling you that Mora is your man."

"I've met him. He's nuts, a fucking iceberg, and a murderer to boot. Hell, everyone is scared half to death of him, including me. How can you even think of suggesting such a maniac? Have you looked at his eyes? If he isn't freezing you, he is staring at you like you are a rabbit, and he is the fox. I think he may actually be crazy."

"He has a pile of awards for bravery. You think our voters don't admire him? They love him. He's like some old-time hero. Sergeant York. Wyatt Earp. You'll see. He'll be at the Policemen's Picnic. Watch how people react to him. Did you know that he was a champion bronc rider, too? He resigned effective Saturday night and has a good plan for the future of Las Cruces police work. Eric Andersen called me right away, suggesting Rick, and it resonates. Keep an open mind. You may be surprised."

"Come on, Larry. He is an uneducated hick from, where is it? Pine Flat?"

"Juniper Springs. And, he is about to marry Luke Kozlowski's niece, the granddaughter of one of your predecessors. One of your beloved predecessors, I might add. I have known Rick since he was a teenager, and if it weren't for his courage and quick thinking, I would be just another body bag occupant from Iraq."

"Anyhow, let's get going. It is a long drive, and you are scheduled to stop halfway down at the Sierra County Fair for a few handshakes and photos. Please, for God's sake, wear your boots and jeans. These small-town folks are not necessarily impressed by designer suits."

"Mora wears designer suits."

"No, he wears custom-made suits. Let's face it, Leo, you have the build of a snowman. Better to look like a fat old country farmer than ...."

"Oh, shut up!"

Chapter 46

"Do you want room service, July? We have a nice room."

"No, I want hot crispy waffles, and bacon, and orange juice, and coffee. I don't want to wait for room service." She was steadier on her feet now, and her speech was clearer. "Let's just go to the coffee shop."

He hesitated, wanting to persuade her. Marietta of the big boobs would be working in the coffee shop. She always worked the breakfast shift. He realized that encounters such as this were inevitable, given his alley cat history, and he wasn't ready for it yet. But he couldn't hide either.

"Okay, July. Coffee shop it is." He mentally braced himself.

July slipped into the first available booth and waved at the waitress. Sure enough, it was Marietta who hurried over to them with cups and coffee pot in hand.

"Oh, Doctor Sullivan, I am so happy to see that you are okay! Do you remember me? I had those plantar warts?"

"I do remember you. I guess they are better now. You certainly aren't limping like you did."

"All gone. I can't thank you enough." She poured a coffee for July. "Do you know what you want to eat?" July gave her order.

"Captain? The usual?" He nodded. "Do you know what happened to your coffee?"

"No, what?"

"It got mugged."

He groaned. "Oh, bad one. You know what happened when I went shopping for some camo gear?"

"Yup. You couldn't find any." They both laughed, and Marietta hurried off to place their orders.

July was giggling. "Is that some kind of competition?"

"Yeah. She's a very bright girl. Good with words. Going to be a good lawyer." He blushed, hesitating. "I didn't know that you knew each other. I was afraid that Marietta and I would be embarrassed, and you would be angry."

"You are a very attractive bachelor, and she is a very attractive young lady. It's only natural. Besides, I don't own you. It's really none of my business, is it? What is that saying of Uncle Luke's? Something about chickens eventually coming home to roost?" She grinned and poked him in the chest.

Marietta smiled at them. "So nice to see you two together," she said as she served their breakfasts. "You are both wonderful people, and you make such a cute couple."

"Cute couple? Really?" Rick laughed. "I never thought I would hear that. Thanks, Marietta."

July wolfed down her breakfast and was tempted to order more, but started feeling sleepy again.

"Come on, babe. Time for a rest before we go shopping." He left a generous tip and waved at Marietta to put the bill on his tab.

The beauty of their room distracted July momentarily. She oohed and aahed over the view, the thick robes in the bathroom, the reclining chairs on the balcony. It was a quiet morning, smelling of roses, and birds were singing in the pecan groves.

"July." He lifted her onto the wide cement rail of the balcony, where she was eye-to-eye with him. "Something happened to me in the mountains, and it changed me. I am just not who I was." He took a big breath. "I made some big changes. I need to be here for my family. I don't want you or Grace to be endangered, tainted, by association with this crazy ass Mora guy. And something else happened, too. This spirit came to me in the mountains. A big old bull elk spoke to me somehow, and the insane coyote that I am shrank down to half his normal size. The different parts of me are doing battle for my soul or my heart or something, and I can't see myself in the same light as before. I want to be your hero. Instead, I've been exposing you to more dangers. I didn't know what to do. When you attacked me, I realized that, at some level, I didn't want you to get better because then you would leave me. I don't understand it. I don't need anyone, at least not since I was about ten. You turned my life upside down, and I have to admit that I am not as strong as I pretend to be because I need this little wabbit in my life."

She didn't answer, but the way she tipped her head told him that she was listening.

"I didn't kill myself because then you might have to fight your battles alone. I couldn't try to make you my own because you might have given up your hunt for a new career. I was torn to pieces by the two sides of me. You were my unresolvable problem. So, there I was with no clue how to handle things, and I felt helpless. I try not to be the boss, but you are so damned illogical sometimes that you need protection from yourself. I'm trying to change. Really, I am. I want to do things differently. I want to build instead of destroy, like Luke said. When I'm away from you, I feel like looking over my shoulder to find you. And when you aren't there, I get this stab of anxiety. Where is my July?"

"I don't understand. Rique. I am trying to, but...."

He smiled. "I don't understand either, babe. I can't seem to get the right words together. But, right now, you need a rest. We can do something fun later. This is karaoke night at Blue Bellies, or we could go to a movie, or we can stay right here and play Scrabble or watch TV or sleep or whatever you feel good enough to do."

His grandmother's ring was burning a hole in his pocket, but this wasn't the right time. Or maybe it was just that he was too scared of what she would say.

Her eyes were closing, but she jerked them open. "I'm fine if you want to do something now."

"Well, I am kind of sleepy. Can we take a little nap? The sun feels kind of good today, and these lounge chairs are great."

It was only a few minutes until July was sound asleep. Rick picked her up, settling her on the closest bed. She instinctively curled into her little ball. He arranged her arm on a pillow, then lay beside her, one heavy arm over her, protective and comforting. In a few minutes, she relaxed back into him without ever waking up.

Chapter 46

Rick's dad and Luke had never been to a karaoke night, and July thought that would be fun. Gisele got a phone call as they were getting ready. She was laughing with delight.

"Guess what? Suzanne is coming for a visit! You go get her, Enrique, El Paso Airport. There is no need for her to rent a car when I can loan her mine. We'll meet you at the bar."

"Okay, Mom. You will like Suzanne, July. She is lots of fun. I'll be back in about two hours."

The rest of the crew went on to Blue Bellies. Kate and Gisele got into the spirit of things right away, singing *Respect*. They had the audience laughing and clapping as they added a spontaneous dance to their act. They did a great job. There was a fairly large crowd, many from law enforcement or other officers of the court. Luke and Kate found some friends and were chatting with them, so there were vacant chairs at the Mora's table. Judge Kendrick joined them.

"Hey, Gisele. I didn't know you were such a good songstress. You are the source of Rick's musical talent I guess."

"Oh, he is infinitely better than I am. I often wish he had made a profession of it. But, you were right to push him into law enforcement."

"He is one of those guys that thrives on adrenaline," Rafael added. "Never would have been happy running the store."

"Where is your wayward boy tonight?" the judge asked.

"He went to pick up a friend at the airport. And see the little redhead over there with Eva Shannon? He is going to buy something special for her, too. Something he saw at the jewelry store. That is July Kozlowski, Luke's grand niece, and the love of my boy's life. He is crazy about her."

"What? Really?"

"Oh yeah. Head over heels. He has been trying to work up the courage to propose for a month." Rafael laughed. "She has turned Rick upside down and inside out without even trying."

The judge was surprised.. "Well, she has a tiger by the tail, doesn't she?"

"She is pretty much of a tiger herself, when she's not feeling shy. Those two have been seesawing back and forth all summer. It has been interesting. I am seeing a side of my son that is new to me. Enrique can hardly keep away from her. He hovers."

They watched July chatting with Eva and some other young folks. "She is a very pretty girl," the judge commented. "But knowing your son, there must be a lot more to her than that. I remember when he was doing security detail for that singer, Marnie Mayne. She's real pretty, too, and she was all over him. Wanted him to travel with her. He could have his pick from lots of pretty women. It's interesting. The left side of his face, with those scars, make him look pretty rough, but the right side is really charming. Kind of like his split personality, isn't it?"

Just then the door opened and Rick breezed in with a beautiful older woman on his arm.. There was no missing his presence. He looked like he owned the place.

"Holy Mackerel!" the judge exclaimed. "Is that Suzanne Gooden? I haven't seen her since she went off to Hollywood. I still think of her as Suzanne Karras from Hooper, no matter how famous she has become."

"She worked at our store all through high school, and was Rick's music tutor."

July spotted them immediately, and as soon as he saw her, he grinned that lopsided grin, his teeth flashing white. He left the lady with his mom, and started toward July. He looked so handsome dressed in the same denim blazer, black jeans and open necked white shirt as the day when they first met in the hospital. July no longer saw the scarring on the left side of his face. She laughed to herself. *Oh, my Rique, you are so devastatingly sexy. Now I know what swooning means.*

People turned to speak to him, but he only had eyes for his girl. One pretty young woman stepped in front of him, placed a hand on his chest, and said, "Are you free tonight, Captain Mora?"

Rick paused, thinking that a few months ago, he would have been happy to buy her a drink before he screwed her. "Thank you, Miss, but I was never really free, just cheap and kind of sleazy." He smiled and went on, weaving his way through the crowd. He was just in time to hear some young fellow, insisting that July dance with him.

"Thank you, but I am with somebody." She looked past him at Rick working his way toward her.

Well lubricated with alcohol, the young fellow didn't notice her lack of interest in him. "What?" he said. "Those old guys you came in with? I don't see them dancing. Come on." He took her arm.

"Let her go."

The man turned, startled, and looked Rick up and down with a growing grin. All he saw was a medium-sized fellow with bifocals and silver strands through his hair. "You speaking to me, Pops?" He sneered.

"You channeling Robert DeNiro, kid? Can't you see that the lady has an injured arm? Let go of her."

"I just want to dance with her. Is that's your business or something?"

"Yes. It is. Leave her alone."

"And you are going to do what?"

Rick felt the coyote starting to rise from his stomach to his chest. *Not in front of my July. Not again. Be an elk. Be an elk.* "Look, son, I don't want to fight you. Okay? It's simple. Get your hands off my woman. There are plenty of ladies here who might want to dance with you."

"I picked this one. Beat it, old man."

"Hey! What do you think I am? A prize in a pissing contest?" July tried to pull away.

Rick's eyes sparkled with anger and he grinned. It was not a friendly grin. "So, you have had a few too many drinks and you are feeling like a tough guy. I understand. I did the same thing when I was your age. But you will not win a fight with me tonight. And Dr. Kozlowski will not be your dance partner tonight."

"You think you can take me?"

"You think you could speak in something besides cliches?"

The young fellow's face flushed, and he let go of July, who stepped back rubbing her wrist.

Rick looked at July. "You hurt, babe?" But before she could aswer, he saw a sudden movement from the corner of his eye. He caught the oncoming fist before it could connect. In the blink of an eye, he had the kid in a reverse wrist lock, forcing him backwards onto a table.

"I can either dislocate it or break it. Your choice, sonny."

"Fuck, man! Let me up!" His other arm flailed at Rick, who ignored the blows.

Rick applied more weight, twisting that elbow joint until the kid howled. "In this bar, ladies' choices are respected. Always. Got it?" The only response was a sob. "Got it?"

A panting sob. "Okay! Okay! I get it!"

"You get it...what? Show some respect for your elders."

He mewed. "Sir! I get it. sir!"

Rick let him up. "Get smart, kid, or you'll get seriously hurt."

The music stopped during the little altercation. Rick's guest, Suzanne Gooden, had started her singing career in bars. She stepped up on the stage, knowing how to get the festive mood back.

"Hi! I'm Suzanne." She was drowned out by whistling and clapping as the crowd recognized her. "And I started singing in joints like this one. I still prefer it to acting, I think. None of those 5 a.m. makeup or costuming calls here!" The crowd laughed and applauded.

"I bet you all can't guess what my first real job was." People called from the crowd suggesting a model, a waitress. "Nope. It was at the farm store in Juniper Springs, working for Rafael and Gisele Mora. At first I ran the cash register. But I was studying music, and they had this little boy that was always messing with his mom's piano or violin. He was an obnoxious little brat, and now he is larger but just as obnoxious. And he needs to come up here now."

Rick and July were just joining the family at their table. Rick swung around to scowl at her. "Aww, Suzanne," he said. "Come on!"

She laughed. "You come on, you little rug rat. Up here. Have some respect for your elders."

July laughed. "Well? Go on. Don't disappoint the audience."

"Aaarrgh," he said, but he went, jumping up on the stage beside his old friend.

Suzanne was saying, "I invested five years in his musical education during my high school and college years, and did he continue it? What did he do with it? He became a cop! I bet you have heard him play his guitar?" Whistles and claps. "He could be doing musical theater on Broadway, or touring the world as a concert pianist, but he always wanted to be George Strait." She shook her head, and pointed to the piano. "Sit." He sat.

"This is what he could have been. Give us Rachmaninoff." He looked at her expectantly. "*Concerto No. 2*," she added. It is a very dramatic piece and he was playing it beautifully, from memory, when she interrupted.

"*West Side Story*." He segued into a medley of tunes from the play. "See? He could have gone pro!"

"Hell yes, " Rick answered. "I could have been a lounge lizard, and lived off tips in joints like this." Laughing at Suzanne, he played and sang *Piano Man*.

"Did I do a good job of teaching?" The crowd cheered her and their Captain, most of them surprised by his versatility.

"Now, one more, then back to karaoke. Is July Kozlowski here? Come up here, dear, because this numbskull is going to sing you a song."

July blushed, but did not want to embarrass either Rick or his famous friend by refusing.

"Rick has been telling me about his friend, Governor Kozlowski's granddaughter, and how she is a terrific doctor, and an incredibly brave woman. There is something he needs to say to her that might come out best in a song." Suzanne sat down at the piano, and played *There Were Bells on the Hills*. It is very romantic, and she had to play the intro twice before he got his voice under control enough to sing.

He had never thought about the meaning of the words. Now, they hit him hard, and he choked up. He took July's hand, his cheeks flushed with emotion. As he sang, he unconsciously lifted her hand, holding it over his heart. As he finished the lyric, he realized that the time was now. He jumped down, lifting his July from the stage.

"Doctor Kozlowski, may I have this dance?" he said.

Suzanne smiled down at them, pleased with what she had pushed Rick into doing, and continued, "Who wants to sing that duet from *Dirty Dancing* with me? Come on up here, Lieutenant, " she called, as Q's hand waved at her.

"You know, in all the years I have been coming here," the judge said, " I have seen Rick break up fights, and get in fights, a hundred times, but I never saw him dance. He usually just leans on the bar. I didn't know he could dance. They're kind of perfect together, aren't they?"

Rick was looking down at July, holding her gently. "This feels so good, having you in my arms. Do you remember the day when you said that I am your man? Am I still, July? Am I still your man?"

"Always, Rique."

"Remember that story about what happened when the wabbit kissed the toad?"

"The princess, silly. And it was a frog. The princess kissed a frog."

"Toad."

"Frog!"

"Okay. Then do you remember what happened when the

princess kissed the amphibian?"

"Amphibian?" Startled by the incongruity of his response, she snorted, "I suppose that he croaked."

Rick laughed at that. "But I don't want to only be a toad. I need another persona, so you won't get bored with me. Let's see." He squinted at the ceiling, pretending to ponder. Then eyebrows raised in mock surprise, he said, "Wait! I know! If you could learn to spell it, maybe I could succeed as a gerbil?" .

"A gerbil!" She doubled over with laughter. "You remembered that?"

"Of course I remembered. You were angry, and frustrated, and kind of scared. I probably fell in love with you right then."

"What? Rique? What did you say?"

He cleared his throat.

"I said, I fell in love with you then. But I was afraid to admit it, even to myself. I was so afraid that you would change my life, and I would lose control." She was looking at him, wide-eyed. "That is exactly what happened, you are the reason why I changed my life, and I'm glad. I am. Really. I want to be more than extended family. I want to be your husband. So, I resigned, and I stopped drinking."

July opened her mouth to say something, but was so stunned that no words came out. She didn't know what to say. She leaned into him, looking up, studying his face. "I...I...are you sure? You're very popular here, and there are all these women to pick from." Then her eyes narrowed and she poked him with a sharp fingernail. "Don't you tease me, Bubba."

"I am not teasing, my Wabbit. July Marie Kozlowski," he spun them around in time with the music, "will you marry me? I have my grandmother's engagement ring burning a hole in my pocket."

She just stared at him for a minute. "But Rique, you wouldn't even kiss me."

"I told you that I couldn't kiss you because I was afraid of what else I might do. But that one time, July, when we were on the hill above the house? That kiss was earth shaking for me." He raised an eyebrow and pretended to twirl a mustache, like the wicked character in a melodrama. "Heh, heh, heh. Come my little wabbit, to the gerbil's den, where you will be kissed to a frazzle."

She laughed. "You are so silly. Oh, Rique. I do love you, so very much. Don't you dare back out on me!"

"Does that mean yes, July? Can you stand me long term? Sleep beside me? Hold my hand?"

"Yes, Enrique Mora. I have been in love with you since at least 4th of July weekend. Yes!"

He stopped dancing right there in the middle of the room, reached into his jeans pocket, and brought out a square cut emerald on a platinum band. He didn't notice that others around them had stopped dancing, too, and were watching Old Stone Face Captain Mora smiling at this girl, and slipping a ring on her left hand. He leaned as though to kiss her but suddenly jerked back, noticing the audience.

"Okay, okay, you guys. You can stop staring now."

"Without an introduction to this young lady, Cap?" Ralph, the bartender, said. "Where are your manners?"

July laughed. "You can wait to kiss me, Gerbil. But you could introduce me."

He looked so happy. "I want to keep you to myself. But Ralph is right, Where are my manners? And I guess we should say something to the folks or Mom will kill me. Our folks. Yours and mine. Ours. Isn't that great? Ours, babe!"

July giggled, leaning on her man. "Where is my stoic tough guy? Is this a new you? Or just a side you kept hidden? And yes, Rique, it is totally great. Totally."

Rick jumped up on the stage, reached down and lifted July up beside him. "This is the biggest, best, most wonderful day of my life, ladies and gentlemen," he said. "Friends, and probably a few enemies." He looked out over the crowd and spotted a very young face. The cop in him took over for a minute. "Denny? You old enough to be here?"

"Yes sir, Cap. My birthday was Tuesday."

"Okay, son. Behave yourself." He cleared his throat, and with a huge grin, said, "Ladies and gentlemen, may I introduce Doctor July Kozlowski, who has just agreed to marry me." He put an arm around her, and the crowd couldn't help but notice how he unconsciously puffed out his chest.

July looked at the family, and this strange man she loved so much. "Can we get married right away? Before I wake up from this dream?"

Rick's brow furrowed. "I hope so, but Mom might want to plan stuff and...." He looked over at his parents sitting there with Judge Kendrick, and the brow cleared. "How about here? Now?"

July's jaw dropped. "Really? I didn't think quite *this* quickly." But then she smiled, caught up in Rick's excitement. "Well, why not? I am willing to love and honor, but that obey thing?"

"Knowing you, definitely not. How about love, honor, and uh...." Rick groped for the right term. From the audience hanging on their words, young Denny called, "Negotiate!"

Laughter spread around the room in ripples, then waves.

It was quickly accomplished. "Congratulations," the judge said, "It is about time. You may kiss your bride."

"Oh yeah, but not here. Free drinks all around, Ralph. I am feeling like a wealthy man tonight." Turning to their folks, he said. "I'm sorry, Mom. I didn't give you time to do the whole wedding thing. I just, you know, all of a sudden I couldn't stop myself." Rick was apologetic. She waved him away with a laugh, delighted that at last she had a daughter.

Luke shook Rick's hand and kissed his grown up little girl on the cheek. "See you tomorrow, July. You are giving me a son and a granddaughter all in one swoop. Thank you, sweetie."

It took time to make it to the door. Most of the crowd were cops and their friends who had known Rick for years. Through hand shaking and back slapping, they finally made it to the parking lot, but instead of handing July into that old Ford as usual, he turned her to face him and pulled her into his arms.

"Are you doing your macho intimidation thing? I'm not intimidated, you know."

"I know. I'm doing my anticipation thing. I put on a good show, but I'm really just putty in your hands." He rethought that. "Or, well, uh, something." He laughed.

She pressed even tighter against him. "That doesn't feel at all like putty. Definitely more like woody. I know a quotation for this moment. It's about too, too solid flesh."

"You mean Hamlet? That is not quite what he meant, but I like the idea of you melting this solid flesh for me." It seemed like his legs were buckling. He could barely stand up, he wanted her so badly. The memory of her naked body was so sharp, every dimple, every contour from rosy nipples to those smooth inviting thighs.

"Your wife is a crazy wild tiger, Rique. Indestructible, insatiable. All the endorphins will be good for me. How fast will this old truck go?"

"Insatiable? It can go pretty darn fast."

The door of their room was still closing as he unzipped her pants and unsnapped her blouse. He kicked off his boots, and still had one leg in his jeans when she pulled him down. He proved his virility more than once in that next hour.

Slick with sweat, Rick collapsed beside his wife, laying a possessive hand on her belly. "You know, there's been this dark thing in my chest. It was kind of like that big rock in the stream, the one with the moss on it?" She nodded. "And it pulled on me. I could feel it dragging me, inch by inch, into a bottomless abyss, like something Dante would have created. An inferno. You know, the city of woe, eternal pain, and all that. It sounds crazy, but that black thing felt real to me, and now it's gone. Just gone. You erased it."

July smiled. "You know what is crazy?" He shook his head. "Thinking that I have ever read Dante." She ran her fingernails up his thigh.

"Are you trying to attack me again, my wild tiger? Umm, at my age, I probably can't manage...uh...oh, yeah," he groaned. He could. He did.

They slept soundly, barely waking as dawn light filled the room with a blushing glow. Eventually, Rick's phone alarm rang, reminding him that July needed her medication, and they had an appointment before the Policeman's Picnic.

"So, now, for the first time in my life, I get to take my wife on a shopping trip. I thought men were supposed to dread it, but I am kind of excited about it."

"I thought we were shopping for Grace's new doll."

"That and a gown for you to wear to the Ball."

She looked down, hesitant, her face kind of pale.

"What's the matter, babe?"

"I don't know how to behave at a Ball, Rique. I don't know how to dress or do makeup and all that feminine stuff. I'm afraid I'll embarrass you. I should have learned all that, but I didn't want the attention of men until I met you." She looked away, trying not to shed childish tears.

"July," he paused, not knowing how to begin.

"I'm sorry, Rique. I don't know how to talk to important people. I only know medical stuff. I know how to do jeans and boots, not ballgowns and such. I will embarrass you."

"Honey." He felt helpless. "You are beautiful and smart and fun. Any man would be delighted to take you to any event. This is just a Las Cruces annual fundraiser. But I would take you to meet the queen or the pope or whatever."

Was it an attack of shyness? Fear? Regret? The last thought sent a spear straight into his heart. But he was just as stubborn as she was. They would get to the bottom of this. He picked up his phone.

"Suzanne? Where are you now? Could you come over here right now?"

He wrapped his arms around July. "You didn't have a mom or aunts or a grandmother to support you when you were growing up, but look at all you accomplished. You are an important person. You were offered that fellowship, July. How many people can brag about that? How many people have you helped? And you have a great sense of humor. You are fun to be around. You are the whole package, my girl. The whole package. Don't cry, baby. Don't cry. Where is my crazy wild tiger woman?"

They heard a knock on the door, and there was lovely Suzanne Gooden, the actress, singer, dancer. She gave Rick a hug. "Hey, rug rat," Suzanne said to Rick, "what's up?"

"Honestly, Suzanne, are you ever going to see me as an adult?"

"Oh, I think I'd rather keep sticking a pin in that inflated ego."

"You know what I always like best about you, Suze?" Rick said, turning on the sarcasm. "It's how supportive you are."

"Hey, July. It looks like this idiot has made you cry. What's wrong?"

"What's wrong is the Ball, Suze," Rick explained.

"Why? What happened?"

July swallowed, her eyes huge in her pale face. "Well, Rique is this important person, and... and I am just the wabbit. I will be an embarrassment."

Just the wabbit? I did this to her. Rick was mortified. He knelt in front of her chair. "No. No. This is my fault. You don't really remember the wabbit thing very well, do you? What did you do? Climb the fence to get on you horse?" She nodded. "And got halfway to town before you fell off old Patches."

Suzanne laughed. "Patches? That was the best old horse. He babysat me for years. Did you know that Luke bought him from my dad?" July shook her head.

"You were so tough, July." Rick went on. "What other little kid would have cussed and kicked and bit someone three times her size? I call you wabbit as a, as ... as an expression of my admiration for that smart, strong little girl who is still smarter and stronger than any woman I have ever known. And utterly gorgeous, too. I am so stupid and insensitive. I didn't understand. We don't have to go to the Ball."

Suzanne took over immediately. "Go away, Rick. I know all about this. It's stage fright. We all go through it. I backed out of auditions a dozen times before I finally learned to cope. No, don't go yet. I am going to give you a shopping list. What were you going to wear to the Ball, July?"

"I don't have anything. I don't really know about clothes and makeup and stuff."

"We are going to Erlene Shattuck's shop this afternoon," Rick said.

"Good choice. Can I go along?"

"Sure, Suze. Mom would love it."

"You don't need much makeup, dear. You are stunning without any artifice at all. But we can make a few features stand out." She gave Rick a shopping list and told him where to get what they needed. "Bring me back a Starbucks while you're at it."

"Now tell me about yourself, July." Suzanne fairly gushed over the importance of July's medical degree and how proud everyone had been of her, and on and on. "You know," she said, "most of those supposedly important people who will be at the Ball never did anything of value in their whole lives. You are definitely one up on them. And, Rick will bust that fat head of his with pride. You are not just a great doctor, you are a very significant person. The wife of Enrique Mora is someone to be reckoned with. Don't worry about what these folks think because in the long run, they are not so important. A lot of them are just all wrapped up in their image and there is nothing behind it. You know, we used to laugh about the false front at the Hooper Café, the way it attracted the tourists. But what's behind it? Just another rundown old building. Their food is good, and that is what counts. What's inside. You have a solid core, You matter. It will be fun. I promise. And most of those folks will envy you. Women because you are so pretty and accomplished, and men will wish you were their date. We are going to have fun."

By the time Rick returned, July's eyes were sparkling again.

"Guess what, Rique? That actor who plays the alien in the Galaxy Wars movies? Guess where he is from? Roswell! Really!" She laughed.

Rick hugged her, looking over her head with gratitude to his friend, Suzanne.

"Okay. Let's go find you a ballgown."

Erlene was ready for them at her exclusive shop. Gisele and Suzanne had done some advance planning over the phone with the shop owner, and she had a few options ready. They picked an emerald green gown with a cream-colored, off-one-shoulder, lace bodice. There would be nothing else like it at the Governor's Ball. July loved it, and Rick kept himself from blinking when Erlene handed him the bill. It was worth it. It only took a few minutes to transfer a little more money from his money market account to his checking account.

Rick was amazed at how elegant his little wabbit looked, even with one arm in a cast. "Look at you, July Marie. No one is more lovely than my wife. I don't care if you are in jeans and boots, my old shirt, or this gorgeous gown. You are special, and everyone who is anyone can see that is true."

While some fitting was being done, he called the shop he had quickly visited last night before joining the family at Blue Bellies. "When will it be ready? Can you have someone bring it to the hotel before the Ball? Thanks!"

Chapter 47

Down at the picnic, Q and Sharon had the band equipment set up and ready to go. "What took you so long, man?" Q was sweating from hauling instruments and equipment from his van.

"Oh, we just did a little shopping. My wife will be the most gorgeous, accomplished woman at the Ball." Rick was grinning as widely as his facial scars allowed.

They sat at the Chief's table, with Eric's wife, Laura, waiting until it was time for their gig. July was feeling a little loopy with the medication and fatigue. She cracked jokes to cover it, keeping them all laughing.

"Well, those folks are sure having a good time," the Governor commented, as Eric, host of the event, joined him at his table.

"That girl is cute. Very smart and determined, too. You would never guess that she saved his life a couple of days ago."

"Who's? That guy in the black tank top? The one kissing her?"

"Yes. Enrique Mora."

"Really? I didn't recognize him from the back. I have never seen him laugh. And I have never seen him without a suit. Geez, he could be someone from one of those muscle magazines. How old is he?"

"Forty five. He works hard at staying in shape. One of the reasons Rick is still alive is that he is quick, strong, and very observant. Not easy to kill."

"So, is that the Kozlowski girl?"

"July Kozlowski Sullivan. Now July Mora. The Kozlowski's and the Mora's jointly own a big ranch above Juniper Springs. If you want to swing the rancher's vote, Rick is your man. He is kind of wild and difficult to deal with sometimes, but he is honest to the core. If he screws up, he admits it. And he is very, very smart. I like sending him to conferences because he puts most of those hot shots with all their degrees to shame. Don't think you can fool him."

"What? So, you are lecturing me? I didn't have anything to do with that scandal."

"Didn't stop it either, did you?"

"Who the hell do you think you are? I am your Governor!"

Larry spoke up. "Easy, boys. This is not the place or the time. Cool down. Let's have a beer. They're getting ready to start the music."

Your Worst Nightmare played and sang for the next hour, obviously having a lot of fun, telling jokes about each other, members of the audience, and local politics between songs. July had never seen Rick perform like this. He was a great entertainer, wowing the crowd with fancy finger work, laughing as he spontaneously came up with new lyrics for some tunes. She was so impressed, so proud.

"Well, boys and girls," Rick said. "I am hanging up my spurs, and starting on a new life with my amazing wife, July. So, here is my song for you." It was not intended for a baritone, but his rendering of *We Are the Champions*, was terrific. He had the audience on their feet, cheering, stomping, singing along on the chorus as Rick made up verses about LCPD.

"Wow! Good enough to go pro," the Governor commented. "He has great, what do you call it? Stage presence? Charisma? I never imagined that this man was hiding inside that scary Captain Mora."

Larry spoke up. "Governor, I am telling you, and the Chief is telling you, that Rick is the right one. Yes, he is tough, stubborn, difficult, crazy. But he is an excellent manager and a hard worker. I have known Rick since he was seventeen, the youngest, and by far the smartest soldier in my platoon. And he is an authentic hero with a

Silver Star. Wait and see. You know I would never steer you wrong because I have too much skin in the game. If you don't get re-elected, I am out of a very cushy job. He is staying here in the hotel, in the room you usually rent overlooking the river. It seems that Rick has done more for the manager than your presence ever did." He laughed at the Governor's swearing.

"Well, I guess this is it," Rick said to the crowd. "Two more days, and I am officially retired. The chief will tell you all about a reorganization, and new opportunities. Farewell! Be well!" There was sustained applause as Rick led July toward the exit.

Chapter 48

"Catch him!" The Governor ordered his aide. Larry leaped up, hurrying after the couple.

"Listen, Eric. I talk big, but I meant it when I said I'm scared of him. I saw it once. Remember that day when the skinhead shot at that Senator? Mora was terrifying. It was all so fast. He made mincemeat of the shooter in seconds. He looked crazy. I mean it. Insane! Mora doesn't fight. He massacres. He nearly killed the guy. Are you sure he is the man for this job?"

Eric replied. "Rick is dangerous, but he is also the real deal, Governor. He can still bust out a bronc. He is observant of the least little details that no one else notices. When I was his Sergeant, I saw Rick track a killer through the desert out there at a trot when the rest of us could barely spot a single track. And he has caught accounting discrepancies that the rest of us missed. He has a brilliant, analytical mind, and he speaks four languages fluently. Imagine what he can contribute to international trade deals. He's a fantastic negotiator, too."

"Geez, Eric, you sound like a schoolgirl with a crush!"

"Rick saved my boy's life with his quick thinking fifteen years ago. Did you know that he is the grandson of Juan Pablo Mora, old Iron Horse himself?"

"No. I didn't. Wow! That would pull a bunch of votes to our ticket, huh?"

"Indeed. And, he stopped drinking, cold turkey, because July was worried about his health."

"So, it is likely to become his ticket in three years."

"That would be up to you. Rick is apolitical. I don't think he would be very interested in campaigning, money raising, all that stuff."

Rick and July were just entering the hotel elevator when Larry caught up to them.

"Congratulations, Rick and Dr. Mora. Great that you are looking so happy, man. Never thought I would see you laughing and joking like this."

"Hey, Larry. I have never before felt quite like this, you know?" His eyes sparkled with joy. "I feel like I can barely keep my feet on the ground. Speaking of which, look at you! You got a new foot?"

"Yeah, a better one. It's titanium and has a spring to it. Works great." He smiled at July.

"July, this is Larry Elkins. He was my Sergeant in the Army until he took some of the force of that IED." He hugged her to his side, and Larry noticed again that he unconsciously puffed out his chest with pride as she extended a small left hand.

Larry gave a very slight bow, and said, "Pleased to meet you. I never met your grandfather, Governor Kozlowski, but I have heard many good things about him and your Uncle Luke. Your husband is too modest to mention that he saved my life, and six other men, in a firefight in Iraq. That is how he won his Silver Star at the grand old age of nineteen."

"Really? A Silver Star? From when they blew up the transport?" She leaned back, looking up at him, and he looked away, clearly embarrassed.

"I shot so many, babe, and I still can smell the heat from my rifle, and the dust, and piss and leaking guts. I try to forget it, and the Star reminds me of that day."

"You should be proud, Rick," Larry said. "I don't mean of the combat, but proud of the lives you saved. After all, it was your own team that asked the Army to consider the award. We all agreed."

July studied him for a minute. "You should appreciate their appreciation, shouldn't you?"

"My blood was running all over his lap while he tried to keep me from bleeding out. If you hadn't thought so fast, Rick, I would not be here pestering you."

"If you didn't have such damn slippery arteries, it would not have been such a problem. What a mess that was. Don't know how you bore the pain, Larry. You are one tough guy."

"Nah, just too stunned to feel much until I got into the MedEvac. Then I hollered until they knocked me out. You were hurt a lot worse. I was out of the hospital in two months. You were in there for what? Three months? Hell, man, it's a miracle that you survived that round rattling around through your chest. You should wear the Star, Rick. It's our way of thanking you."

Rick grimaced. "I understand your point. I am a self absorbed twit, aren't I?"

"No, you are a guy with a callous outer shell and a sensitive soul. That is who you really are, and you are terribly, incredibly, amazingly wonderful!" July hugged him with her good arm.

He laughed. "Well, I am glad my wife feels that way." He quickly changed the subject.

"Still playing footsie with the Governor? Which foot do you use?" Rick asked Larry.

Larry chuckled. "Depends on how far up his whatever I want to kick something. Yeah, I like dealing with problems that won't shoot at me. And, I know this is awkward, but he would like to talk to you. Now."

"Now? Why?"

"I should leave that to him. But I can say that it was Eric Andersen's idea, and Eric is still your boss at the moment. Right?"

Rick snorted in disgust. "Right. July...."

"It's okay. Eric must think it's important."

"Alright, but the Governor needs to come to our room, where I am in charge. Who is he using for security these days?" The two men just looked at each other. "That's what I thought. That little creep can wait in the hallway. Tell them to come now."

Larry dialed the Governor, relaying the invitation. Or was it an order? Rick unlocked the room, and July collapsed into a lounge chair.

"Too tired for this, babe?"

She shook her head. "Nope. You are the one who should be tired." She wiggled an eyebrow, making him blush.

There was a knock. Rick took his weapon from its place on his belt before opening the door to the Governor and another fellow, big and heavy but soft looking. After checking the hallway, Rick spoke a welcoming word to the first man, then started to close the door on the other guy.

"Not you, Mikie," Rick said.

"Hey, I am security for the Governor." He tried to push through the door. Rick suddenly pulled the door open. Mikie stumbled partway in. Rick grabbed him while he was still off-balance. "Sure, and you are doing a great job." He took the man by his shirt front and threw him across the hall. "Out! Try doing your job for once."

"The perfect example of why nepotism is a bad idea, Governor. He didn't even bother to see who is in here but just let you walk in undefended. Get some honest to gosh security for a change. Your sister needs to find a different job for Mikie. Maybe hoeing weeds on the farm, like a real man."

"Did you think we are a danger? Why did you answer with a weapon in your hand?"

"There is someone still on the loose who might want to harm July. I can't let anyone target my wife. She has endured enough. And, I am very unpopular with the cartels and many other people. It will be a while before the bad guys know that I am retired. So, what is so important that you have to talk to me right now?"

He sat beside July, concerned that her effort to keep her tired arm elevated was failing. "Put that cast up here on my shoulder, July." He gave her another of Mo's pain pills and turned his attention to the Governor, raising a brow in question.

"How did you do that? Mikie must outweigh you by a hundred

pounds."

"Sir Isaac Newton."

"What?"

"Governor, this is not the time for Rick to give you a lecture on Newton's *Principia*," Larry said.

"Of course, Larry." The Governor shifted around a bit, exposing his discomfort. "You know about the scandal in my administration." He sighed in disgust. "The Lieutenant Governor resigned and may face prosecution. I need a new Lieutenant who is honest and respected. Your Chief and Larry recommended you. That's it in a nutshell. I admit that I am concerned about your reputation as, as, uh." He looked at July.

"It's okey dokey. I know about the reputation."

"Okey dokey? I think the pill is starting to take effect already. July had surgery on this arm, which she re-broke when she saved me from being shot. My hero! But, do you mean to say that you want to appoint me as your Lieutenant Governor? Why? I am pretty much apolitical. Plus, I have that nasty s.o.b. reputation, I am un-educated, and I am a small-town hick. So, why?"

The Governor hesitated a moment, staring out toward the river. "Look, Rick. I don't know much of anything about science, let alone physics. I am finding that you are intimidating me, and you aren't even trying. So, be patient, okay? You just showed up my expensive university education, and you are physically scary. Hell, man, you look like a thug!"

Rick grunted in amusement, but nodded. His eyes crinkled at the corners, and there was a slight lift to his lips too. Suddenly, he looked friendly, and the Governor relaxed a little.

"I know I look like a thug, and I usually admit to it, given our sloppy American use of the word. But, if you consider the origin of the term, it doesn't really fit. I think it is more that I look like a working-class, lower echelon kind of guy, which I always have been. So, what did Eric and Larry tell you?"

"First, never lie to you. That you would ferret out any corruption and would never cover up for any wrongdoing. That your honesty is unquestioned, and if you are on my ticket in three years, I would attract the rancher's vote. Probably the indigenous vote, too. And, I have no idea where the term thug came from."

Rick chuckled. That charming lop-sided smile showed the Governor one reason he attracted the ladies. "Look up *thugee* sometime. But I don't care about that," he said, "and I don't care if you are re-elected or not."

"Yeah. You do care about this state, though. I think that, together, we can do a lot of good.

"Like what?"

"Well, we have this massive opportunity in terms of solar power. We have most of the minerals, the labor force, the engineers, and the facilities that we need to manufacture the newest in solar technology. But we need investors. There is a faction in the EAE debating whether to invest here or in China. But, using a translator to communicate with their engineers makes me look ignorant, incompetent, because the Emir's English is perfect."

Rick nodded. "What else?"

"At least twelve percent of our population is indigenous, probably a lot more if you include the native populations from Mexico. They don't necessarily trust a fat old white guy. That is understandable. But, Iron Horse's grandson? Maybe they would work with you? Plus, you know the border. We must maintain the flow of tourists from Mexico. Most of the many millions they spend here turns over within the state several times. And, just as important, I know there is some corruption. I want it found, but not by me. I don't want to be digging around in the activities of my supporters. I want someone else to do it, and do it thoroughly, like an experienced policeman knows how to do. I would also like to appoint you as Captain in the State Police, so that you have statewide authority to investigate whatever needs investigating."

"I see. I admit that it sounds interesting, but I am determined that July can pursue her career. I fell into mine. She worked hard, against the odds, against guys like us, to achieve her success. If she wants to move to Timbuktu for an opportunity, then I will go with her."

July stirred. "Enrique. It's perfect. Instead of physical challenges, it will be mostly intellectual challenges, but still an adrenaline trip. You know? I won't have to worry quite as much, every time you walk out the door, that someone with a grudge is waiting in the shadows. And, realistically, my arm will never heal to the point where I can be the hotshot that I was. But you know what? I am going to adapt. It is much more important for me to be your wife and Graciela's mom."

"And I guess I may not have to worry, every time you walk out the door, that there is that sneaky bomber waiting in the shadows." Rick gave her a squeeze of affection.

Leo continued. "One nice bonus is that you could live in the Governor's Mansion. We don't live there. My wife, Mariah, spent years planting her flower beds, and is famous for them. I would never pull her away from that. The public rooms are separate from the family dwelling, and there is a lot of space for family and friends to visit. Twenty four hour security, too. All those creeps wanting to harm you or your man, Doctor, will have a challenge there. And, of course, there is a grand piano. It's a classic 1880s Buckstein. Queen Victoria had one like it." He smiled when Rick's eyes lit up.

"Isn't there some famous interior designer up there? Seems like I saw an article somewhere about a lady with a very unusual name," July asked.

"You mean Digna? Digna Otterbach? She is big with the use of metals and leather. I have one of her chairs at my main office in the Roundhouse."

"Rique, weren't you and Maureen trying to figure out how she could do an apprenticeship while living at home? So, why not our home? If Digna is not a part of the Academy apprenticeship program, maybe there is another prominent designer?" July looked at him hopefully.

"After living alone all these years, I don't know if I can stand being outnumbered by three women."

"Uh, huh," She replied, skeptically. "You like to braid Grace's hair, and color with her, and play Spiderman. You will be in seventh heaven being surrounded by women." She poked his nose gently. "And, it is not so damn hot up there!"

"Spiderman?" Larry asked.

"Oh, Luke's old house has open rafters. So, he swings from them making weird noises, and does backflips off the porch rails. Grace and her friends love it when he is silly like that. If he's not acting like the boss, he is pretty juvenile."

"Is this what you want then, July? It sounds just right for us for the next few years. The folks will miss Grace, but we would only be a few hours from home. Maybe I could still be effective in catching bad guys, just white-collar guys more than gangbangers."

"Oh!" she exclaimed. "What about Uncle Luke, though?"

"He and I have been planning, since I didn't know what you would want to do. Wait and see what he decided. I think you will be pleased. So, Governor, Larry, I guess we might consider it as long as I am just a worker bee and not involved in political bullshit. What is the deal exactly?'

"First, I want to know how you got my room? I always stay in this room."

"Well, Stacy and I agreed that you might want to look out at the city, full of your constituents. And, I tip better than you do. But what is the procedure? I might be interested. What's next."

"The AG swears you in, and that's it. Of course, we would like to announce it at the Ball and have you take up your duties on the first of the month."

Rick rose, walking to the sliding doors that looked over the river. The sun was setting, and a cooling breeze ruffled his hair. He stepped out onto the balcony for a few minutes. The sounds of the DJ, hired for dancing at the picnic, came faintly to him. As he moved back into the room, three pairs of eyes questioned him.

"Just doing a gut check." He waved an arm at the city. "When I started as a young cop, this was a very corrupt place. But, over time, a few of us made a difference. So, in some ways this is my city. That sounds arrogant. Well, I am more than a little arrogant, sort of like a politician. If you can cope with that, I'm ready to go to work."

There was a knock on the door. "Room Service!"

"That will be my wife's supper. If you will excuse us, gentlemen?"

"Thank you, Captain Mora. I look forward to our being a team."

As Larry and his boss walked down the hall, Governor Durbin suddenly exclaimed, "Hey! What just happened? I feel like Mora interviewed me, and I was lucky to get the job."

Chapter 49

July could barely stay awake after their dinner. Her arm throbbed, making her miserable, but she wouldn't admit it. She didn't want Enrique to worry. They sat on the balcony, looking over the pecan groves to the rising moon's reflection on the river, and listening as the city quieted for the night. A siren had Rick up looking for the source.

"Going to take a while to get over the habit," he said. "Not my worry anymore."

"Enrique, why does Bebe want to harm me? I don't understand. I know she never liked me, but why?"

"Apparently, from what Kincannon and Q gathered from Roberta, she blames other dermatologists for her husband losing his license. Your instincts about her were right. There is something very wrong with her mentally. She seriously injured a couple of dermatologists at another clinic where Doctor Garner had worked. One of them, Dr. Gammage, died. Rory and his team are still looking, but she is wily. Even the FBI has made no progress yet."

"Roberta also got pregnant, thanks to Buddy. I guess the baby was deformed by the effects of that medication Dr. Garner gave her, and Bebe was exchanging expensive care for the baby boy for Roberta's help in the clinic bombings. Shirley was right on with her suspicions."

July was silent for a while, taking it all in. "How very sad." She sighed, then roused. "Oh, Shirley! We should let them know what happened."

"Done. I hope you approve. Mom hired Abe and Sheena full-time. Shirley will be babysitting the little ones, Gary and Ralph. Luke and I think it would be great if the kids moved into the house with him. What do you think?"

"Perfect," she yawned and dozed off.

Rafael joined them on the balcony, talking with Rick about the past and the future. A chilly breeze sprang up, bearing the smell of rain. Rick picked July up and carried her to the closest bed, carefully arranging her arm on pillows. With the effects of the medications and fatigue, she barely even woke up.

It was late when Rick finally lay down in the other bed, his heart full as never before. Sometime in the night, a small warm body with cold hands slipped into the bed, snuggling against his back. He smiled. What had happened to him? It was just short of a miracle.

They spent the next day with family, Rick mentally preparing to become someone new. Everything seemed different, brighter, cleaner. His former life was fading away, down a long dark hallway. He didn't even object when Rafael carefully arranged medals in the order they were to be worn.

Evening came, and he dressed in his black tuxedo with a waist-coat that partly covered the pistol he wore. "Still a cop, babe," he said, in response to July's questioning look. It took him three tries to get his tie perfect. "Out of practice since I stopped doing private security for the upper classes."

"Did you do a lot of that?"

"Absolutely. Great secondary income. More than my salary, some months."

"Why did you stop?"

He hesitated.

"Oh. Something bad happened?"

"Not exactly. I just got tired of divas and their demands."

He didn't meet her eyes, and July wondered at that reaction. Then it dawned on her. In one of the photos she had seen when investigating Captain Mora, the famous lady on his arm was giving Rick a possessive look. Boy toy?

"Marney Mayne," she said. "And I suppose there were others?"

"Some bring their own security teams, and others hire locals like me."

"It must have been exciting rubbing elbows with famous singers like Marney."

"It was at first, when I was young, but it wasn't exactly elbows that some wanted to rub. I started feeling more like a gigolo than a cop. Then a member of Jamie G's band asked what I did in her bus. He meant what I looked for. Bombs or something."

"And is that some deep dark secret?"

His blush deepened, turning his face to a dark copper color. "I was actually doing Jamie G. I was ashamed that I couldn't answer his question honestly. I have never been a good liar."

"Well, my elegant husband, you look terrific in that tux. I definitely get why the ladies wanted you as an, umm, escort." She laughed at his growled response.

He was helping her with her ball gown when there was a knock on the door. "I have a package for you, Rick," Stacy, the hotel manager, called. He hurried to invite her in.

"Thanks, Stacey. This is the finishing touch. I was thinking it wouldn't get here in time. But you could have sent the bellboy up with it."

"Nope. When Mr. Loran delivers something in person, it's bound to be really expensive. Do I get to see it?"

Rick took out his penknife and slit the paper. Inside was a blue velvet box. And in the box, a square cut emerald on a heavy gold braided chain, with drop earrings. They matched July's emerald ring. And her dress. And mostly, her eyes. She was speechless.

"You will absolutely be the most gorgeous woman at the Ball, Dr. Mora."

"Thank you. I'm feeling pretty nervous," July whispered, looking like she wanted to hide.

"Not tonight. Nothing to be nervous about. Tonight you will be the Lieutenant Governor's lovely wife. Don't worry, Dr. Mora. I have seen a bunch of these Governor's Balls. Just do what Larry says. He will be stationed on the stairs. You won't be the only one new to this formal crap." That helped, making July laugh.

"Thanks, Stacey. Come on, Mrs. Wabbit. We need to hang around being polite for a bit before the grand announcement."

They stood with others on the mezzanine, waiting and chatting. A small crowd began to gather around Rick. Some were surprised to see that the man who was usually silent and watchful in the background was participating in conversations. Some wanted to get a good look at his medals, some at the woman on his arm. They didn't know yet that Rick was married, and July was amused by overheard comments about eye candy and Badge Bunnies. She wanted to see their facial expressions when they learned that she was a doctor and the new Lieutenant Governor's wife.

She peeked over the railing at Giselle and Kate, waiting at the bottom of the stairs as their men fetched cocktails. There were several other ladies there, too. One, chatting with Kate, seemed vaguely familiar. What was it? The way she stood? July ran through the list of gray-haired women she knew. There were not many. But then the lady laughed, and July drew back in alarm. Bebe! It was Bebe in a gray wig, just like Shirley thought.

"What is it, July?" Rick noticed her reaction. She whispered her response to him, trying to be calm. He gestured to the security team member, standing silent in the rear, as Rick had done for so many years. Q was quickly notified, and July was placed safely behind the bulky body of Sergeant Ruhl. Was it possible that if Bebe could not wreak revenge on July, she would strike another member of the family? Like Gisele?

"Wait a few minutes before you start, please, Leo. I need to straighten out a little problem here." Leo nodded, concerned, and gestured to Larry to hold off on beginning the announcements.

Rick moved down the stairs into the crowd, smiling at acquaintances, shaking hands, ending up beside Bebe. Gisele started to introduce her, "Enrique, this is Mrs. Harrigan."

"We have met. Bebe, isn't it?" His voice was pleasant, but those gray eyes were glacial.

Trapped, Bebe reached into the evening bag she was carrying. But before she could get her hand on the small pistol concealed there, a strong brown hand enfolded hers.

"Good evening, Mrs. Garner. How nice of you to join us. Let me get you a drink." Rick's body was before her, blocking her escape, his hand grasping hers. She tried to turn away, but there was Rory Kincannon on one side and Eva on the other. Bebe's eyes flashed with rage as she tried to pull her bag from Rick's grasp.

"Here. Let me help you with that." He squeezed her hand hard. Bebe's fingers went numb, crushed between the metal of the pistol and the force of his fingers.

"May I see your concealed carry license?" Rory asked, and smiled, seeing the realization of her error in her eyes. "Oh, no permit? Yes. That is a felony," he continued softly. "You can make a fuss, but you cannot get away. Your choice." He and Eva quietly maneuvered Bebe through the crowd, and no one seemed to notice except Gisele.

"Enrique? Was she the one?"

He nodded and looked up at July, who was peeking around Sergeant Ruhl. Her eyes were huge in her face, but it seemed more like curiosity than fear this time. Rick grinned at her and trotted up the stairs. "You can start now, Larry."

The quiet, seemingly inconsequential, removal of Bebe, the announcement of various dignitaries as they descended the stairs to scattered applause, was all right out of a movie as far as July was concerned. Rick took the microphone from Larry. "Ladies and gentlemen, thank you for attending this thirtieth Governor's Ball. Many of you have seen me here before. I was on the security team for this event nineteen times. But, for those who are new here, let me introduce myself. My name is Rick Mora. I am fortunate to be the husband of internationally recognized dermatologist, Dr July Marie Kozlowski Mora, the granddaughter of our beloved former Governor, Ezra Kozlowski." He stepped to the side and turned to lead the applause for July, pride in his voice and stance.

July went pale, then blushed, and in the spirit of the moment, took the mic from Rick. It was finally dawning on her that her shyness had been self centered and childish. She was not the center of attention but just one part of the puzzle, one cog in the wheel. There was no reason to be so self conscious, because she was not the focus of attention anyway. This was what Uncle Luke meant when he said she was too immature. Time for a change, and here was the opportunity.

"Thank you," she said, smiling at the crowd. Turning to face Rick, she continued, "Let me introduce this talented, brilliant man, the former Captain of the Major Crimes Division for the Las Cruces Police Department, and now the new Lieutenant Governor of New Mexico, my husband, Enrique Rodrigo Beaupre Mora."

The applause was thunderous. July looked down at her extended family, Gisele and Rafael, Luke and Kate, Maureen and Grace, the Gambino kids. She grinned, and Grace waved at her.

July was struggling with pain, feeling a little faint, but she rallied, leaning heavily on Rick's arm as they descended the stairs. He glanced down at her, concerned. "I'm okay," she whispered. With perfect timing, the band began to play. Rick swept her onto the dance floor, holding her securely against his chest with one arm, the other supporting her cast, easing the pain a bit.

"We can retreat, babe," he whispered. "I didn't realize how much all this was taking out of you. I'm sorry."

"Rique, this might be the most important night of your life. We will not retreat. I am so proud of you."

He flashed that dazzling smile. "No, July, my wife, my girl, my partner. The most important night of my life was when some little wabbit crawled into bed with her cold hands and snuggled against me, where she belongs. And I knew it was forever and ever. Amen."

CPSIA information can be obtained
at www.ICGtesting.com
Printed in the USA
JSHW031344090722
27781JS00005B/18